Natural History

Neil Cross is the author of *Mr In-Between*, *Christendom*, *Holloway Falls* and *Always the Sun*, which was long-listed for the Man Booker Prize. His memoir, *Heartland*, was a top ten bestseller, and he is a scriptwriter for the TV series *Spooks*. He lives with his wife and two children.

Natural History

Neil Cross

SIMON & SCHUSTER

LONDON • NEW YORK • TORONTO • SYDNEY

First published in Great Britain by Simon & Schuster UK Ltd, 2007
A CBS COMPANY

1 3 5 7 9 10 8 6 4 2

Simon & Schuster UK Ltd
Africa House
64–78 Kingsway
London WC2B 6AH

www.simonsays.co.uk

Simon & Schuster Australia
Sydney

A CIP catalogue record for this book is
available from the British Library

ISBN: 978-0-7432-6375-7

Typeset by Rowland Phototypesetting Ltd,
Bury St Edmunds, Suffolk
Printed and bound in Great Britain by William Clowes Ltd, Beccles, Suffolk

*This book, like everything else,
is for Nadya, Ethan and Finn.*

Acknowledgements

In writing this novel, I used a number of sources, but I'm particularly indebted to Jeffrey Taylor's *Facing the Congo* (Abacus, 2001) for the "Colonel Ebeya" and certain borrowed details of Jane's experience in Kinshasa. I also relied on Mike Farrel's *The Killing Ground: A Journey to Rwanda*, for details of Mugunga refugee camp and its surroundings. Farrel's long article and much else besides can be found on the Human Rights Watch website – www.hrw.org.

Along the way, many people provided help and encouragement. Among them, Tom Adams shared his knowledge of the Zoo Licensing Act (1981) and the Dangerous Wild Animals Act (1973). Cris Warren sent me monkey books to help with my monkey book, and never failed to make me laugh. Ian Hand provided me with insight into the running of the British Mental Health Services – he also introduced me to Joy Division and gin, but that was a long time ago. Steve Braunias, an expert in such matters, helped me survive a prolonged assault by vicious baboons. My wife, Nadya, was remarkable in her unwavering support. (But then, Nadya is remarkable in every way – except for tidying shoes. Where my marriage is concerned, I still can't quite believe my luck.

Or stop tripping on randomly abandoned footwear.) And Tim Binding, as ever, was my untiring friend and my mentor. I hope you like this book, Tim.

Because *Natural History* is a work of fiction I've taken many liberties, not least with the geography of Devon. I hope most of the untruths in these pages are deliberate, a way to help me tell a story. Those errors which aren't deliberate are – naturally – my own damn fault.

1

It was only a dead ape. Patrick had seen dozens, one way or another. He'd seen them die naturally, of old age and disease – and heard the war-shrieks as they murdered each other. He'd watched them cannibalize their young.

But this was Rue, who'd been at Monkeyland since 1982 – fourteen years. She'd been rescued after a tabloid ran shots of her, a powerful ape at a travelling circus, cowering in baffled misery while a trainer beat her with a riding crop.

Rue had grown old at Monkeyland. And Patrick, who knew better, couldn't help but think of her as wise. It was her toffee brown eyes, her pursing, grey-haired lips; the unhurried way she sucked at half an orange.

That morning, Saturday, he found her corpse in a far corner of the enclosure. She was twisted up, her face locked in a death grin. The other chimps, alarmed by the spastic violence of her seizures, had retreated to the edges of the compound, leaving Rue alone to die. They were still there – softly grunting, curious – when Patrick arrived.

He knelt to inspect the corpse. Late the previous night, somebody – kids, probably – must have entered Monkeyland and thrown poisoned food into the A Compound. Perhaps Rue, most trusting of creatures, had been alone in accepting it; because only Rue, most trusting of creatures, had died.

Patrick knew that local kids gained entry to Monkeyland through a gap in the northern perimeter fence. One of the groundsmen had told him about it, in the very early days.

The gap was behind the adventure playground, far from the animals. Kids had been using it for years; the gap was fixed, they cut it open again. Sometimes on Sunday mornings you found cider bottles and lager cans and tacky splats of vomit, the occasional condom. It was a pain in the ass, but Patrick had let it slide. There was so much else to do before the next government inspection, so much else to worry about.

Now Patrick wandered along the figure eight of the footpath. But for the animals and the keepers, Monkeyland was deserted. It was closed for renovations and, because Rue had been killed, Patrick had given the contractors the day off.

Walking, he was watched by spindly gibbons that drooped from their rope-draped pillar. He passed the ring-tailed lemurs, the squirrel monkeys and the A Compound where Rue had lived and died. Finally, he arrived at the decrepit adventure playground.

There was a fort of rotting wood, from which hung slimy, frayed old rope swings. Tyres were secured to bending branches that couldn't take their weight. There were rusty slides and a squeaky roundabout.

They'd closed the adventure playground to the public before Health and Safety got the chance. Seeing it depressed him. Always did; it was a waste of space and a waste of time.

He walked over to the wooden seating shelter. It was chicken scratched with graffiti, urine-stinking.

A dozen metres behind the shelter ran an overgrown hedge, which obstructed the hole in the fence. Kneeling at the hedge was Stu Redman, their local copper. He was based at Minehead police station – but Patrick had called him at home that morning, and Stu had come to Monkeyland on his own time.

Patrick said, 'Anything?'

Stu looked up, surprised to see Patrick, or just surprised to be asked. He straightened, brushed himself off. Laconic, West Country, squinting.

'Not much, mate.' He pointed to a muddy footprint. 'One of them was wearing Dr Marten's. If it helps.'

Patrick laughed, sorely. 'Cheers.'

Stu's mockery, friendly enough, waned. He squinted at the drizzle-lashed playground. Toed at a crushed Stella can.

'God knows why they come here in the first place.'

It seemed like such an effort, for such little reward – to drive out here to this gimcrack shelter, just to drink cider and smoke cigarettes and maybe do some necking.

'I was in the desert once,' Patrick said. 'In a coach. No toilet. The way it worked, when enough men needed to go, the driver stopped to let them off. There was nothing around for miles, just sand and the road. And the men – do you know what they did?'

Stu shook his head.

'They turned round,' Patrick said, 'and pissed on the wheels.'

Stu scratched his nose, considering.

'I'll have a quiet word round the village.'

'But you don't think it was kids?'

'Ah, there's a few local bastards, a few tearaways – tattooed

Harries. But, be honest — if any of them wanted to kill a monkey, they'd most probably have brought their dad's shotgun and blown its head off.'

Patrick looked at him, blinking.

'They're not that clever,' said Stu. 'As a rule. The kids round here.'

'Right,' said Patrick.

*

He and Stu walked back, their heads bowed in the rain. They shook hands near the Bachelor Compound, and Stu went home. Patrick crossed to the infirmary.

Jane was there, in the vet's office. She'd been present at the morning's necropsy. She wore faded jeans and shirt, old walking boots. Her hair was in a casual pony tail. She looked dressed for Africa. She always looked dressed for Africa; even in North Devon, in February.

She was slender, tall, suntanned. Years of squinting in the sunlight had left its mark at the corner of her eyes. Her hands were long and callused with hard work. Jane could tie knots like a sailor.

Patrick said, 'So?'

She lifted her cup of tea and sipped. She looked at him from under her brow; shrugged a shoulder.

It meant, *Who knows?*

They didn't speak until Don Caraway emerged, still dressed for surgery; all but the latex gloves. Behind him, Rue lay dissected on a stainless-steel table; unzipped from throat to pubis, still wearing that lurid death grin.

Patrick said it again, 'So?'

Caraway was tall, hunched; sandy hair combed over a freckled scalp. Years before, if Patrick had been told the truth, he'd spent his spare time, and all his money, hunting the Loch Ness Monster. But there was nothing in Loch Ness, except perhaps some unusually large eels.

Caraway said, 'I'm thinking some kind of rat poison – Warfarin, chlorophacinone, diphacinone?'

Jane said, 'We treat for rats every day.'

'Absolutely. We use Warfarin. And rats – I expect you know this – they leak urine, dribble it wherever they go. Scent trails and what have you. So I'm thinking, perhaps rat urine is contaminating the food supply. Perhaps Rue has eaten contaminated food – and she's so old and weak, you know. A healthier chimp could take it.'

'But it's not that?'

'No. it's not that. Rat poison is slow-acting. She'd have shown symptoms – blood in the urine, nose-bleeds, bleeding gums. But she was asymptomatic.'

'So, what was it?'

'Not sure. But the symptoms – the vomiting, the defecating, the violent seizures . . .'

'Yes?'

'It looks like the effects of a rodenticide called Ten Eighty: sodium fluoro-acetate. They use it in New Zealand, to control possums. It's got no odour, no taste, and it's *phenomenally* potent in small doses. A few mils will kill you in a couple of hours. If you're going to poison a chimp, that's the way to go.'

'So where does a kid get this stuff?'

'I don't know if a kid does.'

Patrick scratched his hairline, irritated. Jane patted his shoulder, nodded for Caraway to continue.

'Ten Eighty's a restricted substance. So first, he's got to get hold of it. Then he's got to survive handling it – and it's dangerous stuff. Breathe it in, get it into a minor abrasion – just a scratch – and you're in big trouble. Inasmuch as you're dead.'

Patrick said, 'Don, you've been round here for years. Has anything like this happened before?'

A contrite, curate's grin. 'Dogs blinded with air-rifles. The odd bonfired cat. Sheep with their throat torn out. Someone brought in a fox once – some sod had lopped off its front legs. But dead chimps? No.'

'Jesus,' said Patrick. 'What a day.'

Monkeyland stood on eighty-five acres, close to the North Devon coast. It homed two hundred primates of nine different species – and two aberrant Spanish donkeys, rescued bonebags with slow-chewing mouths and sad eyes, who sometimes skittishly sidestepped when children grew too loud.

But its main attraction was the thirty-nine chimpanzees – thirty-eight, now Rue was dead.

They had chimps from Spain, Greece, France, Holland, Cyprus, Dubai, Israel: chimps that had been experimented on, used as props for beachfront photographers; chimps that had been driven insane by living in small apartments; that had been dressed in sunglasses and baseball caps and featured in TV sitcoms and advertisements; chimps that had been starved and beaten and burned with cigarettes. Several had arrived addicted to tranquillizers.

Visitors enjoyed this; it made the apes seem plaintively human.

Visitors came to gawp, to coo and cluck at their reassuring captivity.

For years, those visitors had been rare, and declining – an endangered species – but still the animals had to be cleaned, and fed, and medicated; and still the people who did the cleaning and feeding and medicating had to be paid.

Monkeyland was failing. It had been failing when Jane decided to buy it, nearly a year before. She'd decided to buy it precisely because it was failing; she was like that.

They'd driven out one weekend. It wasn't a long trip from their unhappy home in Bath – less than a hundred miles south-west – but Patrick soon lost his sense of direction. He unwound the window and smelled the sea. It made him happy. Always did.

Soon, Jane was pulling into Monkeyland's car park. Patrick got out of the car, and anxiety effervesced inside him. It was a mid-June weekend, and there were only half a dozen vehicles in the visitor car park. Three of them were Hondas; old people.

Monkeyland's perimeter wall was cracked and water-stained. The gate resembled a Soviet border crossing.

Inside, they wandered the sanctuary grounds, tracing the main path's Mobius Strip, its eternity symbol.

The animals looked healthy enough, but their compounds were tired, and so were they. The orangs were listless. The capuchins crouched in watchful groups, munching on apple cores. Spider monkeys hung inverted from their beams, strung together like broomsticks.

Then Patrick and Jane reached the first of the two chimp compounds. This group consisted entirely of males.

Patrick watched them for a long while. His shirt-sleeves were rolled up in the sun and he wore sunglasses. He could smell the unease that radiated from the Bachelor Group – a murky air of damage and suspicion and scarcely restrained violence.

'This, here,' he said. 'This group. This has got to be a mistake.'

'Apparently,' Jane told him, 'none of them can integrate with the mixed group. Some of them are quite—'

Dangerous, she was going to say. Patrick had never been inside a prison, but that's what he was looking at: the violent offenders' wing. All those men in there together, left to fight it out alone.

Chimps were stronger than people – seven or eight times stronger. They had denser bones and thicker hides. In play, they chucked and flung, and slapped and playbit one another: a playful chimp could, with ease, badly injure someone it loved. A malevolent chimp could shred a human being like wet paper. And here were a dozen such males, turning their sullen eyes away from the scattering of bored visitors ogling them from behind a high wall.

He knew that such creatures practised rape, sometimes murder. He also knew he shouldn't use those words; he was wandering into perilous territory. He wasn't a primatologist. He wrote old-fashioned, unpublished adventure stories. He was a sidekick.

He said, 'Christ, how do we deal with this?'

Jane grabbed the curved, concrete edge of the enclosure and watched as a small knot of males came together in a throwing, slapping, shrieking scrap that was followed, at some length, by sombre grooming.

'The place is falling to pieces.'

He looked at the cracked and weedy paving, the dense and uncut hedges lining the dreary walkways, the rusting chain-link fences; the jerry-built jungle gyms, the chewed tyres on the pale, bald trunks of dead trees. And he looked at these half-crazed primates.

'Come on,' Jane said. 'I'm bored.'

'I'm bored, too. Let's go somewhere. Let's leave the country.'

'I've spoken to Richard.'

Patrick had a feeling in his stomach, like descending in a lift.

'Richard. Of course you have.'

'He's talking about a show. Two series, maybe three. Fly-on-the-wall. Following Monkeyland as it gets to its feet. A bit like *The Park*, but about the animals, not the boardroom.'

Patrick scratched his scalp. *Fucking Richard*, he thought.

'It's a good idea,' Jane said. 'It can't fail.'

There was no point arguing; this is what Patrick had wanted – change and adventure. And it wouldn't be for long; nothing ever was.

Jane looked around, expansively. 'It was built by some mad old spinster, apparently. Biddie something. Born and died in Devon; never left.'

Biddie Powys – the kind of reclusive old woman who, a few hundred years earlier, might have burned as a witch – had endowed Monkeyland and her family home to an animal charity. That had been twenty years ago, and now the charity itself was struggling. It had offered Jane a good deal. Monkeyland would be hers, outright, and so would the house – situated on the coast, four miles beyond Monkeyland's far perimeter.

In addition, the charity would maintain a decreasing level of funding for another five years.

'That gives us enough time to turn it round,' Jane had said. 'Bring it into profit. Sell it and move on.'

'Yes,' said Patrick, with exaggerated patience. 'But how much will it cost?'

'Everything,' said Jane.

*

And now they were here, and gentle Rue was dead.

Late in the afternoon, Patrick made a nest of Jiffy bags beneath his desk, curled up under his nylon parka, and went to sleep.

Charlie woke him at 8 p.m. Patrick blinked up, into his boy's triangular face; the beardless chin, the high forehead. Charlie had a face which belonged to another age. All the scruffy hair in the world couldn't mask it.

And he stood there now in Army surplus boots, jeans, parka — seventeen, the age Patrick's grandfather had been, when he went to fight.

He said, 'I brought sandwiches.'

'Cheese?'

'Corned beef.'

'Corned beef.'

Patrick crawled out from under the desk and stood. His knees popped, as loud as it was painful.

An icy starfield suspended above them, they trudged the curve of Monkeyland's main footpath, heading for the adventure play-ground. Faecal and urine odours drifted to them; the hot smell of life.

From the macaque cage came a sudden, shocked detonation — a frightened creature leaping to the safety of a high branch, to cower and watch.

Patrick and Charlie walked on, past the A Compound. In the pooled darkness, Patrick saw chimp movement, recognizable even in abstract. And he wondered at the boldness of Rue's poisoner: it was so dark, and the still winter was undercut by furtive snuffles and sniffs, secret whoopings, the articulation of beasts.

Perhaps there was an ancestral memory of the creatures that had once hunted on English soil: wolves, bears, boar. Not chimpanzees. Chimps belonged to a far older habitat, an older region of the mind, and it was eerie, to hear them prowling and rustling and hooting in the Devon night.

He hurried to catch up with his son, and together they passed the donkeys and crested the incline. The adventure playground opened out beneath them.

They found a place close to the tyre-swing and sat. Patrick liked it, heel to haunch in the darkness with his boy.

Another hour of waiting – and they were startled from their meditations by movement; stealthy, sleek, quick. A fox. It came sniffing from the trees, skittering at an angle towards them. Then it caught their scent and stopped.

It stood there – slender and ribbed; a wild animal. Patrick supposed it came here to scavenge easy scraps. He felt for it; he felt sorry that he and Charlie had scared it.

He clapped his hands, once, resoundingly. The fox whirled and sprinted into the undergrowth.

Patrick stood. 'Come on. Nobody's coming.'

That was the problem.

*

Sunday was supposed to be his day off, and he wasn't going to waste it. So he woke before dawn and crept around the creaky, higgledy old house, bundling his clothes under his arm, shivering, trying not to wake anyone.

Jane was in the deepest part of sleep: her cheek compressed on the pillow, her mouth budded open. She was breathing heavily, not quite snoring. He closed the bedroom door and, to pass the kids' rooms, adopted a high-kneed, cartoon-sneak.

Having been up so late, Charlie would sleep until lunch. But Jo was an early riser, a dawn bird, and she enjoyed having a cup of tea with Patrick, the two of them sitting at the big wooden table in the cobwebby kitchen with the absurd and unlit old Aga. So he had to be quiet.

Downstairs, he pulled on his jeans, his walking boots, a sweater with frayed cuffs and a hole in each elbow. He was tall, strong, thickening, turning in places to flab. A bony face, vertically scored and notched. He wore gypsy hair, shaggy curls that tickled his neck. It too had been dark, once; now it was streaked with grey. And still, a pirate's ring through his earlobe.

He grabbed a kagoul from a hook in the downstairs lavatory – a clutter of coats and piled, muddy shoes that always smelled unaired – and stepped out into the morning.

The house stood alone in its two acres, the colour of biscuit, in need of repair and paint. It was old, ridiculously big, and not well-maintained – its limestone was darkening with green lichen and damp and weathering. Two bats, pipistrelles, drew lightning loops and low dives over its crooked chimney-pots.

Patrick didn't feel like its owner, nor even its custodian. He just lived there.

He tramped across the overgrown acre of rear garden, the wild grass wetting him to the knees. Then he stood on the rotting stile and craned his neck. He couldn't see it – not over the hedge and through the bracken and past the oak trees – but he could feel the ocean.

He crossed the stile into the oak woods, through which ran the South-west Coastal Footpath.

Dawn gave the air a blue-cathode light. Low mist clutched at his knees; it caught like gauze in branches and pooled in moss-draped roots. He walked the squelching topsoil, the leaf humus. Low branches, cold with dew, whipped his face. Then he passed through the trees and walked along the open clifftop, the Bristol Channel calm far below. He hiked down to the salt flats, on and into Innsmouth.

Nearest the harbour, the houses were small, lime-washed; many were now holiday homes and weekend cottages which hugged the narrow belt of the cobbled main street. He followed its bends to the harbour.

The boat was at the weir, bobbing softly on the swell, and Captain Harry was already on board, smoking a roll-up and listening to Motörhead on a tinny portable stereo.

Patrick clambered on board and paid Harry in cash, up front. The boat chugged out on the pewter water, luminous with sunrise, and Patrick smelled the salt and the fuel and the fish and oily, half-rotten wood.

They fished for a while, their silence broken by the occasional muttered comment. Patrick caught some skinny mackerel. He gutted them, and Captain Harry cooked them over a Primus stove; the blue flame whipping in the wind.

As he ate, Patrick noticed a disturbance in the water, a wake that moved against the waves. He followed it, and saw two fur seals, swimming by.

He knew seals were closely related to dogs. And that's how he thought of them in the fizzing instant before the water closed over their sleek wet heads: as dogs, swimming home. Because that's where dogs always went, in the end: dogs went home.

2

In the summer of 1979, Patrick was twenty-five years old and a junior reporter on the *Bristol Evening Post*. His Editor had told him to chase up a story on the white tigers of Bristol Zoo. Seventeen of them had been born since 1963, but most of them had died of a disease yet to be identified. Bristol was sentimental about its dying white tigers – so now and again, they made for an uncomplicated, effective bit of weekend copy.

So Patrick did as instructed. He picked up the phone and – after some waiting, some transferred calls, sitting at his desk making paper aeroplanes – he was put through to a zoo volunteer who might be able to help. She was a PhD student called Jane Campbell, and she sounded busy – but she agreed to meet him at noon tomorrow, by the polar bears.

That was a hot day. He'd wandered in shirt-sleeves through the ice-cream crowds, towards the fishy bleach stink of the polar bear enclosure. His dad's old briefcase hung by its long strap over one shoulder.

He found the enclosure and looked around, craned his neck, stood on tiptoes. Then he saw a young woman sitting alone on a bench, arms tightly folded and ankles crossed before her. She'd been watching him. He approached her, a little flustered, breathless in the heat.

'Is it . . .?'

She stood. She was as tall as him. Tanned. Taut muscles under the skin of her forearm. When she shook his hand, good and firm, her skin was rough as pumice.

'Jane Campbell.' She spoke like a soldier; clipped, no-nonsense, with a trace of accent he couldn't place.

He followed her through the crowds. She had a soldier's walk, too – brisk, erect.

They stopped at the tiger enclosure. Patrick had to speak up, over the noise of the punters and the low growl of the exhibits. 'So,' he said. 'Imagine I don't know anything about tigers. Why exactly are they white? Are they mutants or something?'

There were deep lines at the corners of her eyes – years of squinting in fierce sunlight. She was twenty-four, but seemed older. She'd tied her hair back in a pony tail, frizzy with split ends, like a fistful of wheat. She wore a T-shirt and jeans, Adidas trainers.

'Or something,' she said. 'True albinos have no coloration at all. But if you look closely . . .'

He looked closely. The pale tigers were circling on lazy, padding paws; they braided slowly through one another, like cats against chair legs.

'. . . you can see they have blue eyes. And the stripes are chocolatey. So what you're looking at is chinchilla albinism.'

'Spell, please?'

She spelled.

'And how long have you been working with animals?'

She turned away from the tigers. Stood in the English sun, with the English crowds behind her. She didn't belong there, and Patrick remembered that he didn't belong there either. He thought of sitting near the docks, kicking his legs, watching the ships cast off.

She said, 'Why?'

'Background,' he said. 'For the story.'

But it wasn't.

He took her to a pub on King Street, the Llandoger Trow. In the Llandoger, Daniel Defoe met Alexander Selkirk, whom he later recreated as Robinson Crusoe. And it was in the Llandoger – fictionalized as the Admiral Benbow – that Jim Hawkins unlocked Billy Bones's chest, thus discovering a fateful map of Treasure Island. The Llandoger was part of the mythology that clustered and barnacled to this city, these docks.

Patrick had read *Treasure Island* many times. He'd grown up reading such stories – and *Bulldog Drummond* and *Biggles* and *Doc Savage*, too. A child, he dreamed of going to sea – working a passage to the West Indies, or to South America – an innocent among roustabouts and criminals, but a quick learner and a canny fighter.

Instead, he was a junior reporter who wore curly hair longer and shaggier than fashionable young men wore it in 1979 – partly to hide the hoop of gold earring punched through his left earlobe. He wore a navy-blue suit with narrow lapels and carried his dad's old briefcase, brass buckled and scuffed.

And he drank in this pub, which had been bombed by the

Germans, then turned into a Berni Inn. It was itself again, now, though. It had been rescued from the twentieth century.

He bought her a pint of cloudy cider and set it down on the table. Then he set down his Dictaphone and pressed RECORD.

Their eyes locked. Hers narrowed, playfully.

He looked away, at his reporter's notebook; spiral bound. Blank. A biro alongside it, chewed at the end.

He said, 'So. Back to basics. Where did you grow up?'

'Good question.' She leaned back in her chair and knitted her hands behind her head. Stretched. Then she leaned forward again.

'Nepal and Malaysia. Fiji, for a bit. But Kenya, mostly.'

'Why Kenya?'

'My dad.'

'He was Kenyan?'

'Nope. He was obsessed by the Tsavo lions.'

In surprise, Patrick spilled the head from his pint. He cursed and lifted his Dictaphone from the wet. He passed it to Jane, then hurried to the bar for a cloth to mop up the pooling bitter.

She said, 'Are you quite done?' and he nodded meekly, cloth in hand. Jane deposited the Dictaphone back on the table, shining now with drying loops and smears, while Patrick took the cloth back to the bar.

He knew all about the Tsavo lions. He'd read and re-read a book about them, rooted out from a junk shop in Merthyr Tydfil. In 1898, two lions had killed – and sometimes eaten – one hundred and forty men retained by the British East India Company to build a railway bridge. The lions were eerily prodigious predators. Many thought them agents of supernatural vengeance.

And now, before Patrick could think to restrain himself, he rattled off aloud the first passage of that musty, remembered old book:

'*It was towards noon on March the first, 1898, that I first found myself entering the narrow and somewhat dangerous harbour of Mombasa, on the east coast of Africa . . .*'

Reciting it evoked sense memories, of being trapped in the wrong era, in the wrong country: longing to travel backwards in time, across oceans.

And now he was embarrassed, to hunger like a child for the kind of adventure this young woman took for granted. Her life was different, bigger than his.

He wanted a bigger life, too. And thinking it, he blushed. She saw, and acknowledged his discomfort with a tiny candle-flicker at the edge of her lips. 'They're strange-looking beasts,' she said. 'Huge things. Much bigger than normal lions. Longer. And they've got no mane.'

She sipped cider.

'My dad's had a lifetime of obsessions,' she told him. 'The Tsavo lions are just the latest and the longest. So far.'

To be close to the lions' descendants her father – Jock – had acquired a facsimile Georgian manor, erected years before by some nostalgic expatriate. Two years later, he owned and was running a safari park. He named it 'Lion Manor'. And that was where, since she was twelve, Jane had grown up.

A number of famous people had stayed at Lion Manor, but Jane couldn't remember their names. There'd been an American news anchor, some English actors. Perhaps a James Bond.

Patrick drank off his bitter and set down his glass. Then he turned off the Dictaphone.

She said, 'Enough?'

He said, 'Of course not.'

*

Saturday night, he went to dinner at her Redland flat. The walls were hung with tie-dye wraps and cheap Hindu trinkets; they belonged to Jane's flatmate, a woman for whom time had evidently stopped when the Beatles split up.

Later, they went for a walk.

On the street, Jane took his arm. The night-time breeze, summer scented with diesel, blew in her hair. He'd known her for a thousand years. They'd been lovers, spouses, parents, in a previous life.

It was dark. The streets were all but deserted. They walked up to Clifton Downs, an area of high open grassland that overlooked the city. Bristolians would speak – wonderfully, he thought – of going *up the Downs*.

On one side, the Downs plunged into the craggy fissure of the Avon Gorge. A suspension bridge had been strung across it, hung with fairylights like dew on a web.

Here, they were close to the zoo. If they were lucky, they might hear the low rumble of the white tigers, growling.

They stopped and faced each other. They were a little drunk.

Patrick said, 'How long will you stay?'

'Not long.'

He blinked it away. He wished he hadn't met her yet, that she was still in his future, instead of receding already into the past.

He wanted to reach out and grab her, fold her into him. But

instead, he worked his hands into his pockets and blew the fringe from his eyes.

She reached out. Touched his brow.

'All those curls.'

He needed to piss. There was nowhere to go but the bushes, and that was no good. You couldn't piss in front of a woman before you'd kissed her; not if you *wanted* to kiss her.

'So what, exactly, takes you back to Africa?'

She crossed her arms and kicked at the grass. 'Well, most female field-workers are primatologists. Actually, it's the only research field where women outnumber men.'

He nodded and frowned, wanting to look interested, needing to piss.

'These women, they're brilliant. They spend years watching the interaction of chimps, orangs, gorillas. But the data, the long-term observation, it doesn't seem to be the point. It just makes for good publicity – these good-looking white women devoting themselves to their apes. And there's a kind of racist undercurrent to it, a sex thing. It pisses me off, actually.'

'So what are you studying?'

'Hyenas.'

'As in laughing?'

'As in clitorises.' She considered him sideways.

He said, 'So what is it, with hyenas and their clitorises?'

'She's got this huge clitoris. I mean, it's *enormous* – a real schlong – at least as long as the male's. And she can erect it *at will*. Imagine that.'

'Imagine.'

'And she's got a sack of fibrous tissue that dangles down – y'know, *there*.' She nodded vaguely at his crotch; he erupted inside like an upended snowglobe. 'It looks like, it *feels* like, testicles.'

'Fibrous tissue?' He thought about it. 'Why?'

She clapped her hands. Someone – a stage-hand – had turned the arc-lights on behind her eyes.

'Nobody knows! Not for sure. They're used in greeting ceremonies. A hyena erects its dick or its clitoris – it's difficult to tell which is which, even up close – and they have a good old sniff and a good old lick.'

'For some reason, I was unaware of this.'

'Most people are. But they shouldn't be, don't you think?'

'Oh, definitely not.'

So they stood there, knowing it, until he muttered, 'No wonder they laugh.'

She nudged him with her elbow – it was sharp, and she was strong. And then Patrick said, 'Excuse me,' and walked off to piss in the bushes; it was probably okay to piss in front of a woman who'd said *clitoris*, and *dick* and *testicles,* and *schlong.*

She stood with her back to him, unembarrassed, rocking on the balls of her feet, humming a tune he didn't recognize and looking at the shining bridge, until he was finished. And then she unbuttoned her jeans and went for a piss too. She squatted in the bushes; the epicentre of a hiss, a rising cloud of steam, a whisper of relief.

*

On the afternoon of New Year's Eve, they went for a walk in the Mendips, a range of limestone hills south of the city.

They wore bright kagouls and hiked through a low, milky mist to the flat summit of Beacon Batch, carpeted in damp heather, and set down by the cairn. Patrick had a flask of tea in his knapsack, and they passed it between them. He told her about the ancient barrows and forts littered around the grasslands below – the burial places of forgotten kings. He pointed to where Weston super Mare would be, were it not so foggy.

He knew she wouldn't care about Weston super Mare; who would? But he wanted to show her things about England she didn't know.

In his pocket, he had tickets to that year's pantomime at the Bristol Hippodrome. It was *Babes in the Wood,* starring Jim Davidson and the Krankies.

Patrick believed Pantomime to be a window onto his nation's soul; he was explaining this as she passed him back the tea and said, 'I'm pregnant, by the way.'

He jerked his head – shocked and birdlike – to look at her. She lurched away, as if to avoid a head-butt.

'Sorry?'

She excavated a pack of barley sugars from her kagoul pocket, popped one into her mouth and crunched it to shrapnel. 'I'm keeping it. And blah blah blah.'

'What about your field study?'

'No change. I leave in February.'

There was a noise in his head like a vacuum cleaner.

'You're having the baby in *Africa*?'

'People do.'

He laughed out loud, because she was better than him. It was a glorious feeling. Liberating and exhilarating. She finished her barley sugar, pleased.

He said, 'You're unbelievable.'

'If I want a baby, I'll have one.'

'Do you want one?'

She hugged her knees. 'Actually.'

'Wow.'

She touched the back of his hand. 'This isn't your problem.'

'Is it a problem?'

'I don't know. Is it a problem?'

'I don't think so. I don't think it's a problem.'

They had their backs to the cold stone of the cairn; England was spread below them.

He thought about Jane's bedroom.

Its walls were bare, and she had thrown away the dank old carpet to expose the floorboards. There were bookshelves, an ugly Oxfam table on which sat a beautiful, beetle-green Underwood typewriter.

And there was an old trunk. It had belonged to Jock's father; it was a dead man's chest, manufactured in 1919 by Oshkosh of Wisconsin, and it was scaly with travel stickers. Patrick liked to sit on her messy bed and stare at them; they were sun-faded and half-peeled – *Hotel Richemond, Genève. Cook's Nile Service. Saigon Palace Hotel. Cunard White Star Lines Cruises. Train-Bleu.*

In Patrick's favourite adventure stories, there was always a sidekick. And now he knew that's what he was – not Alan Breck Stuart but David Balfour; not Holmes but Watson. It was heady, finally to learn this. Sidekicks never instigated adventures. They were drawn into them. And here was his; after all those years of waiting.

They'd climbed this hill together in silence. Jane had worn a secret on her face which Patrick pretended not to notice, it was a happy look and he'd been happy too, to think he might be the cause of it.

But now he knew what she'd really been thinking. Before they even reached the foot of the hill, Jane had known that he'd go with her, to Africa.

*

Charlie and Jo were born in Kenya.

They were fine years. Patrick used the Underwood to type Jane's research notes, and his unpublished adventure novels. And when the kids were old enough, he home-schooled them.

At first, he spent time chasing down books which followed the English curriculum – buying them from the English schools in Kenya, ordering them in from London. Then he gave up and made up their education as he went along. It was a good way to teach, and a good way to learn: Jo and Charlie spent time with each other, with their parents, and with all the people around them; and everyone they met contributed in some way to their schooling – the PhDs from Europe and America, the Kenyan men and women who worked with them.

Patrick was proud of his kids, and proud of the life they were leading. He liked to watch his barefoot son kick round a soccer ball with barefoot black boys and ginger-bearded zoologists – and he liked to sit with his daughter, outside, and watch the vast and uninterrupted night sky.

In 1984, Jane secured funding to study the Tsavo lions. Patrick suspected she did it to please her father, but he said nothing, and went with her.

But the post didn't last long, because Jane, Patrick and the kids had to move to Lion Manor.

Jane's father had been leading tourists on horseback bush tour when he suffered a God-almighty stroke and died at the edge of a dried-out water-hole, propped by a panicking tourist against a fever tree.

Lion Manor was Jane's inheritance; they stayed for three years, preparing it for sale. They leased one of the Manor's several islands to a chimpanzee rescue charity, then sold the Safari Park as a going concern and, eager to be free, spent the money part-funding a palaeo-anthropological dig on the coast of Kenya. But all the dig proved was their inability to handle finance. And so, eleven years after leaving, they returned to Britain.

By now, Jane had acquired a small reputation for unusual field projects, which was how she secured a position studying a colony of Tuatara living in freakish isolation off the North Welsh coast. Tuatara were a lizard species unique to New Zealand. Nobody had the first idea how they'd come to be on the wrong side of the world.

The family lived in a coastal, whitewashed cottage. Patrick loved to be near the sea, and at least Wales wasn't England. The kids went to the local school. In spring and summer, they walked or cycled. In winter, he drove them in the old VW estate – leprous with Greenpeace and WWF and surfing decals, rusted round the wheel-rims, orange as a lollipop.

Jo wanted to be an astronaut, and because astronauts had to be fit, she and Patrick went on after-school rambles and beachfront sprints.

Patrick kept house, wrote books, sent them to publishers, kept the rejections. He grew vegetables. He compiled and typed-up Jane's notes, first with the old Underwood, then with a computer bought second-hand from the local Classifieds. He kept on top of Jane's correspondence. He travelled to local libraries, historical societies, document collections, searching out mention of some local traveller's return from New Zealand with a basket of exotic lizards. But he found nothing.

While they were living at this very cottage, in something not far from poverty, Jane took a call from a man called Bob Todd.

Todd worked for a West Country safari park that had just been taken over – and he knew what Jane had achieved, turning round Lion Manor. So he drove his shiny Rover all the way to the little whitewashed cottage on the Welsh coast, just to meet her. Bob Todd was just about as keen as mustard.

He and Jane sat in the little kitchen and talked. Bob Todd showed her a folder, full of glossy photographs and bullet points. And he offered her a proper job, with hours and a salary and sick leave and holiday entitlement – her first, ever. Then Bob Todd drove away again, with a cheery toot of his horn.

Jane took the job. They needed the money; it wouldn't be for long.

Patrick wanted to go back to Africa. He missed the light. He wanted to write a novel about pirates. Instead, they moved to Bath, where the light came in weaker, dissipated, at an English slant, and it was impossible for him to write much of anything.

*

Bob Todd had permitted a fly-on-the-wall documentary crew to film the park's management takeover: they'd record the slumberous boardroom combat, the behind-the-scenes crises, the ear-tugging, the glance-averting.

The Park was a moderate hit, at best; four half-hour episodes tucked away on BBC 2. But Jane was bigger than it. Viewers liked her; they liked her unsentimental devotion to her animals, and they liked her khaki shorts and Caterpillar boots.

In episode four, during a marketing meeting, the camera lingered on her face as she struggled with her contempt. All around her, fat men with five o'clock shadows and cufflinks pronounced balderdash and bullshit, their nervous eyes flitting sideways to the single recording lens.

The episode faded out on that same face, stoic as the vet administered a lethal injection to a sick lion. Jane's jaw was clamped and her eyes didn't waver from the table. Intended as an arch editorial comment on the state of the safari park, this was the moment that made her television career.

That Christmas, she appeared in a popular woman's magazine – the kind you buy at the supermarket checkout. She was wearing a party dress, smiling for the camera. *TV's Jane Bowman says* LOOK AT ME NOW! She was laughing and twirling; showing some leg, some teeth.

She said to Patrick, 'Why not?'

'Why not?' said Patrick.

In 1991, she was invited by *The Park*'s producer to co-present a series of wildlife documentaries. The producer's name was Richard.

Jane resigned her post at the safari park; it was doomed anyway. She said, 'What the hell.'

'What the hell,' said Patrick.

So he and the kids remained in cultured, decorous Bath while Jane and Richard – and his two-man crew – went to Morocco,

Gibraltar, Spain, Greece, Turkey, filming hungry donkeys, sad-eyed spider-monkeys, traumatized baby chimps – and Koukla the bear.

Jane and Richard had the kind of on-screen rapport that cannot be faked. They wandered, side by side, affecting to ignore the camera. It was called *chemistry*; the show was called *Zoo Under-cover*, and it was a big hit.

More was to come.

3

Three years later, because Jane's celebrity had given rise to some difficulty in their marriage, they decided on the move to Monkeyland. This was 1995. They wondered how to tell the kids.

At thirteen, Jo was conscientious, scruffy, unpopular and by far the tallest girl in her year, or the year above that, or the year above that. She was skinny and knobby, her long body full of corners, and she had sulky eyes and big feet – that, and a dandelion clock of frizzy hair.

At ten years old, she had exceeded Patrick's ability to teach her. Now she spent time showing him patterns and symmetries and mysteries.

'Take a river, right? Any river.'

He imagined a river.

'Now take a point, any point. And measure along the curves of the river until you meet the sea. Okay?'

Cunningly, he said, 'But where ex*a*ctly *does* a river meet the sea?'

'That's an arbitrary decision. Go on – pick a point.'

'Done it.'

'Okay. Now – starting from the same point, draw a straight line to the sea.'

'Yup.'

'Now, divide the second number by the first. And what do you get?'

'I don't know.'

'Pi!'

'No!'

'Yes!'

He sat back in the chair. 'How?'

'Nobody knows!'

Like much that interested her, this seemed more than a mystery – it hummed with the magical. It re-entered Patrick's mind when he found himself walking beside the river. But it was slippery as a fish, too. He understood it for a moment, and then it was gone.

The walls of Jo's room were hung with clippings of crew-cut men in black and white, smiling out of unhelmeted space-suits with neckpieces wide as jam jars. Patrick could name Yuri Gagarin, Neil Armstrong, perhaps Buzz Aldrin – but there were many more. The crew of the Space Shuttle *Challenger*, smiling in blue jumpsuits, ready to die.

And there was a long poster mapping out the solar system as a neat arrangement of planets; Patrick had bought it for her. Its scale, she told him, even as she Blu-Tacked it to the wall, was *greatly misleading*.

There were pictures taken by the Hubble Space telescope; a poster of Albert Einstein sticking out his tongue. Books on the birth of the universe, the formation of stars, the theory of relativity, and wormholes and black holes.

On clear nights, she pointed to the stars with a twiggy finger and named them for him. He was hypnotized by her wonder.

One night, she informed him that he wasn't standing on the surface of the planet looking up, but hanging off the planet like a bat; looking down into a limitless abyss.

Overcome with a sudden and terrible vertigo, he reached for Jo's hand. He sat heavily in the grass. He looked at his knees because he was scared, for a moment, to look up; she'd turned looking up into looking down.

Up the downs, he thought.

Patrick and Jane argued about Jo. Jane won: Jo was thirteen. Old enough to be boarder.

She could come home at weekends and holidays. Compared to being in low Earth orbit, boarding school would be a doddle.

Jo said, 'Whatever. Excellent,' and Patrick worried she wouldn't miss them; that he and Jane were superannuated curiosities, like clunky old computers – admirable in context, but laughable too, for their limitations and design flaws.

So Jo didn't come to Devon, and neither did Charlie: Charlie didn't want to go *anywhere,* or do anything but see his friends. They smoked dope round each other's houses, went to Bath pubs and nightclubs.

Patrick supposed he should be happy that Charlie's friends were unthreatening and knowable. But he wasn't; it irritated the crap out of him.

Charlie took a job on a Bristol building site, hauling into skips half-bricks and broken tiles, stained old toilets, useless piping. He wore a baseball cap to keep the hair from his face. He came home in the back of a white van, and he refused to come to Devon.

'I'm just sick of moving.'

Patrick said: 'I thought you hated Bath.'

But Charlie's world had contracted to a few friends' houses, a building site, half a dozen pubs, a few nightclubs – and the ghost of a girl on a bridge.

Patrick had seen them together, once; an early summer evening, not long before.

He was sitting outside the pub, surrounded by much younger people, nursing his third or fourth pint and reading *The Man in the Iron Mask*. And over the road, heading up from Pulteney weir, Charlie passed by. He was with the girl. She was tall, skinny, bleached blonde, in army boots and ripped jeans.

Patrick laid down his book and watched them, greatly moved by something in his son's countenance.

They were *sixteen*, this boy and this girl, and it was *summer*. Bath was pink-washed in the sunset, and they were headed to a nightclub, where they would listen to loud music and maybe dance, and spend time with their friends, and maybe have sex and wake hungover and happy. And they were wasting it, walking with solemn distance between them.

The girl paused and dug out a pack of cigarettes – a green pack, menthols – and offered one to his boy.

Charlie took it, and offered the girl a light. She tilted her head, brushed aside her limp fringe and stooped to the flame. And as she did, Charlie took a secret, heartbroken scent of her.

Charlie closed his eyes. His delicate eyelids. His girlish lashes.

Then the girl straightened, puffing, and they walked on together, without exchanging a word

And now Charlie packed his stuff – some clothes, some records, not much else – and left, to live in a squat.

It would be a genteel kind of squat, Patrick supposed; it was in Bath.

Early autumn 1995, they moved to Monkeyland.

*

Biddie Powys's old house was big, ramshackle, higgledy as ginger-bread – it would've been too big, even filled with the noisy motion of the four of them. Now it drummed out its emptiness like a slow-beating heart. Patrick and Jane had never lived together without children.

On a cool September night, they waded out into the wild acre behind the house. Jane was barefoot, barelegged in his parka.

He unzipped the parka and she lay down and they fucked in a flattened patch of grass, the ice-twinkling universe upended above them.

*

Richard's two-man camera crew was there to record the first, faltering days at Monkeyland – the strained meetings, the worried staff, the flexing stress commas at the corners of Jane's mouth.

They took many shots of Patrick, in his frayed sweater, stirring mugs of milky tea.

Patrick liked the camera crew – Sound Mick and Camra Dave. They were disinterested and professional and jovial; and they told sniggering jokes about Richard, about his perfect hair, his clothes, his background as a quiz-show presenter. They made Patrick snicker, like a schoolboy at a resented teacher.

Sometimes, Patrick joined them as they ranged Monkeyland, collecting shots to portray it in the bleakest possible light. They called it *Going Ukrainian*. They told Patrick that Going Ukrainian had never been such a doddle, and clapped him fraternally on the back.

They shot lonely chimps wandering through cold compounds, wall-eyed gibbons and sad-eyed orangs, munching away. The empty cafeteria, the windblown gift shop. And just the sheeting, grey rain, blowing across the deserted public spaces. The picnic area, the adventure playground.

Patrick stood with them on a grassy mound that overlooked the Bachelor Group, watching as they filmed weather billowing in from the west, soaking the skinny, miserable donkeys.

He laced his hands behind his head and said, 'Fucking hell.'

Camra Dave shifted the unit on his shoulder.

He said, 'I don't envy you, mate.'

Patrick slept six hours a night and woke energized and refreshed. Sometimes in the morning, he did an hour's writing. More often, he went out; he fished, did some running, pounding along muddy tracks in shorts and hooded top. His suburban headaches cleared up.

Then he drove over to Monkeyland and the despondency returned like toothache.

He began every morning with a staff meeting. The staff were unhappy; they feared for their jobs. Patrick feared for their jobs too. He, Jane and the senior keepers spent many hours in planning

meetings – detailing the cost and logistics of refitting the enclosures; discussing how to enrich the chimps' environment without
bankrupting the operation.

The Head Keeper was Harriet. She was from London. She called
moving to Monkeyland a *lifestyle choice*, and she squinted one eye
balefully at Patrick when she said it, as if anticipating a challenge.

Harriet was short, five foot one in her DMs, thirty-five, blonde,
florid, and good at being Head Keeper. She knew what she was
doing, and Patrick didn't. And yet he was her boss. The first time
he met her, he made a joke about her job title. 'You're the Head
Keeper? Great! Where do you keep the heads?'

She did not respond, and now Patrick was slightly scared of her.

*

Sam had been Charlie's girlfriend for three months.

She was American, from Washington DC, and she'd been living
in England for three years. So she understood what it was like,
to speak the same language but not quite understand the jokes – to
miss the undercurrent of astute cultural reference: quips about TV
shows he'd never seen and songs he'd never heard, because he'd
been living in Lion Manor, or in some research camp, or on the
north coast of fucking Wales.

She was older than him – eighteen. And they liked the same
music. Not just the same bands, or the same albums, but the same
songs. Sometimes, they just sat in her room, not moving or
speaking; just hugging their knees, listening to the songs.

Now she was going out with a bloke called Robin, who was the
singer in a band called Quadrophobia.

The first band Charlie liked – the first band he'd been in a position to like – was Nirvana. He was still wearing the checked shirts, the tired jeans, the haphazardly laced, fucked-up old Chuck Taylors. But already, those clothes were out of time.

In the squat were some Goths and a couple of misplaced hippies; but Goths and hippies, like cockroaches, would probably survive a nuclear war. Mostly, everyone was listening to different stuff now. All of it was English – Pulp, Blur, Elastica. It was possible to go on a pub crawl, drink one pint in each, and hear nothing on the various jukeboxes but Oasis.

People scoffed at the John Major's desperate evocation of a counterfeit England – a country of long shadows on country grounds, warm beer, old maids bicycling to Holy Communion. It was Tory sentimentalism, reactionary floundering – because a change was coming.

But everyone Charlie knew was indulging in the same phoney patriotism. They said it was ironic, but it didn't *feel* ironic, not in the late summer of 1995, when people in the pubs and clubs in their Fred Perrys and Adidas were pogo-ing and swaggering home together, football-chanting 'Some Might Say' or 'Champagne Supernova'.

Charlie couldn't yearn for a lie he'd never been raised to cherish – Patrick was always muttering about how much he loathed England. And anyway, Kurt Cobain had schooled him in how to despise such dangerous fables.

But – of course – Kurt was dead. He put a shotgun to his beautiful face, because he couldn't stand it any more.

*

Most weekends, Quadrophobia was playing a shitty support slot in some London pay-to-play toilet; there was talk of them signing to Island Records. But, on occasion, Sam and Robin could still be observed at their old habitats, like exotic birds on dreary salt flats.

Entering any pub, any nightclub, Charlie scanned the crowd looking for her, and his insides always dropped away when she wasn't there. He'd spend another evening drinking and talking; one eye always on the door. He didn't want to see her, and he didn't want to speak to her – but he phoned her three times a night, from the call box on the corner. Usually he hung up when someone, anyone, answered. Then he dialled again.

Other nights, he walked past her house. You couldn't see her bedroom window from the road; it was round the back, over-looking the long garden. But he walked past anyway; went miles out of his way, alone, at night, to brush the furthest edge of her force-field.

And one night, in December, Charlie saw her. She'd changed. She wore very new trainers and smart, tight, indigo jeans. Her hair was much shorter – an asymmetric bob that hung over one eye, like Twiggy. She was wearing make-up.

Robin was there, too. He wore hair like John Lennon and circular sunglasses with blue lenses. He walked with an affected proletarian swagger; three years before, he'd been playing prop forward in the university's first fifteen. People crowded round him because he was the singer in a band that might get signed, that might be on *Top of the Pops*.

He stood with his beefy arm around Sam. She dug him with a bony hip.

Charlie had always been careful not to be *clingy*. He knew girls hated that. And there she was, clinging away, nuzzling Robin's neck and laughing too loudly at his boorish jokes. And when she looked away to light a cigarette, her face became sad.

Charlie couldn't bear to look at her. He ignored her.

He went to get a drink, a fiver clutched like a flower in his skinny fist. And Sam didn't look at him – not even a furtive, side-long glance in the long mirror that ran behind the bar. Charlie knew, because he kept checking.

In the toilets, he scored some speed and stirred the wormwood powder into the last quarter of his pint. Drank it down.

Back in the noisy club, Jake said, 'Mate, she's not worth it.'

Jake was Charlie's best mate. They lived in the squat together. Like almost everyone else in the club, Jake had recently changed the way he dressed. He wore a crushed velvet smoking jacket and lank hair and Chelsea boots and heavy-rimmed geek glasses. But Jake was overweight, always had been. He was squashed and shoved and rolled into his clothes, and the effect of all this effort was comical, and tragic.

Charlie glanced over again, and saw her. He wanted more than it seemed possible for it to be six months ago.

His hands were shaking.

He said, 'I'm all right, mate. I'm fine.'

The music was very loud. It was battering his ears; it seemed to be inside him. Sweat ran into his eyes. The club was small and dark. Sam and Robin were in the far corner, being badgered by sycophants.

Sam always loathed sycophants. She'd rage at them; the

sycophants, the pseuds, the Pod People. And there she was – a Pod Person! It was like a nightmarish pantomime, where Cinderella yielded at once to a vainglorious Prince Charming. And here was Charlie, in his rags; Charlie was Buttons.

He hated being Buttons. He wanted to rescue her; to wake her with a kiss. Her eyes would open wide and clear, and she would take his hand and they would escape this place.

Charlie stood. He walked very quickly, shouldering people to one side. They veered and twisted and stopped, to watch him; all these dicks in their Oasis T-shirts, their Jarvis Cocker spectacles, their jaunty Damon Albarn fringes.

Only Sam and Robin were oblivious to the pocket of silence working its way towards them like a stormfront: a high-pressure system. They were snuggling in the corner, her hand round his waist, fingers dipped in the back pocket of his vintage Levis.

Charlie passed through their snivelling courtiers, their slimy toadies.

Seeing Charlie's face made Sam smile. She'd told him that, once: no matter how sad she was feeling, the thought of his face made her smile. But she wasn't smiling now. She stared at him like he was a smear of cancer on a glass slide.

Seeing that, seeing her disgust, Charlie started to cry. He couldn't help it.

He said, 'You fucking lying bitch.'

Two bubbles of snot popped in his nostrils. He wiped them away, and with the snotty hand he punched Robin in the face.

Robin grabbed a fistful of Charlie's hair and wrenched. Charlie lost his footing. Robin punched him three times in the ear. Charlie fell over, down among the trainers and the Dr Martens

and the Caterpillars, the fag ends and the beer residue. Robin began
to kick him.

By then, the bouncers had arrived. Three men in monkey suits
chugging pompously through the crowd.

One of them chested Robin into the far corner. Robin held out
both hands. His mouth was open; his nose was bleeding.

Two more bouncers, one white, one black, pinned Charlie to
the floor. He struggled. He was screaming about killing Robin. But
there was a knee pressed to the back of his head. His arms were
yanked up behind his back.

Then he was pulled to his feet and rushed away, past his friends,
his acquaintances, a few strangers. He thought of a cow being led
to the slaughterhouse.

And then they reached the main doors and the bouncers threw
him outside. The air hit his face, cold on the sweat. He windmilled
his arms and fell to his knees.

One of the bouncers came outside with Charlie's coat. He helped
Charlie to his feet. His face was pink and round as a Bazooka Joe,
and he wore a bleached blond flat-top.

He said, 'You all right, mate?'

Charlie brushed himself down. He had no anger for the
bouncers. Bouncers were a force of nature.

He said, 'Yeah. Yeah.'

'Fair play to you, mind,' said the bouncer. 'He's a big kiddie.'

'Yeah.'

Charlie looked at him. The bouncer's chest, big as a pigeon's,
filled his vision.

Charlie put on his coat.

The streets were jammed with people leaving clubs, couples

snogging in shop doorways, dry-humping, stooping to get into minicabs. His heart was an engine.

He walked down to Pulteney Bridge and leaned his elbows on the wall, overlooking the weir. Saturday night was happening right behind him; but he watched the water.

Now and then, someone called out, *Don't jump!* and he obligingly turned and grinned at them, raising his cigarette in salute.

He wasn't thinking about suicide, though. He was thinking about being a kid in Africa; about the people he'd met and the places he'd lived and the things he'd seen. Growing up around lions and hyenas, baboons, monkeys, jackals, wild dogs, leopards, cheetahs; and the giraffes and the duikers and the zebras. All the predators and all their prey.

He couldn't explain any of it to anyone. He thought of the wide, dusty corridors of Lion Manor, where he had run, unfettered and barefoot. His mum and dad in the mahogany office, making sense of disordered yellow paperwork.

He leaned on the wall for a long time, smoking, thinking about it; then he turned round and walked to the squat. Everyone was out, or asleep, or stoned.

He went upstairs, to his little room. He threw some clothes into a bag and weighed the bag on his shoulder. He looked at his CDs. They were too heavy to take with him. He stared at them for a long time. They were a diary. But they were only songs, and he knew they would never sound the same.

He slung the bag over his shoulder and left.

On the corner, he went to the phone box.

She answered on the second ring, like someone expecting a call. She said, 'Charlie, just leave me alone, okay?'

He said nothing.

'I mean, get over it, for God's sake.'

A big, foxy leer.

'And stop calling me. Really. It creeps me out.'

He growled, softly. That would be all she heard.

And he hung up.

The first words Sam ever spoke to him were: 'Excuse me.' She'd been squeezing past his table, to get to the bar.

And the last words she spoke to him were: 'It creeps me out.'

That was good; to know the ending. You had to know the moment when things ended. He thought of Kurt, dead on the floor of that big house – a place he should never have tried to inhabit.

Bath was deserted. Overnight, it had become another place where Charlie used to live. He felt no connection to it.

Shifting his bag on his shoulder, he left the phone box, went to a greasy spoon and ordered breakfast. Eggs and sausage, fried bread. He wasn't hungry, but it was the last fiver in his pocket. It was important that he spend it or throw it away.

By sunrise, he was hitch-hiking.

Eventually, he was picked up by a lorry bound for Exeter. He endured the same old stories about the insatiable, hitch-hiking girls the driver had fucked – none of them older than eighteen and all of them *gagging* for it. He thought of Sam; he thought of the trucker fucking her in the toilet of a filthy pub. Her long white legs locked around his hairy arse as he pounded into her; her skinny-rib T-shirt rucked above her pure little tits; his stinking hand pressed over her mouth to keep her from crying out; her teeth clamped down on his oily fingers; his greasy cock in her mouth.

Charlie was aroused and frightened. They sat in a fag-stinking fug of sex. The way the driver talked, Charlie knew he had an erection too, and that recounting stories of these imaginary girls was a kind of foreplay. When he reached Exeter, the trucker would pay some pale junkie mother to suck him off.

Charlie felt old and bitter, crippled by fetid lust.

Outside Taunton, he was picked up by a curly-haired man in a rusty old 2CV that leaned on its springs, such that Charlie sat higher than the driver. The car screamed and shuddered.

He dropped Charlie near Washford where, closer to his destination than he could endure, he waited for many hours.

It was dark by now, and surgically cold, and there were no cars. The few that actually passed did so with a wary grunt of acceleration. Charlie was working hard to look cheerful and harmless, but he looked deranged – grinning from the side of the road, jogging on the spot to keep warm and cradling his busted hand in his armpit.

His teeth were chattering and his feet were numb and there was a dull, dehydrated thump behind his eyes. His hand was tender like an abscessed molar. He wanted to lie down, sleep, never wake up.

But in the darkness close to midnight, a Mini hissed to a stop. Two blokes, on the way home from the pub. Charlie hobbled to the car, shivering.

They dropped him two miles from the house. He hated them for it. He was sick, and he *looked* it. Pale, purple round the eyes, shivering. And two miles was *nothing* to them, in their warm little car.

But he got out at the junction all the same, and thanked them, and stood there, not believing it, as they drove off.

Then he trudged down the dark lane for a long, long time. The rhythm of his footsteps entranced him, and he almost passed the house. He'd only ever seen it in a photograph.

*

Patrick opened the door – and there was his boy.

He was thin, hugging himself, babbling with cold and fever. Patrick half-carried him inside while Jane ran upstairs to draw off a hot bath. In the living room, Patrick mixed a large shot of whisky with hot water.

Charlie sat huddled on the sofa, draped in a heavy blanket like a boxer.

Jane knelt to examine his hand. She turned it round in hers. She stroked the swelling with a forefinger. Charlie yelped.

The whisky made him light-headed, then they frog-marched him into a hot bath while they got his bed ready. Neither had asked a single question.

His new room was long and narrow, into the eaves at the end of the hallway. His bed was in there, and his old bedroom furniture. It was as if he'd gone home, but home had changed shape.

The comedown and the exhaustion twisted his perception. Shadows menaced; cold patches made him shudder. It was a very draughty old house.

He wriggled under the covers, curled into a ball, and soon he was warm. He masturbated, and soon after that he was asleep.

He couldn't eat breakfast; and anyway, it hurt to grip the spoon. Jane took him to the nearest GP, and from there to casualty in Barnstaple.

Two knuckles on his punching hand were fractured. Diagnosing a punch fracture, the doctor looked down his nose like a man driving into the sun, and Charlie came home with his forearm in plaster.

Wednesday, he drove to Monkeyland with his dad.

They found the bachelors surly and bored. Knuckle-walking. Grooming. Sucking on orange halves.

Patrick said, 'So what are your plans, mate?'

Charlie huddled in his coat and walked on, down the hill, Patrick following.

They went to the A Troop. They too were sucking oranges, grooming, listless and watchful in their rotting jungle gyms.

Patrick said, 'It looks bad. Everything looks bad, in winter. But we'll make it better.'

One of the chimps was down by the moat, washing off an apple quarter.

Patrick said, 'That's Rue.'

She was slow and arthritic, dignified with it. Feeling their scrutiny, she raised herself erect on bandy legs. Her coat was grey-flecked and her beard was white, and her eyes, beneath heavy ridges, were moist and chestnut.

Charlie said, 'I could work here. For like a year or something. Get my head together.'

Patrick hadn't known that kids still got their head together. He felt closer to his son, and farther away.

He said, 'You'll be shovelling monkey shit. Cutting up oranges. All that.'

Charlie nodded. Triangular face pale beneath his long, dark hair.

*

He started before the plaster was off. There he was, in his nylon anorak and his Wellingtons, his hair tied back. Cutting up food, dumping it in tin buckets, carrying it to the enclosures; distributing it for the chimps to forage.

When they saw him coming, the chimps whooped and slapped the floor. Charlie smiled. To a chimp, a smile could be a sign of fear. But it could be a sign of happiness too.

Rue approached him and squatted. Charlie gave her half a pear. She extended a slow hand and took it, clasped it to her chest.

When Charlie was done feeding the group, Rue loped up and closed a leathery hand around his spindly wrist. She pursed her lips. Made quick, soft, appeasing vocalizations.

Charlie put down his bucket. He hunkered down. And, with great deliberation, Rue began to groom him.

*

And actually, Jo *didn't* like the school, and she *did* miss her mum and dad.

She didn't like getting up in the morning, surrounded by stinky people; she didn't like girls borrowing her tampons (as if a tampon could ever be *borrowed)*. She hated the lack of privacy.

Separately, most of the girls and most of the teachers were all right. But en masse, she disliked and feared them.

She worked hard at athletics and netball and hockey, knowing it was important for an astronaut to be physically fit. She ran track at all possible angles, like an emu with big, flapping feet. It wasn't tenacity she lacked, or – obviously – the ability to calculate the elliptical trajectory of a descending sphere. The odd thing was, she had problems with concentration.

Usually, she found it easy to concentrate. But on the sports field, she became unfocused. Once, suddenly diverted by the rolling, fractal edge of a white cloud in a blue sky, she took a hockey stick in the guts. She'd seen the cloud for what it was; a large, sky-sailing agglomeration of water vapour.

She was lucky the stick hit her in the belly and not the head, where it might have done some real damage. But it still made her throw up, and she still had to be carried off the pitch.

Now, she only got to go home at weekends, and it wasn't even home, not really; it was just her mum and dad's new house in Devon. But a family bathroom, even an old-fashioned and dirty one, had never felt so private. At the Higgledy House, she slept late and had long baths and made wholegrain toast with honey and ate it while lying on the bed with the curtains open, listening to the sea and the radio, and reading.

She missed Charlie, and didn't know why; for a long time now, they'd barely acknowledged each other's existence. They rarely spoke, or ate together, because usually Charlie was out somewhere, smoking weed in some spotty dork's bedroom.

When they lived in Bath, they rarely found themselves in the same room at the same time. And when they did, Charlie affected a mostly benign indifference. But once, after one of his friends – Jake – made some cruel joke about the state of Jo's teeth, Charlie giggled uncomfortably, and moved the conversation sideways. He looked away, when Jo looked at him.

And two days later, Charlie came home with a present for her.

'What is it?'

'Open it and see.'

It was a CD called *Nevermind*. Its cover showed a naked baby boy swimming underwater, apparently in pursuit of a floating dollar note.

Jo had no interest in Nirvana, who were a noisy, smelly boys' group, but she accepted the gift with a swell of gratitude. She knew that, for whatever reason, *Nevermind* was the most important thing in Charlie's life. Charlie went to *Nevermind* like the pious went to the Bible; Charlie went to *Nevermind* like Jo went to the night sky. Giving her this copy, he was giving her the best thing he could imagine.

Pressing it, ineptly wrapped, into her hand, he was bumbling and shy, and she was proud of him. She felt the beginning of tears, but didn't show it.

What she did do was thank him, and ask Patrick if they could play her new CD on the old boom-box in the kitchen; neutral ground.

They sat at the kitchen table while Charlie told her what *Nevermind* meant. He pressed *pause* to explain the significance of a particular lyric or image –

Monkey see, monkey do. I'd rather be dead than cool.

Not since he was a blond-haired child, her adored big brother, had Jo seen his eyes shine like that – and that was a long, long time ago, in Africa.

It hadn't occurred to her that Charlie's absence could make this new home feel so strange, but it had. It was a variable, one of those surprise vectors that can sneak up behind you, if you're not careful, upsetting an entire equation.

She wished she lived there, with Patrick and Jane. She wished they all lived together. But they didn't.

Oh well, whatever. Never mind.

*

Patrick came to pick her up and drive her home for the Christmas holidays. She was excited, to be spending three weeks with them. She dumped her bag on the back seat and belted herself in.

'Home, James, and don't spare the horses.'

Pulling away, Patrick said, 'How many ears does Captain Kirk have?'

'I don't know. How many ears *does* Captain Kirk have?'

'Three. A left ear, a right ear – and a final, front ear.'

She pinched his arm. It was an old joke, because Jo liked *Star Trek*.

On the way, Patrick flicked the indicator lever, paused at a junction, turned, and said, 'Did you know Charlie's back?'

'What? For Christmas?'

'For good, apparently.'

Jo turned cold with betrayal and fury. Now she was the only Bowman not to live at the draughty old house, a few miles from Monkeyland.

Patrick told Jo how well Charlie was doing, how much he was enjoying his new job. He looked at her sideways, hands on the steering wheel.

'What's the matter?'

'Nothing.'

She folded her arms, because the car was always cold. Patrick had never got round to having the heater fixed. He drove with woolly gloves on, the kind with the fingers cut out of them.

She felt bad when they arrived at the Higgledy House, because Charlie was waiting there to greet her. He ambled over and took her bags.

He said, 'I like how you took the best room.'

'Best room for the best person,' she said back, but her heart wasn't in it. She felt sick. She followed Charlie inside.

And then, about two days later, Jane drove her all the way back to Bath, to go Christmas shopping. It was because she knew the shops there; it would be easier. Jane was a bad, impatient shopper.

They wandered round Bath, cold in the crowds. Before they'd bought a thing, Jane took her daughter for a cup of tea and a jam doughnut.

The café was full of Christmas shoppers, their carrier bags spreading like compost on the wet floor. Jo and Jane took a seat in the far corner, near the fire exit. The teapots were those stupid metal ones: Jane poured, and spilled tea over the table.

Jane took some Handie Andies from her bag and dabbed at the wet patch, then scrunched up the tissues and dumped them in the ashtray. They unfolded in jerks, like flowers blooming in time-lapse.

Jane said, 'What's so funny?'

'Nothing.'

Jane lifted the teapot and looked underneath it; Jo didn't know why. Then she said, 'It's so lovely, having you home.'

Jo smiled, although she wanted to cry. She remembered lying in a cot, or something like a cot, looking at high, thin clouds. Birds slow-circling in the sky. And her mother's celestial face, bright as the bright sun. The sandbar creases in her forehead, etched there by worry and love.

Now she was saying, 'So how's school?'

Jo poured milk into her tea. She stirred. Watched a galaxy revolve. The Milky Way.

'You're not enjoying it, are you?'

Jo was still stirring, watching the vortex; imagining it was a tornado seen from low Earth orbit.

'Not really.'

'Why didn't you say?'

'I didn't think you wanted me to.'

Jane pressed her lips together, and Jo saw that she was working hard not to cry. She took the wet Handie Andies from the ashtray and began, meticulously, to rip them into scraps.

'Do you want to come home?'

'Yes.'

'I mean, to live.'

'Yes!'

Jane encased Jo's hands in her own.

'Come home, then,' she said, 'silly fool,' and Jo did.

4

Every time Jo saw Monkeyland, it looked worse – ramshackle and peeling, like a wintry ghost-town inhabited by clusters of baffled Cro-Magnons.

She looked around. 'Wow,' she said.

There were no paying visitors, just men in hard-hats, pushing wheelbarrows, carrying bricks, lengths of thick rope, fireman's hose, chains, timber, mugs of tea and cigarettes.

The A Troup were being confined to quarters while the contractors erected their new jungle gym. Their enclosure was built into a natural slope, so the far side was slightly elevated. And up there, Jo saw Patrick and Meredith. They had their arms folded and they were looking down at the jungle gym, nodding like boys pretending to be men in deep agreement.

Meredith had a long face and little rimless glasses. He wore his hair in a pony tail, and a Peruvian waistcoat under his workman's kagoul. He was an architect who'd worked in zoos all over the world. He'd been friends with Jo's parents for a long time.

Patrick looked over at Jo and waved. Then he tapped Meredith's shoulder and pointed, and Meredith grinned and waved, too.

Jo liked Meredith. Once, when he was staying with them in Bath – he was doing some work for the safari park – she had asked him to explain his project. He told her to wait, went to get his blueprints and when he came back, he unrolled them on the kitchen table and spoke to her for more than an hour. He explained the nature of the contract, the decisions he'd taken and why, the cost of materials and labour. He taught her some interesting words that, so far, had proved completely useless – words like *imbrex* and *tegula*.

But he'd used these words in a broader context – to show that zoos didn't have to be pretty, or noble. What they had to be was *brute-proof*. And *that* term had come in useful many times.

She hadn't seen Meredith since, so now she wandered up the slope, towards him and Patrick.

Meredith said, 'Hello, chicken.'

'Hello.'

'Back from school, then.'

'Yes.' She pointed into the compound. 'Did you do this one?'

'I had a hand in it, yeah.'

'Is it brute-proof?'

The new jungle gym was a series of higgledy-piggledy walkways and gangplanks and tyres swinging on heavy chains. It was designed, she knew, to maximize what Meredith called *environmental stimulation*.

Wild chimps had large territories to roam and borders to patrol. Their habitat changed, day by day and season by season. But few of these chimps had even glimpsed a rainforest, that alien, humid universe of fruiting trees and termites and occasional monkey meat.

Monkeyland was an unnatural environment, but it was intended as a sanctuary, an asylum, a place where they could behave like real chimpanzees – even though real chimpanzees isn't quite what they were any more, except genetically. So Jo felt weirdly happy, watching the jungle gym going up, because it was people putting right bad things done by other people.

Content, she mumbled goodbye and walked down the slope.

Richard was at the lower end of the compound, interviewing Steve the Builder. Jane was there, too, watching. She had her arms crossed against the cold.

On Christmas day, Steve the Builder had become a father, so he made for what Richard called *solid human interest*. And Richard was asking – how did it feel?

Steve was sipping from a mug of tea, embarrassed to be on camera, talking about it. Jo stood at Jane's side and watched.

Richard was very handsome, with his glossy hair, his easy smile. He was winding up the interview, shaking Steve's hand and congratulating him, and Steve raised his empty mug in salute and wandered off.

And now Richard turned and said, 'Hello, sweetheart,' and kissed Jo's cheek. She had to stoop a bit, for him to reach.

The kiss burned, and Jo blushed. Turning, she saw Patrick and Meredith again. Meredith was pointing at something, but Patrick wasn't paying attention. He was looking at Jane and Richard.

Jo waved, once, and Patrick – surprised – jerked, then grinned and waved back. Then he turned in the direction Meredith was pointing. He buried his hands in his pockets and nodded, to show how carefully he was listening.

Richard was saying something to Jo. She turned back to him, still frowning.

He was saying, '. . . home for Christmas?'

School was all anyone ever talked about. It worried most adults that, if Jo talked about something that actually interested her, she'd make them look stupid.

An adult's willingness to look stupid, she had noticed, decreased inversely to their actual intelligence. Patrick, for example, didn't mind looking stupid at all. He spent half his day wearing an ignorant, frustrated scowl; his monkey face. And when Jo told him something exciting, he crossed his arms and tucked in his jaw and closed his eyes and concentrated.

Sometimes, when he was almost getting it, he nodded along, as if to a song in his head. That made Patrick seem powerful. She thought of him, eyes closed, concentrating; his shaggy hair, his raggedy-sleeved sweaters, the hard muscles in his arms and shoulders.

And suddenly Jo felt sorry for Richard, with his worked-on handsomeness, the drudgery of his excellent grooming.

Avoiding his question, she said, 'How's the filming?'

'It's going well.'

'They filmed me driving up to the door in a Land-Rover,' said Jane. 'And getting out, as if it was my first day.'

'The first episode establishes the *drama* of Monkeyland,' Richard said; it was a recitation. 'We'll show how rundown it is, the size of the job your mum's got to do.'

'And Dad.'

'Absolutely. And then we'll introduce some of the characters, human and monkey—'

'Ape.'

'Human and ape. Which will all lead up to the grand re-opening.'

There was a silence. Richard folded his arms and scratched at the corner of his mouth.

'Tell you what . . .' he said.

Jo had a funny feeling inside. She didn't even know if it was nice or horrible.

'What?'

'How would you feel, if we talked to you? For the programme.'

'About what?'

'Oh, I don't know: everything – living here, your mum, your brother, your dad. Monkeyland.'

'Space?'

'Quite possibly, yes.'

She shrugged and ran her tongue over her braces. When she was speaking to Richard, they always felt oversized and conspicuous – her mouth crammed like an urban canal, with old wire shopping trolleys.

Her eyes flitted to Patrick, up there on the high side of the compound. He wasn't looking at them, but he knew they were there. Jo could tell, by the quality of his movements.

Then she looked at Jane, standing next to Richard.

Behind them all, the contractors worked away on erecting the jungle gym.

She said, 'If you like.'

*

The film crew arrived, in their puffy anoraks and faded jeans and big, muddy boots, and began setting up in the kitchen. Jane was in the corner, programming numbers into her new mobile phone.

The cameraman was called Camra Dave. He had fuzzy ginger-ish hair, balding at the crown, and a red beard. Sound Mick was very tall. He had a deep, slow voice with a Bristol accent. He spoke like a Somerset mountain god.

When the stuff had been set up – the bright light, the reflective umbrella balanced in the corner – the crew had a cup of tea and then Richard arrived. He took off his rainy coat and said hello to everyone, then he hung the coat over the back of a kitchen chair and made himself a cup of tea. He brought it to the table and sat down, opposite Jo.

'How we doing?' he said.

'Good.'

'Outstanding.' He looked at Sound Mick and Camra Dave. 'Ready to go?'

They were.

Jo became aware of how she was sitting. She shifted, and it felt wrong. She cupped her mug, half-full of cold tea.

Richard said, 'So, Jo, tell us a bit about yourself.'

She made a panicky face, and Richard told her, 'Relax. You can't do it wrong. We'll edit out any mistakes, or any bits you don't like.'

Jo glanced at Jane. Jane nodded her encouragement.

'Well,' said Jo. 'I'm thirteen years old. I used to go to school in Bath, but then Mum and Dad moved here. My favourite subjects are maths and reading. My favourite books are books about space. My favourite writers are Douglas Adams and Arthur C. Clarke, who was born in Minehead which is near here.'

'And what do you think of Monkeyland?'

Again, her eyes shifted to Jane. Jane shrugged with one shoulder, still programming numbers but watching Jo, too. The shrug meant, Go on.

'It's nice,' said Jo.

'And are you animal bonkers, like the rest of the family?'

She looked at the table, feeling caught out. 'Not really, no.'

'Not even about the chimps? Everyone loves chimps.'

'They're all right.'

Jo felt guilty and exposed for not caring that much about chimps. She could feel every centimetre of her giraffe neck, every strand of Afro hair, every freckle on her forearm and every pulpy, chewed fingernail.

She took her hands off the table and sat on them.

She said, 'Chimps are just a bit noisy, really. And a bit smelly.'

She smiled, not because what she said had been funny, but because she regretted doing this, grinning like a halfwit on camera, and looking like a freak with her horrible hair and her horrible nails and being thirteen with no boobs to speak of, talking about smelly chimps like she was some kind of idiot.

She could have looked directly into the lens and recited Pi to 50 decimal places (with a few days' practice). She could have articulated some of the apparent paradoxes within the theory of relativity. She could have explained how NASA calculated the flight-path of a Space Shuttle, or how much fuel was required to launch a kilogram, or a tonne, or 100 tonnes of matter into low Earth orbit. She could have recited the names of every NASA astronaut who had ever flown, in what order, and a good many cosmonauts (although she was not confident about the pronunciation of their names, never having heard them spoken aloud). She could have told them about the Rings of Saturn or the surface of the sun. She could have described in a way that made them fall silent the unspeakable distance to the very nearest star. She could have told them about the night sky in such a way, they would never be able to look up at it again without a shiver of awe.

Instead, she squirmed and said, 'And a bit smelly,' and everyone had hysterics and Richard clapped his hands and said, 'Excellent!' because Jo making a twat of herself was good *human interest*.

And later, the crew disassembled the equipment and everyone seemed happy. And Jane slipped her mobile phone into a pocket, with all the numbers programmed in, and Jo sat there with it all going on around her.

*

The end of January 1996.

All day, Sound Mick and Camra Dave had been following Charlie. They took footage as he played with some of the apes in the A Compound. (The ropes he swung on were fireman's hoses, heavy-duty rubber and canvas.)

And always – as Charlie played, pant-grunted, hooted, slapped the ground – Rue watched, serene and good-humoured. It was great for the camera, this relationship between the quiet, pretty young man and the sage old ape; the way she offered him food and groomed his hair.

In the afternoon, Charlie sipped from a bottle of Evian and talked straight to the camera. As he spoke, Rue tugged at his earlobes, his necklace. She ruffled his hair, chucked away his baseball cap. A greying, infirm old coquette hungry for the boy's attention.

Ducking and flinching, Charlie said: 'The bachelors can get scary. I wouldn't go in there alone, not even if I was allowed.'

He nuzzled the coarse hair on the back of the gentle chimp's flat skull. And she pulled her lips back from her teeth, in a clacky, half-mad yellow grin, soft-grunting and smacking her lips. Her merry, coffee-bean eyes.

After the interview, Charlie sneaked out of the sanctuary to have a quiet cup of tea and a roll-up beneath one of the oak trees overhanging the car park.

In their shadow sat a dozen contractor's vehicles – beaten-up vans and painty flat-bed trucks. In the north corner were the staff cars and mopeds. And that's where he saw Jane and Richard. They were standing head to head, outside Jane's white Land-Rover Defender. Richard was holding a sheet of paper – perhaps it was a plan of Monkeyland, or a printed-out spreadsheet.

Their conversation was brief, muttered, intense. Then they stepped back and away from one other, and Richard rolled up the paper. Jane said something and turned away. And as she did, Richard reached out a hand and patted her twice on the arse.

She glanced over her shoulder and said, 'Idiot.'

It was the only word Charlie heard –

Idiot.

– before Jane saw him. A squatting figure in the blue shadow of the oak, rolling a cigarette. Watching Richard pat his mother on her arse.

She called his name – 'Charlie?' – and made it a question.

He finished making his cigarette, then took his time to light it, because his hand was shaking. Then he exhaled and raised a hand in careless hello.

Jane shaded her eyes – the sun was low in a clear sky – and muttered something else to Richard. He stood at the door of his car, holding the handle. He seemed to be looking at Charlie, but he was too far away for Charlie to see the expression on his face.

Charlie exhaled through his nostrils, the horsey smell of fresh tobacco. He squatted, heel to haunch, his back to Monkeyland's exterior wall.

Jane walked up to him. 'I didn't know you smoked.'

'Two or three a day. Just to chill.'

'Just to chill,' she said, trying on his words. She toyed with her necklace. It was a chunk of meteoric iron, set in silver. Jock had given it to her. The meteor had punched into their land, in 1968.

'Well, don't be chilling with one of those in the house.'

He took a defiant, squinty drag. 'Whatever.'

She was still toying with the necklace. 'So – you okay?'

By now, Richard was at the wheel of the stationary Land Cruiser, reading something. But he kept looking up.

Charlie said, 'Are *you*?'

She tucked hair behind her ear. 'I'm fine. I spent all our money on a monkey-house that's got approximately sod-all chance of survival. And if I fail, I'm going to do it on television. Who wouldn't be fine?'

Perhaps things no longer felt quite real to her, not until she could see them played back on a monitor.

Perhaps Richard hadn't touched *Jane's* arse. He'd touched the arse of a woman who had been transfigured by appearing on television. Charlie understood how women could be transfigured that way. He thought of Robin and Sam, parochial demi-gods in that low-ceilinged nightclub. And he thought of the erection he'd endured as he imagined a filthy lorry driver rooting her in a stinking toilet – how he'd taken horrified pleasure at the thought of her being defiled, his grimy hands palpating her little tits. And her humiliation, even as she revelled in it; biting on his hairy shoulder to keep from crying out.

He said, 'You're happy, though?'

Her eyes were a curious light grey, and they met his, unblinking, for several seconds. Then she held out a hand and hauled him to his feet. The strong muscles in her forearms. The freckles on her nose and cheeks.

'I'll be a lot happier when this place is up and running.'

Charlie stood with the roll-up in one hand and twisted at the waist to dust himself off.

Jane clapped his shoulder, fraternally, and walked away.

Inside his shiny Land Cruiser, Richard made a show of stuffing whatever he'd been reading into the glove compartment, starting the engine and reversing out of the car park.

And Jane wandered through the open gates of Monkeyland, her self-selected kingdom.

*

Sound Mick and Camra Dave weren't given permission to film Jo meeting her prospective new personal tutor, even though Richard wanted them to, for *human interest*.

This was 3 February 1996.

The tutor lived several miles from Innsmouth, in a small white house which stood far back from the twisty, hedge-lined road. Its path was bordered by winter-naked rose bushes.

Jane knocked on the door and they waited while, within the silence, there was a sense of something stirring. And then Mr Nately came to the door. He was younger than Jo had expected – no more than thirty. He looked like a Spitfire pilot; boyish and pale, with a lick of strawberry hair.

Jane kissed him on one cheek and said hello. Patrick shook his hand and said, 'Hello, John.'

And then Jane said: 'So! This is Jo. And Jo, this is Mr Nately.'

Mr Nately smiled at her. It was a lepidopterist's smile; a contented squint.

He said, 'Pleased to meet you, Jo. Come in.'

Inside, the cottage was antique and orderly and it smelled of beeswax and lavender. The furniture belonged to an older person – stuffed armchairs with antimacassars, dark wooden tables with lions' feet.

Mr Nately had laid out tea and biscuits. He poured them all a cup of tea, the colour of the furniture, and told Jo, 'I teach all the usual subjects, up to A level. Everything except Physical Education.'

'How big are the classes?'

'Oh, one at a time is all I can handle, I'm afraid.'

Jane told her, 'Mr Nately tutors Gifted Children.'

Jo looked around the room – an old lady's room with no old lady in it.

'My last pupil left me in August,' said Mr Nately. 'He's gone on to bigger and better things.'

'Oxford,' said Jane. 'He was only sixteen.'

'And about the PE thing,' said Patrick. 'What we thought we'd do – a couple of times a week, you and I could go swimming together. Or running. The roads are quiet round here.'

Jo nodded, 'Okay,' and the grandfather clock ticked four times.

Mr Nately said, 'So. I understand you're interested in astronomy.'

Jo waited for him to say, *golly*, or *gosh*, or to make a popping goldfish mouth. But Mr Nately just put his hands in his pockets and said, 'Do you know Hyakutake?'

'Sorry?'

'Hyakutake. A few days ago. a Japanese astronomer – Mr Hyakutake – he sighted a new comet. He's a lucky man, actually. He was browsing the same patch of sky where he'd found *another* comet, a few weeks back. A much smaller one.'

'The same patch of sky?'

'The same patch of sky.'

'But a different comet?'

'But a different comet.'

'What are the chances of that?'

'Astronomical.'

Flattered by the joke, Jo asked him, 'What magnitude?'

'Eleven. It's going to come close.'

'How close?'

'Nought point one.'

Patrick leaned in and asked, 'Nought point one what?'

'Astronomical units,' said Jo.

'That's a measurement of distance,' said Nately. 'The average distance between the earth and the sun –'

'– a hundred and fifty million kilometres.'

'Which is pretty close, actually.'

'Pretty close,' said Patrick.

Jane nudged him with her elbow. He stepped back, towards the corner, and clasped his hands behind him, like Dixon of Dock Green.

'And it's going to be night-visible,' Nately said. 'It's a serious comet.'

Patrick coughed. Jo and Jane both looked his way, now – identically irritated.

Patrick said, 'So, this isn't the comet Jo's been going on about? The big one, coming in?'

'No,' said Jo, meaning *obviously*.

Nately said, 'I expect you mean Hale Bopp. That's coming later. So we're getting two great comets in one year. That's actually pretty unusual.' Then he turned to Jo and said, 'Do you know when the last great comet arrived, Jo?'

Jo thought about it. And, all at once, she noticed how the stranger Mr Nately had been, a few moments ago, had been replaced, like a genie leaping through the hatch in a stage floor, by a teacher.

'Comet West,' she said. 'Nineteen seventy-six.'

Mr Nately nodded, and glanced at Patrick and Jane.

Behind her, Jo felt her parents relax.

Mr Nately held lessons in the back room, which overlooked the garden with its vegetable patch and curiously modern shed. The garden bordered an orchard – always moving in the corner of Jo's eye.

The room was equipped like a proper classroom, with a grey desk and school chair, and a wooden desk for Mr Nately. There were posters on the wall – the Periodic Table, Gandhi, the Moon, a mass of white birds taking off from the surface of some lake, a computer on a stand. Instead of a blackboard, Mr Nately had a whiteboard. He wiped it clean with an old Pink Floyd T-shirt. Jo did not comment on this. She pretended to think it was a proper whiteboard-erasing cloth; for some reason, the scrunched up Pink Floyd T-shirt made her hurt on Mr Nately's behalf.

Once in a while, Mr Nately walked or cycled to the village, where he did most of his shopping. He had his milk, his bread, and *The Times* delivered. He grew his own vegetables and some of his own fruit. He made jam and apple sauce and cider. He hung his laundry on a creaky old rotary line that stood in an overgrown and sunless corner of the back garden. And in the evening, he took it inside again, still damp and smelling of laundry powder.

Make yourself at home, he said every morning, as she lolloped her stuff to the classroom.

And she did – although there was nowhere less homely than Mr Nately's house, with its mixture of old people's things, chairs and cookers and kettles, and antimacassars and china animals.

That and the back room with its Apple Macintosh and its school chairs and its TV and VCR, and the creepy orchard that bordered the garden, making a sound like the sea.

*

MONKEY BUSINESS!
US BRITS ARE ANIMAL CRACKERS, BUT HAS TV'S
JANE JONES FINALLY GONE APE?

Jane Jones – the animal-loving babe dubbed THE PHWOAR OF THE JUNGLE *by cheeky fans of her trademark khaki shorts – is worried she's bitten off more than she can chew . . . by taking on an ailing chimpanzee sanctuary in the wilds of Devon!*

'Monkeyland is the biggest challenge of my life,' confesses the jungle temptress.

Monkeyland's star attraction is Rue, the chimp made famous by a 1982 Mirror *exclusive that revealed how cruel circus owner Jerry Lovelock was using violence and intimidation to train his animals.*

*Animal-loving Britain took gentle Rue to its heart after grue-
some footage showed Lovelock beating her with a plank of wood
and shouting: 'You f*****g bitch, I'll sort you.'*

*Mirror experts revealed that, at ten times stronger than a
human being, Rue could easily have injured or killed her crazy
master.*

*Lovelock left Britain following our investigation and now
works as an 'animal consultant' in France.*

*'Rue has been through a lot,' says Jane. 'She's a very special
lady. Her welcome has made us all feel very honoured – especially
my son Charlie, whom she seems to have adopted!'*

In the photograph, Jane wears shorts and caterpillar boots, and
kneels, her arm about Rue's shoulder. Charlie kneels to the left.
Rue is holding his hand.

Patrick read the piece out loud, in the office. He peered at her
over his spectacles.

He said, '"A very special lady"?'

'I didn't say that.'

'I should hope not.'

'They make it up anyway,' said Jane. 'No matter what you say.
So why bother?'

A week later, Rue was killed.

*

To capitalize on Rue's death, Richard arranged lunch in Soho with
a journalist friend, a good contact. His name was Nick Avery, and

he accorded in no way with Jane's expectation of a tabloid journalist; he was well-dressed, plummy, homosexual.

Nick was on his eighth cigarette and his fifth espresso when Jane directed into his Dictaphone the quote she'd written the previous night and rehearsed all that morning, on the train to London.

'The fact is,' she said, leaning over the table, squinting into the cigarette smoke, 'we don't know who's responsible. But the police are taking this very seriously, not just because of Rue, but because of certain threats my family and I received over the course of 1995.'

Richard sat back, arms crossed, job done, while Avery quizzed Jane for half an hour.

Next morning, the banner head on page one showed a picture of Jane – in shorts, naturally – and the legend: TV JANE: 'My Stalker Horror.'

She came home late the next night.

A couple of local reporters were at the gate, and Jane stopped off to speak to them – to offer a wry *no comment* and a cup of tea; they must be cold. They declined. Jane thanked them, went inside.

Patrick was upstairs, reading. Jo was watching *Star Trek: The Voyage Home* on video. It contained a scene where life was given to a lifeless planet – it happened in real time, as the viewer appeared to orbit the alien world.

Charlie was in his room, listening to music with the earphones on.

Jane went upstairs.

Patrick could read her mood by her footfalls. Now he heard restraint, apprehension.

She paused at the door. He measured it, the shape and intention of the pause. And then she came in.

'Are you awake?'

He peered over his half-moons. 'Reading.'

She sat down on the bed. Unlaced her boots.

'What a day.'

He folded a page, closed the book.

'How are you?'

'Tired.'

'Me, too. When are *they* going to leave?' He nodded at the wall. He meant the local journalists.

'Tomorrow,' she said. 'Next day. Soon.'

'Why did you tell them?'

'Why did I tell them what?'

'About the threats.' He'd seen the headlines. 'Did Richard put you up to it?'

She crossed her leg and massaged the arch of her foot. 'No.'

He opened *The Three Musketeers*.

'It was *kids*,' he said. 'It was just kids.'

'Probably, yes. Probably it was.' She took the book off him. Then she curled up and laid her head in his lap. She said, 'I was sending a message to him. In case he's out there.'

'Well, he's not.'

She nuzzled his thigh; nibbled it. He yelped.

'It was probably kids,' she said.

*

Because she appeared on television, Jane had always received a certain amount of fanmail.

The very first obscene letter had made her guffaw in shock. It was a Polaroid of a man in a gorilla suit; through a hole in the crotch projected what Jane at first honestly took for a banana – the man in the gorilla suit having taken the trouble to paint it yellow.

But after that, it wasn't funny. The letters, with their inept obscenity, depressed her more than they frightened her. There just weren't enough synonyms for breasts, penises, vaginas, anuses, semen, orgasm. But all those words got used, and used up, and used again and again.

Her agent paid a long-retired corporate PA to filter the fanmail. And for three years this woman, Gwen, spent every Wednesday opening white envelopes and Jiffy bags addressed to Jane c/o the production company, or the BBC, or various magazines that had featured or even mentioned her in passing.

Gwen sorted the DIY porn and the hatemail and forwarded the rest of it – the fan worship, the begging letters, the marriage proposals – without comment; just two loopy initials scrawled on a hand-dated comp slip.

Jane never met Gwen, so she wasn't able to picture the look on Gwen's face, the day in 1994 when she opened the first of the really bad letters.

At a first, cursory glance, the letter resembled an invitation to attend a local function, perhaps high tea at the Lord mayor's house.

Dear Whore (it read)

> *I know how much you love it I know the things you do. Your 'husband' doesn't know, does he. But I do, I know. I have stood close to you I touched your arm I could smell the cum on you*

As well as the letter, the envelope – which was postmarked Bath – contained Polaroid photographs of Jane's house, and Jane in her car, and Patrick walking Jo to school.

They went to the police. A young PC took them to an office. He listened, then read the letter to himself as Jane sat there, squirming. Then he tugged at an earlobe and told them the best thing was, keep an eye out for anything unusual.

'Like what?' said Patrick. 'A pervert in a tree? In my wardrobe? What?'

'Anything unusual.'

The kids knew nothing of this: not the letters, nor the injury it caused to their parents' marriage, because Patrick and Jane made a furtive secret of it all, keeping their frightened arguments, to hissing spats in otherwise empty rooms.

But there was hardly any need for all the whispering and skulking around. The kids were teenagers; Patrick and Jane were little more than fixtures so permanent they'd become morally invisible.

When Jo wasn't at school, she was in her room, reading. Now and again she could be found in the living room, watching *Star Trek* movies on VHS. *The Voyage Home* was her favourite.

Charlie was struggling with some unhappiness of his own. Something was wrong. He alternated, apparently at random, between resentful silence and confrontational malice.

Patrick thought Charlie resented Bath, because he liked it; liking it unsettled him. He'd liked other places, and left them.

So it was Patrick's idea to acquire for him a token of domestic permanence. At Bristol Dogs' Home Charlie picked out a mongrel terrier – a perky bitch called Blondie who sat panting in his lap all the way home.

Blondie never learned the proper place to shit. Every morning, Patrick scooped her curly black turds into a carrier bag, knotted the carrier bag and threw it in the dustbin.

She had not been spayed. That was Patrick's job, and he never got round to it. It was an omission he regretted, because Blondie's oestrus drew to the door a jostling, whining pack of males. This feral presence bored Patrick and infuriated Jane; she equated the dogs' pink, importunate cocks with the obscene letters. Charlie cursed the horny dogs under his breath; he thumped the windows, threw out buckets of water; he ran outside wielding a golf umbrella like a club, breaking up the pack and driving the dogs away.

Patrick disliked Blondie. Secretly, he kicked her up the arse when no one was around; she cowered and scuttled away with her tail covering her genitals. In the garden, safe from Patrick's toecap, she cheerfully ran in circles and yapped at passers-by, her tail springy and erect.

She didn't like being alone with Patrick, yet she was alone with him much of the day. So when she ran away there was no real reason to suspect anything but an escape. Probably her new life of urban scavenging would be cut short by the dog-catcher; or perhaps a speeding car on a dual carriageway. Perhaps, like Lassie, Blondie would come home.

But perhaps not.

A week after she disappeared, someone left a Milk Tray box on their doorstep. A curl of shit had been mashed into the circles and squares of the liner tray; and inserted into the shit like a crippled flag was a Polaroid of what Jane eventually decided might be the foetus of a dog. It lay, curled and purple, on a yellow baby blanket, edged with a wide ribbon of satin.

When Patrick allowed himself to consider this, he grew very scared. Because he was scared, he never discussed it with Jane. She was scared, too.

Charlie had been made happy by the way Blondie clung to his heels, her busy claws skittering on the old tiles and floorboards. So which was worse? The likelihood that she'd gone because she wanted to? Or the slight probability that Blondie had been taken by a stranger who wished his family ill?

Neither Patrick nor Jane knew the answer to this, and they kept silent. The guilt made them angry with each other.

The letter that followed contained a photograph of Jane on the doorstep, peering into the Milk Tray box, and Patrick, lost in the shadows behind her, his daylit hand on her shoulder. Jane's face, however, was blistered and melted, because someone had burned it with a cigarette lighter. Then, using a sharpened, orange pencil – in many places, it had scratched away the surface of the Polaroid to reveal the white paper backing beneath – they had circled on exaggerated breasts and grotesque, elongated nipples. With the same pencil, they had punched a hole through Jane's crotch and drawn tear-shaped drips down her thighs, pooling between her legs. Piss, semen, blood? – who knew?

One day I'll cum on you and in you and over you I'll roll you in cum I'll stuff your fucking mouth with it.

Now Jane and Patrick shouted at the police, but there was still nothing the police could do; not until a crime had been committed.

Britain had no anti-stalking laws, and no privacy laws either.

Jane contacted the National Anti-Stalking and Harassment Campaign. They told her that most people assumed 'anti-stalking' had something to do with animal rights activism. Jane laughed down the line, and hung up. And then the letters stopped.

There was a tentative, hopeful month. Perhaps the writer had moved to another target, one that was easier to terrorize. Perhaps he was in prison for something else, or in hospital. Perhaps he was dead.

It was easy to say all that, and to say it all again and again, murmuring it over breakfast, and over the telephone, and in bed, and in the bathroom, as Jane pissed and Patrick cleaned his teeth. But it wasn't so easy to believe it.

It was preposterous, after those years spent researching real beasts, to be so disturbed by an inadequate man with a word-processor and an erection – someone who probably still lived with his mother. And after that, to be equally terrified by his silence.

For many months, being afraid had made them unhappy. They squabbled, and squabbles became arguments. They stopped having sex. They argued about that, too.

Sometimes, Patrick hated to be in the same house as her, the same enclosure. He sat in the pub, reading novels by Edgar Rice Burroughs and H. Rider Haggard – novels Jane loathed for their racism and colonial presumption; novels Jane loathed because they had been written for children in knickerbockers and stiff collars; children who were dead long before Patrick was born. She hated Patrick for hating England, and for falling back upon childhood romance – dreams of hazard and deliverance; tales where the villain, in the end, could always be confronted and destroyed.

*

To break the impasse, Jane booked a family holiday; the first they'd ever taken.

They spent a month on the coast of Barbados. The ocean crashed and boiled on jagged black rocks. They laid towels on spiny grass in the midday heat. They hired a car and drove round the island; Patrick stopped to join a game of cricket on a parched village green. Jane bought a flowing, tie-dyed cloth to wear knotted at her hip. They lunched on flying fish sandwiches with hot sauce. When the kids were asleep, Patrick and Jane played Scrabble, got drunk, made love.

They visited a wildlife reserve, and were surrounded by slow, convulsing tangles of copulating tortoises. Occasionally, a male would stretch his sinewed neck and groan in the tectonic agony of orgasm.

Patrick laughed, looking sideways at his kids: Charlie said, '*Gross,* man,' and Jo mimicked him and tickled him under the armpits and he said '*Oi!*' and tickled her back and they ran, chasing each other through the mating tortoises.

They flew home, and Patrick hated Bath and he hated their house. It felt like a pair of shoes a stranger had been wearing. He'd never liked it: now it made him cooped up and furious.

He tore open his suitcase and stuffed clothes, dirty and clean, into drawers. He kicked open internal doors; jammed on taps with a savage twist of the wrist.

And then – as she'd been planning in Barbados, but could never find the right time – Jane told him about Monkeyland.

She took him to Beacon Batch. It was a hazy spring day, and at the same flat summit she stopped and slipped her arm through his. With her other hand, she pointed.

She said, 'There's Weston super Mare.'

He chuckled, because that conversation had been sixteen years ago. He'd never thought she might remember it – or at least that part of it. So much had happened since then.

He felt there were four of them up here: the people they had been, and the people they had become. They were breaking like clouds and passing through one another and merging.

She rooted in her daypack and took out a flask. Flasks had come on in sixteen years; this one was silver, and tough – you could drop it from a high cupboard and it wouldn't smash.

She poured a cup of tea and they passed it back and forth. Above their heads, two kestrels hovered on the muscular updraught. Patrick could see their power and control; how they corrected first in one direction, then the other.

He looked at the pale blue dab of Weston, at Bristol Airport, at Bristol itself; and at the other walkers, ascending the hill. The last time Patrick and Jane were here, they came alone – except for Charlie, and he was still a secret inside her. And they had been very young.

Patrick wondered if the closing of this circle meant their marriage was over, and he thought of it spiralling up on the thermals, disrupting the balance of the predating kestrels.

Jane said, 'We need a change.'

It was true.

'Look at you. You're caged.'

That was true, too.

'You'll go mad. Like one of the polar bears.'

Since the day they met, Bristol Zoo's polar bears had been diagnosed as psychotic. Their compound was too small. They wandered up and down all day, vanilla yellow, waving their heads like dead geraniums.

'You're trying hard. But look at you.'

He nodded, too scared to speak.

'There's a chimp sanctuary. In Devon.'

He looked at her.

'It's miles from anywhere. It's on the edge of Exmoor. It's peaceful. Next to the ocean. You could walk, dive, cycle. Burn some of it off.'

All that pent-up energy, she meant.

'Come on,' she said. 'It'll be an adventure.'

5

Late in the evening of 24 March 1996, Jo and Patrick stood at the far end of their wild garden in North Devon, knee-deep in grass and early dandelions, and she showed him Hyakutake – the first of that year's two great comets. By now, it was among the brightest objects in the sky.

Emission of diatomic carbon made it shine blue-green, but Patrick's colour vision was poor and, when he looked up – following her pointing finger and her instructions – he could see only another bright, white dot. But he cried out, 'I see it!'

Behind the comet followed a haze of tail which, she told him, stretched across thirty-five degrees of night sky.

'Thirty-five degrees,' he said, whistling.

There was a silence. They watched the sky.

Then, without looking at him, Jo reached out and took Patrick's hand. She held on for a second. Her hand was thin and long and dry. She squeezed once, hard, and let go.

Patrick realized that soon he would lose his daughter. She would grow up and away and love someone else.

The dark stadium of sky curved overhead. He could still feel the warmth of her hand. This was their last moment, he thought – watching the great comet in the back garden.

He wished he could see the blue-green of it.

As he blinked, a white line arced across his field of vision.

He said, 'Did you see that?'

'I saw it.'

'Shooting star,' said Patrick and, next to him, Jo nodded.

'Shooting star,' she said.

The next day, she was allowed to stay late and observe the comet through Mr Nately's telescope.

Hyakutake would be moving very rapidly – about the diameter of a full moon every half-hour. That was fast enough for its motion to be detected by the patient but unassisted human eye.

In the dark kitchen, woolly hat on his head, Nately said, 'Shall we?'

Jo pulled on her own hat, knitted wool, striped like a bee; it made her hair stick out like a clown's. She followed Mr Nately into the garden, the universe wheeling overhead, spattered like milk. It was cold enough to see her breath.

Mr Nately unlocked the heavy brass padlock on his shed and stepped inside. Then there was a loud noise, amplified by the silence, as he rolled back the roll-off roof. Jo thought of a cafeteria opening for business, rolling up its vandalized metal shutters.

Inside the shed was a reflecting telescope, wide as a barrel – a Dobsonian mount that Mr Nately had made himself, right down to grinding out the primary mirror. Shoved in behind it, there was room for a single office chair, and Mr Nately let Jo take it.

She sat and put her eye to the viewer. Mr Nately placed a pale hand between her shoulders. She could feel it there. Now and again he murmured an instruction, his voice quiet in her ear, but he allowed her to make the adjustments herself, to familiarize herself with the equipment. It took some time to locate Hyakutake, and to get it in focus, and to learn how to follow its fizzing trajectory.

As she did this, he spoke to her: 'Ancient people knew the heavens much better than most of us today. And something changing up there was scary. Eclipses, meteor showers, comets – they were always met with dread.'

'Well . . .' Jo was squinting like Popeye '. . . they were primitive.'

'But when Halley's Comet swung by in 1910, the press reported that Earth would actually pass through its tail. This was not long before the First World War, remember; there was a lot of anxiety about poison gas. So newspapers caught hold of the story, just like modern newspapers latch on to health scares, or Satanic abuse. What they didn't print is what the astronomers said, that the tail was too vaporous to be harmful. So newspapers got sold and conmen sold anti-comet pills. People boarded up doors and windows.'

'People are silly, though.'

'Well, yes. But at the same time, every few million years a comet actually *does* hit the Earth. Perhaps it was a comet that brought us water. No water, no life. Or maybe a comet brought life in the first place. And maybe it was a comet that wiped out the dinosaurs.'

Jo screwed up her eye, even tighter. It helped her to concentrate. Hyakutake was very bright, and moving so quickly. It was so close. It would never be closer.

Mr Nately said, 'I think our fear of them is coded right down in our DNA. Just like the fear of serpents.'

*

Later, she dozed on Mr Nately's sofa. He laid a scratchy, clean blanket over her – it smelled faintly of lavender. Almost asleep, she listened as he pottered around, locking and double-locking the windows and doors, hiding the keys from sight in drawers and cupboards.

Perhaps, she thought, Mr Nately was protecting her from the werewolves and witches that nightly sprang up like mushrooms in the ripe darkness of the forest.

Perhaps it was simply a habit, because he lived alone, far from anybody, overlooking a creepy orchard on one side and a lonely lane on the other. Perhaps he did it every night; locking the doors against the woods. And perhaps he slept safely under wool and lavender blankets, overlooked by his ranked and silent books – his histories, his textbooks, his science.

Jo was asleep when Patrick came to collect her. He lifted her, still asleep, into his arms and carried her to the Land-Rover. She had half a memory of it, a broken dream of being taken from the cottage in the arms of a great, slow giant, and carried to the thin, cold air at the top of a distant mountain.

And that was Jo's best day, ever.

6

Jane wasn't good in the morning. She was furiously disorganized and irritable – and every day, being late took her by surprise.

She stomped round the house, turning off or re-tuning or stealing radios. When it was Charlie's turn in the shower, she hogged the bathroom mirror, scowling, yanking her hair into a pony tail. When Patrick needed his morning dump, she sat on the closed lavatory, tweezing ingrown hairs from the blade of her shin. When Jo wanted to make muesli and yoghurt, she used up the entire kitchen, trying to find a clean butter-knife to excavate her burned toast from the toaster.

And every morning she stood, exasperated, at the door, yelling for them to for God's sake *hurry up*.

And then, as they filed out, she remembered something she'd forgotten – her keys, her wallet – and ran inside to find them.

Patrick and Jo and Charlie waited in the car in defeated silence, knowing she was ransacking the already ransacked house, cursing whatever eluded her and knowing that, whatever it was, it was probably in her bag or on top of the fridge.

Eventually, Patrick said, 'Look. I've been thinking. It might be easier if you took the VW in the mornings.'

She frowned at him over her reading spectacles. 'Why? Don't you want me with you?'

'Of course I do.'

'It's time together.'

'I know.'

But she kept frowning and he grew uncomfortable. So he said, 'It's just that, sometimes, I get the impression we're in the way. That we're – you know – annoying you.'

She put down her book. 'What do you mean, annoying me?'

'Well. You're busy. In the morning. You've got – y'know – a lot on your plate at the moment.'

She removed her spectacles and placed them, upended, on the book. 'Jesus *Christ*, Patrick.'

He thought she was about to cry, and he didn't know what to do. In nearly twenty years, he'd cried far more than her; he cried at the end of blockbuster movies and sentimental advertisements for disposable handkerchiefs. Once, he had boasted that he would never trust anyone who failed to weep at *Bambi* – but Jane had not wept at *Bambi*.

She was about to weep now, though. She was in the sitting room, legs curled beneath her, while their teenage children slept upstairs, and she was beginning to cry.

He said, 'Hey, hey. Come on.'

She sniffed and wiped her nose on her sleeve and said, 'I'm fine,' and next morning, she took the old VW estate to work.

Patrick and the kids said nothing. But, as he turned the ignition in the too-quiet Land-Rover, Patrick already wished things were back the way they'd been. Their chaotic, snappy mornings seemed lost and precious, and that evening, over the dinner table, he said: 'The VW.'

'What about it?'

He tore off a chunk of bread. Dipped it in his soup. Said, 'I think Charlie should have it.'

The kids looked at him. Jane didn't.

'He needs his own car. Living out here, in the sticks and whatnot.'

Charlie nodded solemn agreement, and the car became his moral property.

Next morning, they returned to the routine. Jane, harried and bad-tempered, made them all late. Nobody said anything about it. They were frustrated and bickering. On the way to work, Jane touched Patrick's knee and squeezed.

*

Monkeyland opened on Easter Sunday, 1996.

Camra Dave and Sound Mick were waiting at the gates, in their jeans and kagouls and knackered trainers, to film the family's arrival – and later, the stiff, nervous speech that Jane delivered to the staff.

Off camera, Patrick started the applause. It splattered like the first spots of heavy rain on a windscreen, and then caught.

For the cameras, Jane opened the gates on the stroke of 9 a.m. to admit a small rubbernecking gaggle of local pensioners who entered cautiously, as if unsure of their welcome, and visibly conscious of the recording camera.

Patrick took Jane's hand. 'They'll come,' he said.

She stood looking at the gate, the geese-like pensioners.

He said, 'Come on, let's get on with the day.'

'You go.'

He lingered.

She said, 'Honestly. I'll be along in a minute.'

He wandered off to the office, to run through his day's itinerary. But first, he kissed his wife. He knew Camra Dave wouldn't fail to capture the moment, and he didn't mind; not really. Camra Dave wasn't morally responsible, any more than a Spider-Hunting Wasp, which paralysed its prey before allowing its larvae to eat them alive from the inside out. Camra Dave and the Spider-Hunting Wasp just did what they did, and that was that.

Jane went to the gift shop, newly supplied with Monkeyland branded pencils and plastic rulers and mugs and T-shirts and posters and key-rings and embossed key-wallets. She took a fluffy lemur from the shelf, inspecting it. The shop assistants looked silently and anxiously on. Camra Dave recorded their skittishness. It would be intercut with Jane's frowning inspection.

Then Jane went outside, to check the weather. She walked to the A Compound, where Rue had lived, and looked down at her animals.

They were lazily knuckle-walking and climbing and playing and grooming in the fine English drizzle, and the wind caught a rag of her hair, trapped it in the corner of her mouth – and the clouds broke and the sun came out. And within the hour, the punters began to arrive.

At the end of the day, the staff gathered to toast their success with inexpensive champagne. Jane poured. The mousse fizzed and ran over her hands. And they stood in a circle and raised their glasses and said, '*Cheers!*'

Patrick watched, enjoying her relief, and knew that tomorrow they all had to get up for work, and do it again, and the day after that too. And one day the camera crew wouldn't be there; it would just be the staff, the apes, and the visitors, if the visitors kept coming.

But he said nothing, and in the evening Jane curled up in the armchair, reading a novel, a glass of wine on the table beside her.

She said, 'What?'

'Nothing.'

She fiddled with the front of the shapeless cardigan she wore against the night chill – the house was always cold. Then she put down her book, took off her glasses and pinched the bridge of her nose. 'I was talking to Richard.'

Patrick's good mood left him. 'And what did Richard have to say?'

'He's had an idea. A good one, I think.'

'How good?'

'There's an unknown primate species.'

'An unknown primate species where?'

'Zaire.'

'Oh, Christ.'

'It's called the Bili Ape. People have seen it. Photographed it.'

Patrick enlarged his eyes and said, 'Wooh!'

'Six weeks,' said Jane. 'And not until July. Monkeyland will be solid by then.'

He spluttered in protest.

She said, 'Oh, come on. We've done the really hard work. And it's not till *July*. We've got to plan a schedule. You can't just throw these things together, not in a place like Zaire.'

He said nothing, because what he wanted to say was childish – and if he was childish she'd pick up on it and use it against him. It was one of her weapons, and usually it was clinching.

He said, 'There's no way this thing even exists.'

'You're sure?'

'Pretty sure.'

She grinned with one side of her mouth – it was her grin of triumph. It was Napoleonic. It gave her away when she was playing cards, and Scrabble. He'd never told her.

He said, 'Don't talk to me about the coelacanth. I know about the coelacanth.'

The coelacanth was an ancient fish, long-believed extinct – until 1938, when a living specimen was caught off the coast of South Africa.

'This is different,' said Patrick. 'It's not a deepwater fish, it's a big fucking monkey. Somebody would've noticed it.'

'Like somebody noticed the coelacanth,' and Patrick groaned theatrically, because she'd mentioned it. She raised her voice to continue, waving him silent. 'The local fisherman knew about it. They called it the *gombessa*. And what about the Megamouth shark?'

'What about it?'

'Some boat caught one off the coast of Hawaii. Some research vessel. This was in the mid-seventies. Seventy-five? Whatever. The weirdest thing you ever saw. Fifty rows of teeth. The thing's a freak, a *big* freak – twenty, twenty-five feet. Bigger. The size of a bus. And I find it hard to believe that nobody, in the entire history of the world, not one sailor, ever set eyes on this thing, not until one happened to be caught by someone who happened to be a marine scientist.'

'Whatever.'

'Come on! It's exciting, isn't it? Actually to prove that something exists?'

'And what next? The Yeti? Bigfoot?'

Her grin of triumph widened and warmed, and when she patted the sofa next to her, Patrick ambled over. He ambled when he'd been drinking, and when he'd lost an argument.

She said, 'Babe,' and rubbed his head.

She said, 'It's been a weird time. A strange couple of years.'

He nodded.

'It's going to take a toll,' she said. 'It's bound to. But come on. Look at us.' She cupped his face in her hands. Her skin was rough. 'We're all right, aren't we?'

He said, 'I want to be bored. Just for one year. For a change. One year of boredom.'

She kissed the tip of his nose.

He laid his head in her lap. 'I like being bored,' he said.

She played with his hair. 'No, you don't.'

Eventually, he fell asleep.

*

She met Richard, Mick and Dave at the airport. Their luggage, on chromium trolleys, seemed ridiculously abundant. She'd brought her grandfather's trunk. It was lucky; as long as she travelled with it, she'd be safe.

Patrick had scoffed when she told him, but he'd never allow her to travel without the trunk. It was his talisman, too.

A week ago, he'd climbed into the spidery attic to take it down. He'd left it in the bedroom, its mouth open, waiting to be filled. She packed without even mentioning it.

Now Mick was helping the taxi driver remove the trunk from the boot. It was still leprous with its patching of old travel stickers – *Excelsior Hotel Rome*, *TWA Transcontinental* – but now she noticed that Patrick had added something to it – a new sticker.

It was a scribble, a primary-coloured portrait of a chimpanzee, and it read: *MONKEYLAND*.

7

They missed her most in the mornings.

Usually, Jo woke Patrick. She was in her running clothes

'Coming?'

He made himself sit up. His head wilted on his neck. He blinked at his lap.

'What's the time?'

'Half-past six.'

'Give me a minute.'

Together, they stepped outside. The sun was up. Low mist clung to the ground. Their footsteps were amplified by the silence. Unseen crows barked and cawed.

The exertion and the cool morning air on his face was good. He ran through a stitch. Jo ran at his side, all sharp points and acute angles. Her feet flapped sideways. Her legs helicoptered from the knees down. Her elbows jutted like chicken wings.

They ran to the corner of the main road and stopped, they rested together on the wet grass. It was an overgrown corner by a roadside junction. Behind them, a fence marked the limits of a field. No cars passed. Their arses got wet. Patrick's discomfort began to leave him: weightlessness rose in his chest, a low euphoria.

He stood and grasped the metal pole supporting a road-sign. He looked like a captain at the mast. Jo squatted, forearms on knees. Breathing high and laboured.

She wheezed, 'How do you feel?'

Patrick spat. 'Good. Terrible. You?'

'Good.'

Eventually, he tapped his wristwatch and they began to run back again, slow and steady until they were home, the mist burning off in the sunrise, and when they got back, Charlie was up.

They took turns in the bathroom, took turns preparing breakfast. Patrick was happy to have the Radio 1 *Breakfast Show* blaring tinnily in every room. Then they piled into the Land-Rover.

They dropped Jo at Mr Nately's, and she stood waving goodbye from the gate at the end of the luxuriant, blossoming garden. They never saw her turn, let alone walk to the door.

If the roads weren't wet, Patrick let Charlie drive to Monkeyland. It was good, hazardous fun – the windows down and the radio on, motoring down empty roads in the fragile summer morning.

The aura of recklessness deserted Patrick immediately they got to work.

Mornings began with a staff meeting, during which the keepers took turns sipping Nescafé and debriefing the room. It was like running a school; each keeper was a teacher, and each exhibit was a classroom – someone was always ill, someone else was being bullied, someone was depressed and, now and again, someone tried to escape.

After the morning briefing, Patrick sat at his desk and stared at the To-Do list that had been left somewhere conspicuous by Mrs de Frietas, his Personal Assistant. Generally, it wasn't a long list, but he never got to the end of it, since more pressing jobs always popped up during the day. He rarely took a lunchbreak, eating a sandwich en route to the gibbons, the orangs, the Bachelor Group or the capuchins to inspect the enclosures, listen to keepers' gripes, monitor the punters.

When he did get the opportunity for an hour off, he spent it watching the capuchins – cute and very intelligent little monkeys.

Their enclosure, which they shared with the black-handed spider-monkeys, was surrounded by a moat; capuchins couldn't swim and feared water. In the moat lived ducks who swam in lazy circles, trailing strings of happy little ducklings.

What the capuchins liked to do was this: dangle upside-down from a branch that overhung the water, snatch up a straggling duckling, then hustle it to dry land, kill it and eat it.

Visitors who witnessed this were distressed by the panicking duckling, the haughty, oblivious mother, the cute little monkey with duckling blood smeared round its chittering mouth.

If they demanded it, Patrick usually refunded their entrance money. He didn't like dealing with the punters and he didn't really care if they were shocked by seeing a monkey eating a duckling. What did they expect?

But the genius of the capuchins fascinated him. Their compound was like a prison for flesh-crazed mad scientists.

Around 4 p.m. he went to pick up Jo. She'd be waiting at John Nately's gate, as if she hadn't moved all day. She was eating an apple, or she simply stood with a book in one hand, reading.

Whatever she was doing, she never noticed him arrive. He sat at the wheel, watching her – crunching her apple or holding a book before her face, or just huddling in the rain.

She made him smile – she always made him smile. And when he honked the horn she always glanced up as if surprised to see him.

He drove her to Monkeyland and sometimes, she accompanied him as he shambled about his business. But mostly she sat in his office and read books, or wrote essays on Patrick's work computer – which was excellent, because it meant Patrick couldn't access his emails or get to his spreadsheets.

When she grew bored, Patrick sometimes paid her two quid an hour to sort his in-tray. She set the important paperwork in a neat pile on the right side of his desk. Like all neat piles, it soon became invisible.

Now and again, Charlie took her to feed the old donkeys; she liked the warm, straw, horseshitty smell of them.

But usually, she just did her homework at Patrick's desk, or read, erect in his chair with the book two inches from the tip of her nose.

Sometimes, when Mrs de Frietas slipped out for a crafty Lambert & Butler, which Patrick wasn't supposed to know about, Jo answered his phone. 'Patrick Bowman's phone,' she would say. 'How may I help you?'

*

Jane finally called from Uganda, near the eastern Zairean border. She was breathless and excited and hassled, and the line was very bad. So he told her everything was fine, that he loved her and the kids missed her, that it was good to hear her voice, and not to worry.

He didn't say they already had a big problem.

There was a weird mood in the Bachelor Group. In the early morning, when the mist was thin, the chimps were sombre and watchful – as if terrible anxieties had kept them awake through the night. Never relaxed, the group, was becoming schismatic. Small, temporary alliances were forming – chimps huddling like Victorian anarchists, then dissolving, often in shrieking twisters of violence.

Uncle Joe, the dominant bachelor, spent much of his time in furious display. He threw tyres, food. He slapped at the ground. He vocalized rapidly through pursed lips. He pulled his lips back from his teeth and screamed.

One morning, instead of retreating from Uncle Joe's display, two younger apes called Gilbert and Rollo responded by attacking him. There was an unpleasant little squabble – shrieking and thumping and kicking and biting – until Gilbert and Rollo retreated to higher ground (their new jungle gym) and squatted there, sulking, grooming themselves by way of displacement.

Bleeding, haughty, Uncle Joe retreated to a farther corner. Believing himself out of eyesight, he sagged.

'These fucking bastards,' said Patrick. 'I wish they'd all die.'

Harriet, the Head Keeper, gave him a worried look, which he ignored. But she kept squinting at him so he said, 'Well, honestly.'

And he saw it on her face: *nobody* liked the Bachelors.

She said, 'What can I say? They're here, because they're here, because they're here.'

*

A week later, Charlie noticed Uncle Joe, face down by the water under the shade of a chestnut tree.

He and Harriet, who carried a tranquillizer pistol at her hip, entered the compound like thieves, scattering dried mangoes and hazelnuts; unusual morsels to distract the fretful Bachelors.

Many of Uncle Joe's bones were broken. His testicles had been bitten off. While he lay bleeding and helpless, the Bachelors had stamped on him, bitten him, punched him. They had ripped out his fingernails and torn out his throat.

The remaining Bachelors watched Charlie and Harriet from their silent gallery. They were wary, embarrassed, curious.

Mindful of their gaze, Charlie said: 'Who did it?'

Harriet licked a dry lower lip.

'All of them.'

They delayed opening Monkeyland to get Uncle Joe to surgery. But he was dead anyway.

Charlie had Uncle Joe's blood on his clothes and face, and Uncle Joe's blood in his hair and it was beginning to smell.

He went to shower.

Patrick chaired that morning's meeting. Punters were already milling around outside – a little girl eating a 99, her face smeared in chocolate.

Patrick said, 'Be honest, none of us is going to miss that old bastard. So tough shit – he's dead. If I could give the rest of them a containable virus and free up the compound for something more cuddly, I'd do it. But here's the thing: we've already had a high-profile death. And yeah, Rue was a sweetheart. And yeah, the publicity brought in the punters, so God bless her. So – dead

Rue means good for business. Dead Uncle Joe? It's looking like Inspector fucking Morse.'

Harriet said, 'You can't compare it.'

'You can if you're an idiot with a newspaper to fill in the silly season. What happened to Uncle Joe doesn't leave this office.'

They nodded. Patrick shuffled random papers.

He said, 'I hate doing this, but if we want to keep food on the table, if we want to keep this place running, we've got no choice.'

The distrustful keepers reminded him of the Bachelor Group. Everyone agreed, and nobody looked him in the eye. He thanked them, dismissed them, and they shuffled out.

They got rid of the body that evening, and Patrick composed a death notice: *Uncle Joe was one of Monkeyland's great characters and no one who worked with him will ever forget him.*

He had the obituary copied and laminated and put on the information boards outside the Bachelor Compound. They didn't have a photograph of Uncle Joe; instead, they used the new Monkeyland logo.

But Uncle Joe had left no clear successor, and peace didn't settle upon the Bachelors. There were more urgent confabulations, more conspiratorial huddles, more ambitious princes and artful politicians. And there were more deafening displays to amuse and disturb Monkeyland's paying customers.

But the violence wasn't comical. It was explosive and riotous, and the screeches and howls dipped and swooped around the compound like bats.

Women covered the eyes of their baffled children. Men looked on, fascinated and aroused. And they bared their teeth and pointed while, beneath them, in the compound, chimps broke out in rage and hate and anxiety and blood.

And at night Patrick turned over, troubled even in his dreams by the war brewing in the Bachelor Compound.

*

He was watching the capuchins – longing to see them tackle a full-sized duck – when a junior keeper approached, carrying a handwritten message from Mrs de Frietas. The message told Patrick that

1) he had a visitor and

2) he'd left his mobile phone in the office

3) again

He thanked the keeper, scrunching up the note, then headed down the hill, finishing his sandwich. He walked past the new children's climbing frame, erected not far from the entrance, then past the food vans and the visitor lavatories and into the office.

He nodded curtly to Mrs de Frietas, who thought him work-shy and scruffy, and squeezed past her desk into his office.

In there was a woman. She had her back to him, watching the punters eating their hot dogs and cones of chips – and she turned at the sound of the door opening.

Pixie face, pixie hair. She wore tennis shoes, paint-spattered jeans, a man's checked shirt over a Gap T-shirt. And she wore delicate, wire-framed spectacles. The way the light fell, her eyes were half-obscured behind smudged finger- and thumbprints.

From behind one ear, past her clavicle and into the neck of her T-shirt, ran a twisting rope of scar tissue. Its nudity was shocking, but Patrick recovered well enough by moving his gaze to the painting the woman carried under one arm. It was wrapped in brown paper.

She said, 'Hi,' and shifted the painting to offer her hand. 'Sarah Lime.'

He shook her hand. 'Patrick. Pleased to ... you know.' Then, hasty and apologetic, he invited her to sit.

She thanked him and did, setting the painting against his desk. She laced her hands in her lap.

He sat with elbows on the desk, playing with a Biro.

She said, 'Actually, I was hoping to see Jane. Your, um ... She came in – to my shop. A while ago. To have a look round. And she ...' She nodded at the brown paper square. 'She bought this. She decided she wanted it on the spot. It wasn't actually finished.'

'That sounds like Jane.'

'So – is she? Actually around?'

'Actually, no. She's in Zaire, of all places.'

'Zaire?'

'Hunting monkeys.'

She knotted her hands. 'Okay. Well, not to worry.'

'Right,' said Patrick. 'Well, thanks for dropping it off.'

'Right, then.' Sarah stood, putting her bag on her shoulder.

Patrick stood, too.

She said, 'Best be off.'

'Okay. Thanks again.'

'No problem. I expect I'll see you again.'

'Absolutely. I must drop round the shop. Gallery. Shop.'

'Quay Lime.' She jerked a thumb over her shoulder, like someone dancing the hitch-hiker. 'On the front. By the chip shop. Can't miss it.'

'I'll do that.' He spread a hand to show her the small office crammed with old desks and crappy old filing cabinets and dusty piles of paper – stuff he was supposed to have read and never would, stuff he was supposed to sign but didn't bother. 'This place could do with brightening up.'

'Excellent.'

'Excellent.'

She hesitated in the doorway, about to say something, but instead she said, 'Cheers,' and on the way out she struck her hip on the corner of Mrs de Frietas's oversized and malevolent desk.

He heard Sarah's yelp and her wounded apology, and finally the door closing. When she had safely gone, he fiddled with the Biro and let the awkwardness work its way through his system and drain away.

All it was, Jane had bought a painting without telling him. She'd done worse things; spending all their money on a chimpanzee sanctuary, for example.

But, before getting back to avoiding work, he lifted the painting, still wrapped. Probably, the polite thing would have been to examine it in the artist's presence. Instead, he'd shown no interest; and it wasn't Sarah Lime's fault that he didn't get to see villainous monkeys mugging a duck.

Deep in the piles of crap on his desk, he found a letter-opener. Its handle was in the shape of a Scots Guard playing the bagpipes. He'd never seen it before, and wondered briefly where the hell it had come from. Then he used it to saw at the cross of hairy string that bound the painting. When the string had fallen away, he slit the taut brown paper.

It smelled good – acrylic and wood sap and something else, perhaps varnish and white spirit and maybe the brown paper itself, baked on the hot back seat of the car that had delivered it.

He hoisted the painting and rested it on a shelf, elbowing some paperwork out of the way.

The painting had been knifed onto the canvas in pale loops and swirling bruises. It showed a naked woman with a storm rising behind her, filling the sky. The woman was tranquil – either imperiously immune to the storm, or perfectly oblivious of it and about to be swept into its vortex like an autumn leaf.

The painting seemed at once deeply English and very old; as if it had been copied from something disinterred from the soil, or discovered painted deep on the wall of limestone caves.

Taking it down from the shelf and turning it to lean it, face-forward against the wall (where it would remain until Jane returned and decided what to do with it), he noticed the hand-written invoice taped to the rough backside of it, and realized why Sarah had hung around, reluctant to leave but with nothing to say.

He'd acted like a banana republic customs officer as she squirmed and waited and finally gave up and gathered her bag and left, bruising her leg on the way out. She'd been waiting for him to pay for the painting.

———

FROM JANE'S NOTEBOOKS

The city of Goma stands on the banks of Lake Kivu, eastern Zaire. Its northern sky is dominated by Mount Nyiragongo, a living volcano. Inside its massive crater seethes a lake of molten rock. The mountain glows in the dark like a night-light.

The buildings are single-story, cement blocks. The streets are acned with holes and gorged with cars, motorbikes, people, animals, carts, ancient vans, patched-up Volkswagen buses. Young moneychangers wander from car to car with thick wads of cash clasped in their fists. Stands sell hot, seasoned fried dough. Women carry goods for sale under their arms, on their heads, in push-carts. There are barefoot soldiers. And there is a constant snarl of NGO vehicles: UNICEF, UNHCR, CARE, CONCERN.

Goma used to be a tourist town. It's got an airport, it's close to Virunga National Park. It was celebrated for its nightlife. If it's a tourist town now, it's in a different way: since 1994, more than two hundred Non-Governmental Organizations have come here to compete for more than a billion dollars of relief-related contracts. The gang's all here: the United Nations, naturally. And the French, the Dutch, the Swedes, the Germans, the Americans, the Irish, the British, the Canadians, the Australians: World Vision, Care, the Samaritans, Oxfam, Southern Baptist Relief, Médecins Sans Frontières.

Not unlike soft drinks companies, the competing aid groups trumpet their names with logos stamped on vehicles, T-shirts, baseball caps.

They're here because, in 1994, a flood of refugees gushed through this dry city. They were taking flight from Rwanda but, despite what we heard in the Western media, they weren't fleeing the genocide; they were Hutus. Among the many innocent Hutus were thousands of *interahamwe*: Those Who Stand Together. The *génocidaires*.

After slaughtering and inciting the slaughter of perhaps a

million people, the *interahamwe* had been driven out of
Rwanda by a Tutsi army a quarter its size. The humili-
ated leaders of the *interahamwe* then terrified Rwanda's entire
civilian Hutu population into joining them in exodus. The
Tutsi cockroaches had escaped extermination, and now they
were coming to wreak genocidal revenge.

Hundreds of thousands of homeless Hutus fanned out
along Nyiragongo's volcanic black skirts. They brought no
food, no livestock, no carts, no goods. They built hovels that,
shoulder to shoulder, stretched to the far horizon. There was
typhoid, dysentery, malaria; of course, there was AIDs.

The camp closest to Goma is called Mugunga. It goes on
forever, sprawling under the live, night-glowing volcano. You
couldn't make that up. Two hundred thousand people sleep
on rock lava and black volcanic soil. Main streets have risen;
there are markets, bars, barber shops and discos. You can buy
a hand grenade for three American dollars. An R4 rifle will
set you back sixty. The ground is so hard, you can't dig a grave
into it.

Our route took us past the camp, and as we drew near, the
dense roadside crowds thickened and coagulated. All around,
blue plastic sheeting was draped over temporary shelters,
always a sign of UNHCR presence.

Tens of thousands were gathered round the huts; standing,
sitting, trading, eating, talking. The sheer crush of dis-
possessed, bored, watchful humanity was frightening. We'd
hidden the camera and sound equipment. Not all Hutus
appreciate the Western media.

Only when the surly and vigilant multitude began to thin

out did the atmosphere in the car loosen up. And after a few miles, approaching the Hotel Karibu, the masses were thinner still – and we actually began to relax – a little.

The Karibu is a tourist resort whose tourists are gone and whose swimming pool is empty, ringed with green moss. The dim Reception is hung with dried-out animal skins, local art, fading travel posters.

We checked in. I dumped my bags in my room, went back to Reception, called home. There's no landline, just a fervently guarded cell-phone. The desk clerk claimed to be busy, then he informed me the lines were tied up, then he instructed me that the phone was to be used for incoming calls only.

I stood there until he gave up. He passed me the cell-phone – *une dollar per minute, madame* – and I got through to home. But the line was bad and I didn't know what to say. Nor did Patrick, and neither did the kids. It was more like using a ouija board than making a phone call, and when I hung up I felt nauseated and empty, stagnant as the swimming pool outside.

Then Richard appeared and I enjoyed watching him go through the same protracted negotiations, with less success. Richard doesn't have my patience. Richard doesn't know about waiting. He thinks he does, but he doesn't.

Later, in the deserted bar, we met Claude.

He used to be a ranger at Virunga, the vast national park that runs along the Ugandan and Rwandan borders. Virunga is home to more than half the mountain gorillas left on earth; about 350 of them.

As a ranger, Claude's salary was less than 50 cents a month;

even so, he often didn't receive it. International agencies supplied him with equipment, uniforms and a $20 monthly 'bonus' – but that money, along with most of the funds marked for conservation projects, was diverted into the hands of venal officials.

And now, naturally, bloodshed has come to Virunga. In the last few months, four mountain gorillas have been killed. Murdered, said Claude; the first such incidents in more than a decade. Probably, they were shot and eaten by famished Hutus using *interahamwe* weapons.

All this bedlam makes it impossible to monitor the remaining gorillas. A few rangers tried, because these are dedicated men. They disappeared.

————

Late in July 1996, three local kids paid a visit to Monkeyland. They were Robbie Swindon, James Gaddis and Michael Redman – Stu Redman's son.

It was the holidays, they were bored and, because Robbie's mum worked in Monkeyland as a cleaner, they got in cheap.

They were sixteen, and the summer looked good on them. Their clothes were sun-faded and cool: their washed-out combat shorts, their Pearl Jam, Blur and Oasis T-shirts. The hair in their eyes, bleached by the sun.

First thing, they went to the gift shop and mucked around, shouting, throwing cuddly toys to one another. The shop assistant looked up from the crossword. She was Arielle Thompson's mum; she used to work in the bakery in Innsmouth, she knew their names. And by name, she told them to sod off before she called Red's dad. So they filed through the door and legged it to the ice-cream van. They bought 99s with strawberry sauce and began to explore.

They went to the A Compound, where chimps lazed on tyre swings and sucked at sawdusty oranges, looking really fucking bored. Now and again the animals swivelled their nutty-brown eyes in the boys' direction, then returned to picking nits from each other.

The boys passed the colobus monkeys, the spider monkey island, and arrived at the Bachelor Group. By the handrail, a laminated note informed visitors that the boss chimp had just died, and warned them that the group was undergoing a *transition period*.

And there was definitely something going on down there. Little groups, little gangs, huddled in different corners. Other chimps were knuckle-walking, pacing. They looked tense and wary.

'Cool,' said Robbie, making it a three-syllable word.

Red locked on to the biggest of the chimps. It was an ugly bastard. Its head was almost bald and its ears were big and raw-looking; a bite-sized chunk had been taken from one of them. It was panting and muttering like a street-corner nutcase.

As Red watched, it burst into attack – driving away a second, smaller chimp. The fight seemed to pass an electric current through the compound; chimps screeched and leaped, and their hair was standing rigidly on end.

When the fight ended, the chimps split into two groups. Most of them strolled away and began to pick at each other's fur. But a dozen thunderous chimp brows were turned upwards, at the human audience drawn to this noisy compound like wasps to a bin.

Those surly frowns should have been comical, but they weren't – and Red was glad when the moment was broken by some bored-looking head-turning, some grooming, some eating.

But then the ugly chimp stepped forward again; the one with the fucked-up ear. It was huffing and puffing and glaring at them, at the ring of high faces, circling it like a jury.

It waa-barked, showing teeth, and thrashed the ground with a stick, then clambered up the jungle gym and tried to rip it apart. It displayed for a minute, then snuffled and slapped at the ground and, in disgust, turned its back.

Nobody moved. Nobody said much: they were waiting. There was tension in the chimp's arms, and in the hunching of its shoulders, and in its lunatic mutterings.

Softly barking, it scooped a handful of matter from the ground. Then it turned and, shrieking, threw it – a turd missile.

It broke up in the air like a meteor, and scattered over the quickly atomizing crowd; ducking their heads, as if to avoid a sudden shower of rain. Some of the shit got in Robbie's hair. A chunk of it splatted on Red's cheek.

Below, the chimp was pant-hooting. It swatted the ground with the stick, and this time more of the chimps joined in; a shrieking, carnival frenzy. The spectators, imagining a barrage of pulpy missiles – shit and fruit and clods of mud – were mostly jogging away now, almost running – and none of them were smiling. A few kids, toddlers, were crying.

But Red wasn't running. He alone hung back, breathing through his mouth. Shit was smeared on his face, round his eyes and mouth. Particles of shit had dropped down the neck of his T-shirt; more shit had fallen in a clump between his feet.

Red stooped to gather up the shit. Straightening, he re-squashed it into a ball – smaller, but more compacted, like Plasticine.

Now he saw that zoo keepers were rushing in. Khaki uniforms, big boots. He measured their approach, then drew back his arm like a cricketer and bowled the squashed-up ball of monkey shit, overarm.

Before running away, he hesitated, to see if the missile had struck home. The throw was pretty good; Red was a talented athlete. But the clod of shit broke up. All it did was increase the frenzy; the tumult of waa-barking, the pant-hooting, the berserk physical display – the knuckle-leaping, the ground-beating.

The keepers were getting closer. One of them, not much older than Red, had broken away from the pack and into a full sprint. The other keepers were grabbing at him, trying to stop him. But they were older and slower, nowhere near quick enough.

They called the kid's name. But the kid wasn't listening. He ran at Red.

The kid was really fast.

*

Patrick hurried to the Bachelor Compound. He found a junior keeper trying to corral the loitering, craning visitors. The ground was littered with orange quarters, apple cores, splatterings of faecal matter.

Patrick's heart doubled in weight; his pace halved.

On a patch of grass opposite the Bachelor Compound, a boy sat with his back to a hazel tree. His head was tilted and he was pressing something to his nose. There was blood on his T-shirt and jeans. Patrick recognized him as Stu Redman's son. He was flanked by two of his friends. They were shuffling their feet, kicking at the grass, hands deep in their pockets.

On the opposite side of the grass patch, Harriet was having words with Charlie. Charlie was cupping his right hand in his left, massaging it. It was a gesture Patrick recognized at once as the way you rubbed your hand after getting off a really good punch. Everyone was surprised by how much it hurt; that punching someone in the head felt like punching a brick wall.

Patrick approached them. 'So what's going on?'

Harriet jerked her thumb over her shoulder, at the Bachelor Group.

She said, 'Incident,' and Patrick groaned, because 'incident' meant 'report', which meant inspectors, officials, DEFRA, possibly even newspapers. 'Incident' meant a pain in the ass, maybe for weeks.

'What kind of incident?'

'Donnie threw shit into the crowd.'

'Oh, Christ. Did it——?'

'Yep.'

Patrick's shoulders drooped.

'It gets better. The kid threw it back.'

'The kid threw shit at the chimp?'

'Yep. And of course, Charlie sees what's happening. So he runs up and punches him.'

Patrick hated Monkeyland. He rubbed his face vigorously, as if washing it.

Then he said, 'Wait.'

He made himself amble over to the local kids. He squatted at Michael Redman's side.

'How is it?'

Michael tried to nod, but his head was still tilted back.

'All right.'

'I'm going to have to call your dad. You know that.'

Michael Redman closed his eyes in acknowledgment. The other two hunched their shoulders, groaned, dug at the soil with their toes.

'No choice,' said Patrick. He resisted the urge to look over his shoulder, at his boy.

He said, 'So tell you what. You boys wander over to my office. Michael, you be careful of that nose. Keep the dressing pressed tight for another ten minutes. We'll call your dad, and while you're waiting, we'll get you a Coke or something. A bag of chips. How's that?'

He had Harriet lead them away. He waited until they were gone, then went to find Charlie. Someone had taken him to the staff room. He was sitting alone in there, cupping his hand.

Patrick said, 'Does it hurt?'

'Yes.'

'Good.'

Charlie stopped massaging the hand.

'You twat,' said Patrick. 'You dickhead. He's a local. He's the local *copper's* son. Jesus, Charlie.'

Charlie said, 'I was thinking of Rue.'

And Patrick's anger was gone. He sat down, next to Charlie. He examined his hand, front and back, then went to get the green First Aid box.

*

Stu Redman arrived in uniform. Entering the office, he lowered his head and removed his hat.

At first, he ignored the teenagers. They were sitting in a line against the far wall – Charlie and Red gloomy in the middle. Red's nostrils were clogged with blood: his eye was good and swollen. Charlie had his hand in a white dressing.

Stu gave Patrick a private, jaded look. Rolled his eyes. Arms crossed, Patrick shrugged a shoulder.

Stu sat, facing the boys. He spread his legs wide and passed his hat through his hands. His bored and pugnacious gaze lingered on Red, then Charlie.

Robbie couldn't stand it.

'That monkey threw shit. That's illegal.'

Stu said, 'It would be illegal if *you* threw shit, Robbie. But the chimp can't have broken the law, because it's a *monkey*. All right? Not actually a bloke in a suit.'

Robbie flushed and muttered something at his knees.

'What *is* against the law,' said Stu, 'is for Michael to assault an animal. Even with its own turds, as it happens.'

He saw their doleful surrender, the downcast eyes, the tugging at fingers.

'I've spoken to Patrick. He and Charlie are going to sort this out between them. The rest of you, I'm going to take you home. And I'm warning you: I don't want to hear another word about this. Not a single effing word. All right?'

Stu held their gaze. Then he stood and put on his hat.

He said, 'Wait outside,' and Red, Robbie and James shuffled out of the office in a shackled-convict tread.

Stu and Patrick shook hands.

Patrick said, 'Appreciate it.'

'Boys, innit. Idiots. All of them.'

He put his hat on. Straightening it, he faced Charlie.

He said, 'And you, Henry Cooper – you be careful with those fists. Because next time, your old man might not be around to bail you out – and next time I'll have you. All right?'

And then the office was empty, but for Charlie and Patrick.

Patrick sat down and scratched his scalp. He picked up a Biro and tapped the table with it. He put it down.

'Mate, you hit a punter.'

Patrick saw it in Charlie's eyes; the weary desire just to hear it and be done.

He said, 'My hands are tied. I've got to sack you.'

Charlie stared at Patrick. Patrick stared at the desk; the teetering reams and slip-sliding piles of unread paperwork.

'Not that it'll make you feel any better,' he said. 'But you're a lot more popular round here than I am.'

8

We ate before sunrise – croissants and coffee – then loaded up the Land Cruisers and headed off in convoy down the Western Axis, the main road out of here.

Already, people had gathered. We saw the red sun on the black volcanic rock, the blue tarpaulins, gritty dust collecting in its windless folds, the ragged people.

But soon the crowds thinned then eventually disappeared altogether; we were travelling along empty dirt tracks, sky all around. Then scattered villages, where people exchanged smiles and waves.

There's a kind of hope there, in the way the crops are tended, the beauty of flowers round frail huts. The children playing. We were a few miles from Goma, a revision of hell, and here they were, children playing, and seeing them play I felt good and happy and relieved.

*

On the third day, we stopped to ask gathering locals about the Bili Ape. They were familiar with a large ape, they said: *the lion killer*. We passed round photos of gorillas, but they shook their heads. No, not gorillas.

We weren't surprised. The Bili Forest is about 500 kilometres from the nearest recorded gorilla population.

The first night at the Belgian camp, we passed the special photograph among ourselves. It had been taken by a local hunter, a poacher. This is the photograph that brought us to Bili.

Claude was seeing it for the first time. I'd held it back, kept it in my luggage. We hadn't even discussed it. It's a kind of talisman. It has certain properties, which were accentuated by the firelight.

The photograph shows an ape, dead.

The face is gorilla-like: very flat, with a wide muzzle and a heavy, overhanging brow ridge.

The body is that of a chimp.

But the creature in the photograph is two metres tall. It is taller than the hunter who claims to have killed it.

———

Patrick's morning meetings had become even more insufferable, punctuated by the keepers' secret looks and furtive snorts: who could trust a man who'd sacked his own son – and for defending an animal?

Patrick thought of Uncle Joe in his final days; isolated and plotted against. And when Harriet told him about Charlie's goodbye party, he groaned and said, 'I sacked him, Harriet. What's it going to look like if we have a frigging celebration?'

She folded her chubby arms and screwed up one eye. 'There'll be trouble if we don't.'

So they did. Harriet booked the Olde Shippe's upstairs room. And Charlie walked in, alone. He opened a door marked PRIVATE FUNCTION. It was quiet inside, and dark – until someone hit the lights.

Charlie saw the keepers, the grounds staff, the volunteers. They cheered and threw streamers and kicked balloons. Somebody had cued up the jukebox; it played 'I Fought the Law'. No one knew the words, except the chorus, but everyone sang along.

And later, people began to peel off and stagger home, and those who remained became reflective and maudlin.

Charlie was sitting with Harriet, rolling her a cigarette.

She was florid and loud. For the first time, Charlie heard the Lancashire in her accent. She said, 'Next time, break his nose. The little prick.'

He nodded, concentrating on the roll-up.

'Anyway,' she said, 'well done, love. Sorry you're not coming back.'

'One day, maybe.'

'But until then – what's next for Charlie Chuckles?'

He looked up. Stopped rolling the cigarette.

'It's what the girlies call you.'

'It is not.'

'No, love. It's not.'

He got back to the cigarette.

Harriet leaned over and pinched his cheek. She pinched hard, twisting, almost malicious; then let go.

'They call you Cheeky Charlie.'

He finished the cigarette and passed it to her.

She said, 'A mate of mine, Big Clive in Minehead – do you know Minehead? – he's always looking for staff. I could put a word in, if you like.'

'Big Clive?'

She slapped at him feebly, mock-offended. 'Clive's very tall, as it happens.'

'Right.'

She slapped him again. 'Well, do I put a word in, or what?'

'What does he do?'

'He runs a hotel – the Anchorage. Nice place. Do I give him a call?'

Charlie drained his drink.

'Go on then,' he said. 'Why not? Give him a call.'

*

Saturday evening, Patrick paid a visit to Sarah Lime.

He walked through the amber light, then along the harbour, past the new gastro-pub and the Post Office that sold beach toys and postcards and newspapers and camping gear. Tethered boats bobbed on the tide, collided, looked conspiratorial. Tourist flotsam stirred on the greasy water. He smelled rotting seaweed and saw the floating, glove-grey corpse of a seagull.

He stopped outside Quay Lime. It took up the converted ground floor of a narrow old harbour-front house.

He opened the door – a bell jangled – and stepped inside. It smelled of cooling dust and wood wax and oil paint and stretched canvas. The floorboards were bare and the walls were white and hung with paintings – landscapes, sweeps of light, reflections. Indices of fish, of gulls and other birds – local fauna – but as through a distorting lens.

He wandered round, hands in pockets. Now and again, he paused to nod, learnedly. He knew that Sarah Lime had crept in from the back but, admiring the paintings, he affected not to see her. Then he turned, as if mildly startled.

'Oh. Hello, there.'

'Hello.' She wore the same paint-spattered jeans, a man's shirt, defiantly open at the scarred neck.

He put his hands in his pockets.

'Look. This is a bit embarrassing.'

He produced the ripped, shrivelled remains of a chequebook containing a single cheque and a few paying-in slips.

She took a rag and began to dry her hands.

'When you came by,' he said, 'it didn't even occur to me.'

Sarah tucked the rag into her pocket like a handkerchief. 'No problem. I mean, your wife paid a deposit and everything. I assumed we'd settle when she got back.'

'She didn't tell me about the painting. She's always thinking about three hundred things at once. And she's more disorganized than I am, even. We're not an organized couple.'

The tension left her shoulders. She put her weight on one foot. 'Look. Really. It's no problem. Whenever.'

'Anyway.'

He wrote out the cheque on the counter and presented it with a flourish, to cover his discomfort. She slipped it unexamined into her pocket, to cover hers.

'Fancy a glass of wine?'

'Absolutely. Absolutely.'

He followed her behind the counter, through a short passage and up some narrow stairs, the wood blackened with age.

What he saw of the flat – the hallway, the kitchen – was pleasantly disordered. The kitchen was piled with books and newspapers and unwashed plates. The table was almost big enough for two. He sat down. Sarah dug out a bottle of wine and two cloudy, mismatched whisky glasses. She poured him a glass, urine-coloured in the storm light.

Patrick took a sip. Lifted the bottle to examine it; an organic brew from some local vineyard.

'Theresa and Steve,' Sarah told him. 'Steve's a Kiwi. They're good at wine, down there, but Theresa wouldn't leave England. So they compromised on five and a half acres, down Lipton way.'

He turned the bottle by the neck, so the label was facing away. 'Well, you seem very integrated into the local community.'

'With the other immigrants, yeah.'

'But not the locals?'

'But not the locals.'

'Ah. And I thought it was just me.'

'You've got it easy, mate. At least you're providing jobs.'

'Yeah, well. They don't make it *feel* easy.'

She made a noise in her throat, a grim affirmation. And she picked at something on the table – a fleck of paint, or ketchup. She was thinking about it: the locals, the winter. Then she looked up.

'And how's Jane?'

'Haven't heard.'

Intermittent, fat rain exploded on the wonky windows. The storm was ripening overhead. He could feel the wine.

She held her glass in both hands. She was studying him, across the small square of table.

'Do you worry?'

'Worry? Jesus, no, I'm not worried.' And then, regretting his tone, he added, 'The place is eighty per cent rainforest. It's got beasties you don't want to think about. It's – you know, politically it's not great at the moment. But she walks into it like most people walk into a supermarket. If I worried, I'd never sleep.'

She tucked a lock of hair behind her ear. 'Amazing woman.'

'Amazing.'

'And Monkeyland? I hear good things.'

'Oh, I don't know. Summer's been all right. But summer ends, y'know? I just get the feeling – the place is going to die over Christmas.'

'Winter's always bad.'

'For you, too?'

'I teach a few classes, keep the wolf from the door.'

She shifted in her seat, and sat on the back of her hands, and brightened with a sudden idea that wasn't really sudden at all. 'What you should do, you should hold a winter market. Craft stalls, organic food. Art. Clothes. Wine. Whatever. Charge for the stalls. Then you're still pulling money through the door. Not just day trippers – locals too. Christmas shopping and whatever.'

He listened to the rain.

He disliked English market-towns, with their snooty and herbivorous New Age travellers, anarchists, Wiccans and occultists. But he liked the idea of a market in Monkeyland. It might bring in some money. But, better than that, it might give him something to think about, for five minutes, that wasn't fucking monkeys.

They talked about it, and more. They got a little drunk. And later, at the door, there was awkwardness. Should he kiss her cheek, his new friend, or shake her hand, his new acquaintance? They ducked and bumbled and, in the end, Patrick nodded and grunted something, and buried his hands in his jacket pockets and said, 'Okey dokey,' and left.

It was darker now. Strong winds whipping in, off the water.

The town was empty. He walked up the cobbled hill and into the pub. The sudden noise, like a cloudburst. He sat in the corner and took his time over a couple of pints. Nobody spoke to him, and when his last drink was drained he muttered, '*Sod it*,' and decided not to risk driving home.

It was still warm: the insulating, low clouds. Wind was channelled up the valley, through the hedges – and as he left Innsmouth on foot, it whistled like a jaunty spectre at his heels.

Halfway home, on the dark hill, he became aware of his solitude. And now, scared on this pitch-black trail, he felt foolish, half-pissed, an idiot.

He saw movement in the dark, slinky shadows, and heard a low growl beneath the wind. Shaking branches made an eager, voodoo rattle. He considered walking back to Innsmouth, calling Charlie – asking his son to come and pick him up in the orange VW. But it was nearly as far back to Innsmouth as it was to home.

He was persuaded by a volcanic rumble of thunder – and a sudden, violent flattening of the trees, like a cat's ears. He hurried on.

It wasn't a good idea to run, not with a belly full of booze and workboots on his feet. But he ran anyway, and got more scared the faster he ran, and although he ran, he did not beat the rain.

*

The Anchorage was an Edwardian hotel that stood on Minehead sea front, halfway between the high, wooded bluff called North Hill and Somerwest World, which was the new name for Butlins.

Charlie's boss was a giant called Clive – six feet four with a blimp of gut and a pink hock of fist. In order to hold a conversation with him, Charlie had to crane his neck like someone watching an aeroplane; he was treated to a foreshortened panorama of chasmal nostrils, above which Clive's skull seemed to terminate in a point, like railway lines meeting at the far horizon.

Clive had, he didn't let Charlie forget, been in *the business* all his working life. He'd run working men's clubs, mostly in Leeds and Bradford, before moving into the hotel trade. And he'd run some rough old places before moving down south. This, the Anchorage, it was a doddle. On-season, it was all pensioners and shaggers. Hardly any kids – who'd bring kids to an Edwardian hotel, with Butlins two minutes up the road? Nobody. So pensioners and shaggers it was.

Off-season, the pensioners stayed home.

*

Patrick couldn't sleep. Just after dawn, he went for a walk.

Outside, it was beautiful and silent. The wet grass, heavy with daisies and dandelions, swirled at his ankles: dawn mist snagged in the trees. Moisture sparkled on the hedgerows. The silence was sweetened with birdsong.

Patrick swelled inside with it; it felt good.

He tramped to the stile at the far end of the garden and clambered over it. He went through the oak trees, the moss and rot scent of them, and joined the tangled, South-West Coastal Footpath.

Trekking through the woods, he could hear, feel, smell the ocean. In several places, the forest ran down to the highwater mark. Rags of seaweed, glistening green-black, snared in exposed roots; crabs scuttled there.

When the woods thinned, he sat near the edge of the cliff. Yellow gorse pricked his arse. He opened his backpack and took out his breakfast – a banana and a bottle of mineral water filled that morning from the tap; it tasted of the house's old pipes.

After breakfast he wandered until he found a comfortable, sun-warming scoop in the rock. He sat and opened his book. The morning mist had burned off all but the deepest hollows, now – and even there it was loosening, stretching anemone tendrils at the sky.

It was still too early for anyone to be around, even the elderly hikers, the cheerful Tories who hiked this way in their red and blue kagouls, their daypacks. It was an in-between time; light, but not really morning – not unless you were a farmer, or an animal, or Patrick.

He read until the sun began to warm his neck. Soon it would burn. So he folded the page and put the book in his backpack and struck out for home. He was still feeling pretty good.

Accompanied by the sounds of the sea, he thought about England. He thought of his ancestors and saw the stamp of their lives on the fields and hills and coppices, these outbreaks of ancient forest. They would have breathed just like him, on any late-August morning. And perhaps, passing by this place, they had sensed his presence, a ghost of the future.

And then he was nearly home. He was moving through the dappled light under the trees, and he could see the stile, not far ahead – and on the other side of it, his land.

He wasn't quite 200 metres away when a panther, slinky and black as ink, its heavy tail raised like a question mark, padded onto the path and stopped at the stile.

It looked at Patrick. Between them was a moment of perfect recognition.

The panther twitched its tail, once. Then it flowed, unhurried, over the stile – the tip of its black tail disappearing last.

Patrick stood, quite still, for a very, very long time. A ladybird crawled over the toe of his boot. A fly landed on his forearm and fed on something it found there. Sweat ran into his eyes.

He blinked. The sunlight made patterns on his eyelids: sweeping and merging like the Northern Lights.

He listened for the cat.

He thought of it, stalking him through archaic English woodland.

There was no malevolence in it; just ferocious perfection. He imagined the cat dragging his body into the fork of a tree, leaving him there to season, eating him for weeks.

When that thought came – his corpse, still wearing hiking boots and a mini-rucksack, hanging in the branches of a tree, while local volunteers searched the fields and beaches below – Patrick became conscious of his paralysis. He surged with something like joy. He saw that his leg was trembling.

It had frozen in a difficult position, halfway through a step. So he moved, to ease it. And that broke his stasis.

There was a tidal surge of dirty panic, a geyser inside him. The cat had entered his garden.

In the garden was his house.

Inside the house was his daughter.

He took a tentative step. Another. And then he was running, the backpack slamming between his shoulders. Vaulting the stile, he sprinted through the dewy grass (where he and his wife had once made love, perhaps beneath the predator's yellow gaze). He sometimes ran backwards a few steps, just to make sure no low, inky missile had launched through the remains of the morning mist.

And when the stone house had grown close, when he was nearly safe, the panic broke and he accelerated still further.

His hands were graceless and clumsy with it; he couldn't open the kitchen door. And when he'd managed that, he threw himself inside and slammed the door behind him.

And then he stood at the kitchen window.

He drew off a glass of water and stood there, sipping it. Looking out.

In time, he became aware of the kitchen clock ticking behind him. He drained the water, drew off another glass, and sat at the cracked and warped old kitchen table. He began to shake.

He was still sitting there, shaking, when Jo came down. She was wearing a flannelette nightgown that almost reached her ankles and a pair of unlaced Converse.

'All right, Dad?'

He glanced at the window and felt himself furtive and hunted.

'Good, yeah.'

'Do you want to go for a run?'

He had to think about that for a while. He doubted the cat was active during full daylight. But this was his daughter. He imagined her, hauled into the fork of a tree.

'Not this morning.'

She put some bread in the toaster.

Patrick was still looking out of the window. He looked away only when she brought the toast to the table, to spread it with butter and jam.

He picked up the jam jar. There was no label on it, just a sticky square where one had been removed. He thumbed it, absently.

'Where does this come from?'

'Mr Nately.'

'He makes jam?'

'It's really nice. You can taste the fruit. Plums. He's won prizes.'

He said, 'Have you got any plans for today?'

'Not really.'

'Do me a favour, then . . .'

She was chewing toast, half-listening, flicking through the local freesheet.

'I have to go out later, for an hour,' he said.

'Fine.'

'When I'm gone, I'd like you to stay inside. Inside the house, please.'

She stopped chewing, and stopped reading, and looked at him. There was a smear of jam in the corner of her mouth.

'Why?'

'It doesn't matter. But just for today, okay? Read a book. Watch TV.'

'Why?'

'Just do me a favour and do it.'

'Fine,' she said. 'Whatever.' And took another bite of toast, and pretended not to be curious.

He drove to Monkeyland and picked up a flat-folded cage. Erected, it would be large enough for an adult male chimp. He made two junior keepers load the car with it.

On the way home, he stopped off at Greg Woods's farm.

Perhaps because it was Sunday, or perhaps because of Patrick's harried air, Greg forced him to haggle at vexatious length. The ewe was mutton, no good to anyone, and Patrick's voice grew higher and more exasperated with each of Greg's lethargic counter-offers.

But once a deal was agreed, Greg was quick enough to help Patrick manipulate the sheep into the back of the Land-Rover. It didn't want to go. It bleated and kicked and twisted. Patrick fell over a couple of times – flat on his arse in the dried-out mud, the old ewe leaping him like a hummock.

Greg hauled Patrick to his feet, but wasn't shy about his amusement – and eventually, Patrick laughed, too.

But in the end, the sheep went in.

At home, Patrick tethered the ewe on a long rope which he pegged to the centre of the garden. She was an elderly creature. Her eyes were moist and her fleece was yellow and tangled. Eventually she began, with an air of bewildered preoccupation, to mow Patrick's long grass into a crop circle.

He stood with the munching sheep, trying not to think of names for it.

He stripped to the waist, sweltering in his impatience, and

erected the cage inside the shade of the oak trees that bordered his land.

Then he went inside, for a long glass of water.

Jo had been watching from the bedroom window. Patrick had an air she recognized – distraction, impatience, excitement: fear. She wondered why. Obviously, it had to do with an animal; she knew a trap when she saw one. But Patrick and Jane were always so relaxed around animals, even vermin.

Once – this was in their house in Wales, when Jo was smaller – Jane had tracked a rat by sprinkling Johnson's Baby Talc onto the kitchen floor. Next morning, she followed the ratty footprints in the powder and pulled back the old fridge. That way, she found the hole through which the rat was getting in.

She laid out a big, vicious old trap and baited it with peanut butter, and the next morning (or at least, Jo remembered it as the next morning) the rat was captured. It was still alive. Its fur was black with blood. Paler blood was smeared on the floor and the wall. The rat was trying to gnaw off its hind leg. It looked like a cat, cleaning itself.

When it saw Jane, it grew frantic. It gnawed faster.

Jane moved young Jo back into a corner and then knelt a few inches from the rat. She rifled the kitchen drawers, examining potential weapons – knives, a claw hammer (whose weight she tested once, before laying it aside) and finally, in the lowest drawer, an old wooden rolling pin, stained and swollen and cracked. She crushed the rat's skull with a single, precise blow.

Then she slipped on a pair of Marigolds and picked up the corpse. The rat separated from its leg like slow-cooked meat from the bone.

Jane dangled the corpse. Apparently delighted, she said, 'Look — it bit all the way through.'

Later, as Jane tucked her up, Jo wondered why people were so scared of rats. They didn't look so frightening to her.

And Jane told her this: human beings are naturally scared of things that, long, long ago, were dangerous to us. Things like spiders and snakes and rats.

She sat on the edge of the bed and stroked Jo's hair and told her about an experiment with monkeys.

These monkeys were raised in isolation, in a protected, very safe environment. Then scientists took them to a special room and tried to make them scared of things. They did it by delivering electric shocks whenever a certain picture appeared on screen. That way, they could make a monkey scared of pretty much anything they wanted — a flower, or beach ball, or Bob Monkhouse. But it took a long time, and the monkey that learned to be scared of (say) a feather-duster couldn't make other monkeys scared of it. The other monkeys just thought him mad, a loony monkey, screaming in terror at a red bucket, or a handful of tulips, or a yo-yo.

It was much, much easier to make the monkeys scared of something that resembled, for example, a snake — something they'd evolved to fear. A length of garden hose would do, or a piece of rope.

But what was really interesting: it was also much, much easier for the monkey who was scared of garden hoses to spread that fear among his troop. They didn't think he was a loony; show them a hose and the whole group erupted into mad panic.

And now Jo watched Patrick, coming out of the house again, stripped to the waist, erecting the cage.

Unloading it, he'd told her a lie – he told her it was a kennel for the sheep. Jo didn't know much about animals, but she wasn't completely stupid. And when Patrick warned her not to go out alone, he had a strange look in his eye; a crazed look, like someone who's just woken up from a terrible dream.

Bored of watching from the window, she walked downstairs, through the cool kitchen and into the bright garden.

It was a hot day. She winced in the abrupt sunlight. She went to the sheep. It looked at her with trusting eyes. It had a mouth full of dandelions. Absently, she rubbed its head.

She said, 'Dad, what did you see?'

Patrick put his hands on his hips. He was sweating, grubby, shirtless.

'Nothing. Go back inside.'

That night, Patrick carried a kitchen chair upstairs and set it before the bedroom window. On the windowsill, he'd already set out his field-glasses and a 35 mm camera with flash.

He opened the window – he didn't want condensed breath to obscure his view. He wrapped himself in a blanket and watched the sheep, a bone-yellow glow in the darkness.

Sometime after dawn, his head nodded onto his chest. He was woken by the sound of the flush. Jo getting up.

Out there in the sunrise, the sheep was still alive. It was looking up at him.

Patrick remembered it was Monday morning. So he took Jo to Nately's, and went to work.

Patrick and Jo became fond of the sheep. During the day, they tethered it. Each evening, getting home, Patrick was consoled and discouraged to find it still alive. And each night, as he herded the sheep into its cage (to which it quickly became habituated) he felt villainous and full of shame. The sheep trusted him: he was a bad shepherd.

Often, in the early morning, he went out, carrying a heavy stick and the camera. And he sat in a deckchair, waiting. The silence amplified all the noises around him, the sounds of the nearby, invisible ocean, and he was scared.

But the cat did not return.

9

Charlie learned how to maintain the Anchorage as if he were a nurse and it were his patient. He learned how to take reservations, how to clean and prepare the rooms, making the blankets army-taut, the carpets free of dust. He bleached the shit-stained lavatories and emptied bins full of waxy cotton buds and tampon applicators and balls of gummy toilet paper. He learned to wait tables of diffident guests and, in the sweaty and hellish kitchen, to scrub out the gigantic aluminium pots in which their potatoes were boiled.

The nearest he got to a friend was Mad Mervin in the laundry room. Mervin was griping, possibly East European; hook-nosed, vulture-shouldered, wearing a Budweiser cap. He claimed to have been caught in the Anchorage Hotel for twelve years. He never called Charlie any name but *Boy*, which creeped him out: *Come here, boy*.

Other than Mervin and Clive, the staff were mostly temporary and seasonal. The men in the kitchen were skinny, and tattooed. The women spoke only when they formed a smoking gaggle round the back, by the bins – where they were invisible, both to the guests and to Clive.

Charlie liked best to work the bar on a quiet night. It hadn't been decorated for years. The wood was dark; the flock wallpaper was scarlet and blood-red, and the lights were low. Sometimes, he was pestered by only half a dozen customers, nursing their drinks, murmuring across tables, touching knees, playing footsie. Sometimes there were no customers at all, and he was free to read the paper in a cone of light until Clive stomped in and told him to close up.

Charlie liked the Anchorage. He liked to work double shifts – for the money, and also because there was no point leaving. At home, there was only Patrick and Jo, and the house stultified him with its routine and its silence. It was easier to take one of the vacant, inferior single rooms near the back of the ground floor, overlooking the car park and the giant metal bins, and lay down his head.

And so, because he slept there and ate there and worked there, the Anchorage soon began to feel like Charlie's natural habitat.

––––––––––

FROM JANE'S NOTEBOOKS

We talked to the hunters of the Bili Forest. They described two indigenous ape species: *tree-beaters* and *lion-killers*. These apes resemble one another, but lion-killers are much the larger: gorilla-sized.

Threatened by a hunter, a male gorilla will usually charge. It's a stupefying display, absolutely terrifying, and usually it works. Any hunter who wishes to live will back away. I'd consider myself fortunate to maintain bowel control.

But gorillas aren't belligerent, aren't warlike. They charge only to protect, and then move on.

For all their reported gorilla size, lion-killers don't behave like that. Sometimes, the hunters are startled by these giant apes, which fade in like ghosts from the dense foliage. And sometimes, this hushed apparition is followed by an attack.

If these were bluff charges, the apes would be screaming, displaying, shrieking. But the lion-killers are quite silent, utterly purposeful. And very, very big.

Only when they see the hunters' weapons do they stop. Then they just fade back into the forest, like ink onto blotting paper.

This approximates chimp behaviour. Chimp war-parties move quietly. So perhaps these apes are simply chimps: very big, very intelligent, very aggressive chimps.

Several unusual skulls have been taken from the area. The first went to the Trevuren Museum in Brussels, in 1898. So this ape is not a newcomer.

The Bili skulls have a prominent sagittal crest – a bony, arrow-shaped ridge that runs the length of the skull; it attaches to the *temporalis*, which in turn attaches the skull to the jaw of certain mammals.

Sagittal crests can be found in numerous human populations – the Inuit, for example – and in many of our ancestors. They are also found in male gorillas.

But they are not found in chimpanzees.

*

On the first day, we found nothing.

We hadn't expected to, but it was still a disappointment – it's human nature to let hope outweigh expectation. In fact, we had to wait until day five before we found anything at all: not the ape, but evidence of where it sleeps. We discovered a number of large, well-worn ground nests.

Chimps usually bed down in trees – it's gorillas who make nests, but they tend to construct a new one every night. And they hate water.

These nests were on swampy ground, and they showed signs of multiple use. They were abandoned now, though. We took some faecal samples, but they were degraded and old. There was no fresh shit. Whatever had slept here (and kept coming back to sleep here) was long gone.

But it was the first real sign of their existence. I could feel them – feel them in the forest with their flat gorilla faces and their quick, brown, human eyes.

We filmed the nests: even filmed the stool samples we took back with us for analysis. And none of us spoke, not even Claude.

I caught him, staring into the trees as if he felt it, too – the intelligent eyes, wondering who we are and what we're doing, prodding at their beds and their two-week-old turds, averting our eyes and nodding now and again, and sometimes gently vocalizing: the soft, wordless grunts that to a chimpanzee, as to a person, are sounds of reassurance and fellowship.

Perhaps all we're looking for is an isolated chimp population with certain unusual physical characteristics – size, facial physiognomy – and unique behaviour patterns. Chimps have culture. Such an isolated group would undoubtedly develop unique strategies.

Or perhaps the Bili Ape is a hybrid – a descendant of mated gorillas and chimps. Although no one has ever seen this or to my knowledge tried it, in theory the two species are close enough to breed and produce fertile offspring.

If, long, long ago, the Congo Basin had lowered, perhaps ancient gorilla and chimp populations intermingled, both geographically and (somehow) genetically. And, when the Congo rose again, it left behind an isolated, hybrid species in an island of jungle.

Perhaps.

Near the end of our second week, we found some footprints. They looked to come from perhaps eight individuals. The largest was 35 centimetres – bigger than the biggest gorilla footprint. Most of the prints were spoiled – there were too many of them and the mud was churned up. We took casts where we could. We got two or three really good ones.

But we didn't find these footprints in the forest, or in a nesting site.

We found them at the edge of our camp.

They had gathered here, during the night, quite silently. And we don't know why. Perhaps they're threatened by us. Perhaps they're just curious.

Perhaps they were a hunting-party.

Chimpanzee war-parties will patrol territorial borders, and they will beat to death any individual unlucky enough to come into contact with them. It's a bonding experience for them. They enjoy it.

We made funny faces, because we were scared. We have only one gun, Claude's, and anyway only one of us knows how to use it. Richard joked about buying a few grenades, back at the refugee camp.

I thought, We've come here to find this thing – but what if it's the last thing we see? That gorilla face, that chimp body; those human eyes.

————

At night, Patrick kept vigil at his bedroom window and tried not to sleep. But when he did, he dreamed of Jane.

He talked to her. He said nothing of importance or interest. *I broke a shoelace*, he said, and dangled it to show her.

The dreams were memories of a life they had never lived. They were in a supermarket, pushing a squeaky trolley down a bright white aisle; picking up tins of beans and loaves of bread. Or they were in a cinema, sharing a bucket of salty popcorn.

Or they were having sex. There was no phantasmagoria, no role play. They were simply in bed – any one of the beds which, over the years, they had shared – and they were naked and kissing.

But in the dreams he couldn't come and she stroked his face (the rough pads of her fingertips!) and she told him *shhhh*, and he woke frustrated – upright in the hard-backed chair, wrapped in a blanket, and he was ashamed and frightened and unable to remember his name.

He was stiff, from sitting up all night. He stood, and his legs and arms and back hurt. He rolled his head on his shoulders and threw off the blanket and turned on the radio and waited for bad news from Zaire.

But there was no bad news from Zaire: there was no news from Zaire at all. For that, he had to burrow deep into the dreary centre pages of *The Times*. And what little news he got, none of it was good.

The *interahamwe* were using refugee camps in the east of Zaire as a base from which to launch attacks into Rwanda. And also to kill Zaireans; Banyamulenge Tutsis.

Siding with the refugee *génocidaires,* President Mobuto had threatened to expel all Tutsis from Zaire.

Meanwhile, the Rwanda Patriotic Army had entered into coalition with Uganda and Laurent-Désiré Kabila's *Alliance des Forces Démocratiques pour la Libération du Congo-Zaire*. Kabila was a Tutsi, of course.

First, this vengeful coalition would deal with the camps, which meant probable massacre. Then they'd move west, towards Kinshasa.

For all Patrick knew, Jane was far from all this. But was she far enough? Chaos sends out great backwashes, riptides, tsunamis. How could she be safe?

Charlie and Jo never talked about her, and became monosyllabic if Patrick tried to do so. He supposed they were having bad dreams of their own.

And anyway, what was he supposed to say? Their mother was in Africa with a war billowing out behind her like bread in an oven. What could he say, that wasn't a lie?

So Patrick understood the dreams. They were a function of his unarticulated anxiety.

And yet, the day before learning of his father's death, Patrick had dreamed of him; an old man in carpet slippers and baggy old trousers, shuffling around outside, surrounded by an uneasy swirl of snapping hyenas.

He knew then (and he knew now), that this had been a co-incidence, but there was a deep, human part of him – a magical thinker, a maker-of-connections – and that part demanded a link between the subject of his dreams and the object of them.

This part of him knew, too that to dream of Jane was to speak with her.

By day, at Monkeyland, the dreams left him with a dirge of unease. And at night, he kept his vigil: window open, camera ready. Blanket worn like a hooded robe. And he watched the oblivious sheep, a dim globe of light in the darkness – a sacrifice to certain dark gods in whom Patrick did not believe.

He knew that something was about to happen.

He believed in none of this. He believed in all of it. He believed it in the way he knew Jane must never travel without her grand-father's old trunk.

He kept his vigil.

*

Charlie was at the bar. White shirt, wine-coloured waistcoat. He was reading yesterday's *Sun*. The bar was empty, until a woman walked in. Business suit. Kitten heels. Handbag.

He felt weird in the big, empty bar, not knowing where to look.

She looked around. Saw him.

'Where is everybody?'

'Somewhere else.'

The red flock walls soaked up the echoes.

He beamed at her; it felt huge on his face. Customers rarely spoke to him except to order a drink and, once or twice, to try to procure a prostitute.

She spun around, taking in the emptiness. Her heels clicked on the floor. She wasn't wearing a wedding ring. Her shirt was open to the third button. Around her neck, she wore a silver chain.

Her hair was short at the neck; a very blunt bob. He could see the tendons under the skin: the tendons in her thin wrist, her feet, her ankles.

'Does it get any livelier?'

He closed the *Sun*, concealing it under a cloth. 'Not really.'

She perched on a stool and placed her little handbag on the bar.

He said, 'What can I get you?'

'Oh, I don't know.'

She ordered a gin and tonic. Preparing it, his hands were blundering – twice, he almost dropped the glass. He passed her the drink and she took a sip.

'So it's always like this?'

He wondered what to say. He thought of twenty things.

He said: 'Usually.'

'How long have you worked here?'

'A while.'

'It feels longer, I bet.' Her eyes were effervescent, and she wore that delicate necklace and that shirt, open three buttons.

'I lost my old job. I worked out at the chimp sanctuary – Monkeyland, up the road. Some kid was throwing stuff at a chimpanzee. So I hit him.'

She laughed – just once, but loud in the emptiness. The laugh scattered on the ceiling and came down as glitter and the red room became a snowglobe.

'Well, I suppose that's as good a reason as any for losing your job.'

She was down from Manchester, she told him. She was a rep for a Medical Supplies Company. She ordered another drink.

And later, she said, 'So I might go out, grab something to eat. Any recommendations?'

'There's a seafood place on the harbour, but it'll be quiet.' He referred theatrically to his watch. 'It might not even be *open*.'

She grabbed her bag. 'What the hell. Let's see.'

She left a tip.

When she'd gone, trailing perfume behind her, the bar doubled in size, and fungal silence unfolded from the scarlet walls.

He flicked through the *Sun*, but it held no interest – not even page 3, which was always worth a glance. Now it looked stupid; that happy, dumb smile, those perky tits.

In the end, he poured himself a Coke and watched the ice melt until 10.45, when he began preparations to close the bar.

At 10.55, she came back.

His heart made a noise. He wondered if she heard it. The expression on her face implied she had.

She had reapplied her lipstick. It was not red. It was a dark brown. Charlie knew nothing about lipstick. Charlie had never kissed anyone who wore it.

She said, 'Too late for last orders?'

'Not at all.' He began to slice the remaining half of the lime.

She sat down and lit a cigarette. 'It's horrible, eating alone,' she said. 'Everyone looks at you.'

Charlie scooped ice into the long glass and silently agreed.

She said, 'Are you finished for the night?'

'Closing the bar.' He added a vibrating splash of gin over ice.

'Do you do room service?'

'Until two a.m.'

He handed her the glass, and she took it. He thought for a second that she might actually wink. She didn't. He watched her leave the red bar, taking her drink with her, and wondered if she knew he was watching.

He didn't see her again for a month.

————

FROM JANE'S NOTEBOOKS

In five weeks at the camp, we've surveyed several hundred square kilometres of forest, patchy savannah and near-swamp. We've gathered information on more than fifty ground nests and several tree nests.

The way it looks, the dominant males make the ground nests. Females, juveniles and infants prefer the trees.

We think they live in small groups; probably fewer than ten of them. Perhaps there is only one group. Perhaps the species is about to vanish, just before it's officially discovered.

Here is the evidence we've collected for its existence, the Bili Ape: its nests, its shit, its footprints. And the look in people's eyes when they speak of it, the stories they tell.

We haven't seen it. But it's seen us. It's been watching.

We discussed what to do next. We have a great deal of film, but no ape. So Richard suggested that Claude takes us to

Virunga National Park. He wants to film some evidence of poaching: it'll play well, if only as context.

Claude agreed. He cares about the animals, he wants people in England to see what's happening to them.

'People in England will care about the animals more than the people,' I said, and Claude gave me a look that made me uncomfortable.

We took a vote. We opened a bottle of gin I've been hoarding since the hotel. Passed round a tin mug.

It was down to Camra Dave and Sound Mick – whatever happens, they get their fee. If we go home now, it's no loss to them. So we looked at the ground and waited out their silence.

Claude wanted them to film the poachers, even though it might be dangerous – for us, but more so for him. Even though he has the gun.

In the end, Camra Dave said, 'Fuck it, why not?'

And we nodded, and bravely jutted out our lips.

'Fuck it, why not?' said Claude, pleased, and we shook hands. Claude kissed me on the cheek.

———

10

Comet Hyakutakewa was long gone; it had shone brightly for a few days, back in the early spring, and then departed on its vast and soundless ellipse.

But Hyakutakewa had been only the opening act. Now, Comet Hale Bopp was coming. Hale Bopp was the main event; the greatest comet Jo and Nately, or anyone else on the planet, were ever likely to see.

It wouldn't shine at its brightest until next year. But already, if you knew where to look, it was visible to the naked eye. Had been, since the summer. A white point, coming closer.

Mr Nately had been staying up late to observe it. Jo could tell; during lessons he drifted off, yawned, covered his mouth with a fist. Once or twice, as she worked at an essay or a test, his eyes closed and she saw the surprised, waking twitch after his chin had drooped to his chest.

Jo didn't mind; she was tired, too.

The sun was still rising when she got to her desk. The blush behind the dark and fearful orchard at the end of the garden made an oblong silhouette of Mr Nately's observatory.

Mr Nately heated the classroom with a Calor-gas burner whose rippling emanations thickened the light, blurring the space between Jo's eye and the text of her books. She wore layers of clothes and felt languid and unable to concentrate. Her mind was elsewhere on Earth.

At night, she dreamed of her mother, but the dreams were confused – Jane stood on a high rock with her arms in the air, and behind her, the sun rose (or set) behind a vast and lowering bank of stormclouds.

It was difficult to imagine the African heat when waking in a breath-condensing, cold-floored bedroom, or passing the frost on the briars. It was more difficult still to imagine Jane being threatened by a war which, for most people in England, did not exist.

Jo supposed there must be other wars in the world, going on right now, and she wondered how she was supposed to find out about them. The TV news and the newspapers were full of New Labour, and John Major and Tony Blair, and an election that wasn't going to happen for months yet – and she wouldn't be interested in it, even then.

She wondered what made one war matter, and another not. It wasn't something she could ask Mr Nately. He could recite the campaigns of Alexander, or Julius Caesar, or Field Marshal Haig, or General Montgomery. He watched the news and read *The Times*. He knew something about the genocide in Rwanda – more than most people seemed to. But he knew almost nothing about what was going on, right now, in Zaire.

————

FROM JANE'S NOTEBOOKS

The war is coming.

We've decided to head west, fly out from Kinshasa, cross the border into Brazzaville if we have to. We've got petrol: we've got trucks.

And we've got good footage from Virunga: an elephant on a smoking table, being hacked into pieces for transportation; villagers tortured by armed gangs of poachers, beaten and burned for daring to open their mouths in protest.

We've got the bushmeat stalls at Bukavu – the heaped baskets of monkeys; the cakes of blackened meat, the smiling vendor who said they were either smoked elephant or gorilla.

We've got bulldozed trees heaped either side of the logging road; hunting camps at the edge of the floor of a cathedral-like, brand new clearing in the forest. We've got the skinny men carrying panniers hung with duikers and colobus monkeys.

We've got the miserable little camp, a ramshackle collection of palm-frond shelters, and a gorilla's head bubbling in its own juices. There was a burned, sweet undercurrent to its smell, like sugar blackening the bottom of a heavy-based pan. The woodsmoke made our eyes water.

We've got the poacher passing me a huge, meaty hand; a hand with black nails and a leathery palm.

I began to cry and wanted the camera turned off, but of course they kept it rolling because tears are good. Tears will sell it. Tears are *human interest*.

I did a shouted piece to camera, standing on a scar of logging road while huge, yellow lorries, piled with hardwood, passed with a noise like jet engines.

'More than thirty million people survive in the forests of the Congo Basin. These people have hunted here for thousands of years, and had little impact on overall animal numbers.

A few years ago, you couldn't find bushmeat in Zairean cities – not until the European logging companies, mostly French, began to decimate the forests for its hardwood.

They forced animals into ever-smaller spaces, little enclaves, through which more and more new roads are being rammed. And on these new roads come the urban hunters – men who know little, and care less, about maintaining the balance of the forest.

They cut deals with the drivers, to cross the country with bushmeat secreted in their trucks. Thus, they introduced a new taste to the cities. And so, most bushmeat – chimpanzee meat, gorilla meat, elephant meat – isn't used to feed starving people; not the hungry refugees subsisting in the unfamiliar rainforest. It's sold in cities, at far higher prices than beef or goat. It's destined for the plates of the wealthy.'

Anyway. There's enough. The war is coming.

Once we decided, it became urgent: we wanted to get home right now, right away.

We said goodbye to Claude. He's returning to Goma, to work for some Belgian NGOs. The boys told jokes about Belgians, but I don't think boring Belgians are much of a joke on the Congo – not when they're told by white Europeans, anyway. Any more, I suppose, than efficient Germans are much of a joke in Tel Aviv.

I'm scared for Claude. He has to walk right back into it. We swapped addresses: we passed a Biro, a little notepad. He gave me an address where he can check his mail, periodically. I gave him the PO Box of Monkeyland. It looks pitiful, written down: Monkeyland. I cringed, and felt like a coward. England seemed almost comical, when I thought about where Claude is going. After all these weeks together, and all he's shown us, we didn't know how to say goodbye.

In the end, he just walked off. Richard made another joke. Claude turned and waved, and turned again, and that is the last time I think I will ever see his face.

In the morning, as we were preparing to leave, a young soldier found me.

Into my arms he pressed a bundle. It's a tiny, sick bonobo. A week ago, it saw its mother captured, taunted and beaten. Then it saw its mother killed, skinned, butchered and cooked. Then it was chained to the stall on which its mother was for sale, smoked and in pieces.

The soldiers wanted to sell the infant as a pet. But it was sick, and nobody would buy it.

The young soldier could see my anger – this exhausted, rheumy-eyed white woman, sweat-stained. He wanted me to take the bonobo and just leave. He wouldn't meet my eyes.

I was so angry, but we didn't leave. Instead, Dave was quick to get the camera running, hoisted onto his shoulder.

And, on camera, I asked the shy young man with the gun how bonobo tastes.

'It is a little tough,' he said.

Bonobos are found only between the Congo River in the north and the Kasai River in the south.

Unlike chimpanzees, who are violent, territorial, warlike, predatory and murderous, bonobos regulate their society with non-procreative sex. They use sex in greeting, as a means of conflict resolution, as reconciliation – and as favours traded by the females in exchange for food. They are the only non-human creature to have been observed kissing with tongues, engaging in face-to-face vaginal intercourse, oral sex, mutual masturbation between females, and frottage between males.

They do eat insects and sometimes small mammals, but their primary energy source is fruit.

In 1980, there were 100,000 of them. By 1990, that number had been reduced by 90 per cent. And that was before the boy soldiers started hunting them as bushmeat, with automatic weapons.

The soldier slunk away; feeling watched, he was narrow-hipped and insulted, surly as a young Elvis Presley.

The infant weighs about the same as a bag of sugar. It is dark-faced, with coarse black hair, parted in the centre. I took it to the Land-Rover and opened some bottled water.

As I dripped water into her mouth, she struggled to

free her arms from the blanket, then reached out for me. She grasped me tightly – the falling reflex – then she stroked the hair on my bare forearm.

She's not really strong enough to be carried on my back, but it's what she wants – it makes her feel secure. She clings on as best she can; then slides off. In the end, I fashioned a sling for her, from the blanket, and she rests in that. She's thin. She's dying.

I laid her in the back of the Land-Rover. She slept. I watched her for a while.

I spoke to Richard.

'Zaire,' he said, reading my expression, 'is going to fuck. It's a mess. We need to get out, asap. We *agreed* to get out.'

And I am homesick, and scared, and longing for my children. But home doesn't seem real. How can it be real, a few hours' flight from all this – this sick creature which has fallen into my care, in this sick country and this chaos? You can feel it gathering.

I offered Richard a deal. I told him it's a good show: we didn't find the Bili, but we can rescue this ape, this child, from a war-zone. It'll be a quest, a drama, dragging this sick baby across a dangerous country, in an attempt to save its life.

Naming her.

I said, 'We have to give her a name.'

Richard gave me a look. The others sulked. They want to go home. Back to the West Country of England; cider and Glastonbury Tor.

We argued. People stopped to frankly watch; we must have

been quite a diversion, these four white people in filthy clothes, three men and one woman, screaming at each other outside the Land Cruisers.

But finally, we agreed.

Let's get the bonobo to Kinshasa. Let's drop it off somewhere safe, and then let's cross over to Brazzaville, where there is no war, and then let's work out how the hell to get home.

———

Patrick maintained his night-time vigil. But still, the cat did not return, and the sheep lived. He grew to resent it; easy meat, content in her metal trap at night, munching the abundant grass short by day.

Perhaps the cat had been one of the dreams that were infecting his waking life. He remembered it had been early morning, the light unreal in the woodland. Perhaps he had blinked and slept, and made of the mossy English oakwoods a rainforest.

But the fear had been real. He didn't run the way he ran in dreams: his legs weren't treacle-slow, dream slow, dream heavy. He ran like an athlete, and stood in his kitchen and drank cold, limestone-tinctured water.

He didn't know what to think, or to whom he could speak, and sometimes he wondered – sitting in the darkness, shrouded in a coarse blanket, making deals with forces in which he did not believe, to take the life of the sheep as a substitute for his wife – if he might not be going a little mad.

*

As the year grew older, the Anchorage Hotel grew void and creepy. Charlie hated the emptiness; it made the hallways shabby. He feared the blind, numbered doors to empty rooms. He snooped out of guest-room windows and saw winter dust devils travelling the deserted scoop of Minehead beach.

And now it was Friday night, very late in November. Nearly 10 p.m., and Charlie was behind the bar. His only customers were a gaggle of reps, single-room occupiers.

Charlie loathed them for their paunches, their moustaches, their cheap suits and wrinkled socks; he felt corrupted by the braying lewdness of their desire.

And when Chris McNeil walked in, feline and fluid, Charlie was halfway to their corner table, balancing a circle of pints and whisky chasers on a dented tray.

Seeing her, *smelling* her, sent a spasm of shock through him. He had to correct his balance or risk losing the tray – and how great *that* would look, standing there drenched in slopped John Smiths, with a corner table full of piggish old fuckers ridiculing him in their cigarette voices.

Chris McNeil walked to the bar, arching an eyebrow as she cruised past.

Charlie plonked down the beers, one by one.

The reps had gotten to purring and tittering because a woman had entered the bar; a woman alone. These men, in their shiny-arsed suits, with shrivelled purple fruit between their hairy thighs, pretending themselves animals of sex.

By the time Charlie got to the bar, the tray held at his side, she was on a stool, lighting a cigarette.

He said, 'Hello again,' and put down the tray. 'What can I get you?'

She tilted her head, half a degree. 'Who's that lot?'

'Reps.'

She blew smoke. 'Then I'll make it a quick one.'

He wanted to protect her from their polluting insinuations. She saw him glance at them; the hatred in it. Seeing that opened her face, and she seemed younger and sadder. Her face, in that moment, was the most naked thing he had ever seen.

She said, 'You get used to it.'

'You shouldn't have to.'

He muttered it, but she must have heard okay, because she reached out and touched the back of his hand. He withdrew it, sharply.

It hung between them for a while. Her opened-up, naked face. His desire to protect her. Her fingertip heat fading on the back of his hand.

She said, 'It's nice to see you again.'

He got a clean glass and began to prepare a gin and tonic. He worked, hands shaking.

'So, what brings you back?'

'The monthly call.'

'I thought maybe you'd find a better hotel.'

'I like this one.'

His heart made a noise again. There was an eruption of braying hilarity from the reps.

She raised an eyebrow; Charlie raised two. They were conspirators. She had touched his hand.

She waited until the uproar had died down. And then she said, 'We'll get no peace this evening.'

'I doubt it.'

'So. Are you working tomorrow?'

He shook his head. No.

She stubbed out her cigarette.

'All right. Why don't I see you then?'

He was in Minehead early. It was growing cold and he shivered in his jacket. He went for a walk along the sea wall and sat down there for a bit, watching the boats bob and the gulls dive-bomb the water. He could smell rotting seaweed and salt and vinegar.

He waited for a long time and wished he'd brought a book. He looked at his watch. Seven minutes had passed.

He went to an amusement arcade – almost deserted, the cabinets flashing and whooping madly in the emptiness – and spent a few minutes deciding what to play. He found a big, old *Tekken* cabinet and pumped in some money. And then he wondered what Chris McNeil might think if – according to some horrible, inevitable coincidence – she should happen past and see him, bashing buttons, slamming weight on one foot then the other.

He blushed with mortification and skulked away from the arcade, *Tekken* still soliciting him from the corner.

Returning to the sea wall, he sat and waited and it grew fully dark and even colder and the gulls were points of white light on the black low tide, and she was late.

He heard footsteps behind him.

She was huddled deep into her coat and had her chin tucked between her shoulders. 'Hello,' she said.

Then her position changed. She fossicked in her handbag,

looking for cigarettes, and he felt the moment receding. Already he was nostalgic for it: it seemed to mark the end of something.

She offered him a cigarette. He took one. Accepted a light, bowing to the flame, brushing his fringe to one side.

'So.' She crooked an elbow and he slipped his arm through hers. And that would have been enough; that shock of contact, prolonged, even through several layers of fabric.

'Where are we going?'

She showed him her car keys, folded up in her hand. Then asked, 'How old are you, exactly?'

'Eighteen.'

'Eighteen,' she said. 'Eighteen.'

They walked to her car – a black Golf – which chirruped and flashed, and they got inside, and closed the doors with a heavy, night-time sound.

Inside, it smelled of new car and perfume and perhaps an undercurrent of long-ago cigarettes. He looked at her hand on the gear stick: the flexing tendons, the red nail on the thumb. The shape of her knee. The weird intimacy of her ankles, naked beneath the hems of her trousers. The seat belt, separating her breasts. The fine silver chain.

He looked at his jeans, his Converse. Strobing in the sodium light.

They drove past the salt flats. No lights. Just the water, cold silver on the near horizon.

The restaurant was less than half-full. They sat near the window, where they could watch people and cars and buses come and go. He pushed food round his plate and sipped Sauvignon Blanc.

She didn't say much, except that she was glad of his company.

She hated eating alone. Never got used to it. You always got funny looks.

'Men,' she said.

There were laughter-lines at the corner of her eyes and mouth. They were inexpressibly sexy.

When the plate was taken away she lit a cigarette. Offered him one. A light.

He dug out his wallet and opened it, and she chuckled, not unkindly, and touched the back of his hand again. 'My treat.'

As she signed the bill, she kept the cigarette in the corner of her mouth, looked at him from under her fringe, and said, 'I'll claim you on expenses. Entertainment.'

He'd taken the next day off, just in case – so she offered to drop him home; she knew the way to Innsmouth, but after that he directed her through the lightless back road, past farmland and woodland.

His heart beat feverish and thin. But she didn't pull over, as he had been fearing and hoping she might, until they reached the house.

Then she yanked up the handbrake and the car was silent and they sat there in the dark.

She said, 'Well, thanks again. For looking after me.'

She leaned over. He held his breath. She kissed his cheek. Her lips were cold warm on him: the blood beneath the lipstick.

He opened the door. He walked slowly because he could feel her eyes on him and it robbed the strength from his legs.

Her car made a three-point turn in the narrow road then pulled away; the red lights diminishing.

Charlie dug around for his keys, found them and went inside.

When he got back to work in the morning, she was gone.

*

The nearest decent library was in Barnstaple, thirty miles down the coast.

Patrick woke, still propped up in the kitchen chair, still wrapped in a blanket, having decided in his sleep to go there. Immediately, he couldn't wait. He shrugged off the blanket. It was a decision; better than waiting night after night at the open window, shivering and doubting what he'd seen, all those weeks ago. And it was better than praying for the cat to return – just once – to feast on the old ewe and prove him sane.

He called Harriet at home and made vague, muttering intimations of a domestic problem, exploiting her awareness of Jane's absence, his two teenage children. And he dropped Jo early at Nately's. Then he drove south to Barnstaple.

It felt good to be back in a library, hunting – his stomach growling, light-headed, because he'd forgotten to eat. It made him feel like a reporter again, the kind of reporter he had wanted to be. It was an adventure.

He swept through blurring microfiche, but still it took half a morning, searching local archives, to find the first mention of what he wanted. Seeing it for the first time, he wanted to cackle in triumph, like an old witch. But he gritted his teeth and counted down to slow his heart, then began the cross-referencing, the digging up and tracking down, taking books from shelves, accessing national-newspaper archives. He scribbled notes in long-unused, always-familiar shorthand on a spiral-bound notebook, bought fresh that morning.

Then, mid-afternoon, by now queasy with hunger, he took the

notebook to a nearby café. Breaking off to shovel lunch down himself with a fork, he began to compile his notes, to work them into an order.

And when that was done, he scrawled the notes in longhand, and allowed himself wonder, with a self-satisfied smirk and a full belly, if all those nights at the window, watching the sheep survive, had been wasted after all.

In 1976, the last Labour Government had passed the Dangerous Wild Animals Act, which controlled the private ownership of, among other things, big cats.

It had long been rumoured that, rather than surrender their darlings to the ignominy of a public zoo, or death, the decadent wealthy who kept such creatures – the pop stars, the actors, the junkie aristos — preferred to set them free, to fend for themselves.

This had never actually been proven. But, in 1983, a farmer down in South Molton – Eric Ley – lost a hundred sheep, all of them to throat injuries.

It was the *Daily Express* that first named this predator 'the Beast of Exmoor'. It offered a reward for its capture.

No luck.

Then, in 1989, following the loss of more livestock, the Royal Marines were sent in. Plenty of them saw the beast, or said they did – but always briefly, without sufficient time to execute a decent shot; none were fired. Eventually, the livestock attacks died off again, but only until the Marines were sent home – by which time the government had designated the Beast a myth, a hallucination, a hoax.

Such sightings were not confined to North Devon. Alien Big Cats had been spotted all over the United Kingdom. In 1980, a

Scottish farmer trapped a lynx. He called it Felicity; it died in captivity.

Someone else – on the Isle of Wight – shot a leopard. He'd imagined a fox must be responsible for the death of so many ducks and chickens. Seeing what he'd killed, he kept silent for months, fearing that he'd harmed a protected species.

Patrick snorted, joyously, at the poor sap's folly.

And then he transcribed the notes which told him that, of all the big cats, leopards were the most adaptable. They were common, especially in dense forest. And, of course, they had once been popular with private collectors. This was particularly true of melanistic leopards, often known as black panthers. Very chic, a black panther. Very showbiz. Very Jackie Collins. In the right decade, in the right context.

Leopards were most active at dawn and dusk. But they would hunt in the day, too.

Patrick had been right to be cautious, and right to be scared.

In the late 1970s, a lynx had been captured in Barnstaple itself – not far, in fact, from where Patrick had just eaten a belated breakfast.

He thought of the beast in the woods – the hot, slinking predator who did not belong there – and he was overjoyed not, after all, to be mad.

11

The *Colonel Ebeya* arrived. It is a disintegrating hulk, the rusting corpse of a cyclopean water beetle. A horde of barges and pirogues is fastened to it: they float and meander like rotting lilies. They're loaded up with flesh to sell: fish, pork, crocodile, and fruit.

Every surface throngs, hums, with life, human and animal: the *Ebeya* is home to 4,000 people: merchants, children, soldiers, prostitutes.

The four of us – the five of us – share one cabin during the voyage, for safety.

The heat and humidity are unendurable. Elephantine roaches scamper the riveted walls. Mick and Richard share a terrified, girlish loathing for them. And there are rats. I hate rats.

We forced open the porthole window, but there's no relief – just the wide, flat river, like milky coffee, fog drifting along its surface, and the far, far banks and the forest on either side, green-black, broken only by low villages.

We have become sick and silent, like prisoners.

We feed the bonobo on fruit bought from the visiting pirogues, but every day it grows weaker. It clings to me now in constant mortal fear.

Dave wants to get shots of the decks out there, but Richard won't allow it. There are too many people, too much un-certainty, for Dave to go swanning around with a valuable camera mounted on his shoulder like a parrot.

My sickness is made worse by my knowledge of the fearless rats in the bathroom. I have to take someone with me when I shit – Camra Dave or Sound Mick or Richard hold my hand as I squat and the liquid squirts out of me in bursts and spasms.

In my turn, I hunt out the roaches, which like to mass in the gap between mattress and slimy bulkhead wall. These are big creatures, and fast. I kill as many as I can.

In the evening, the torchlight attracts insects in their multitudes and we sit in a queasy snowglobe of flickering moths, Camra Dave and Sound Mick and Richard and me and the sick bonobo, which they have come to despise, and it seems that there is nowhere else on the planet; that everything – cups of tea in china cups, clean socks, Marks & Spencers – has been a feverish dream.

After five long, long days, docking at Mbandandaka was barely a relief. The mash of bodies, moving in different directions, not moving at all. The soldiers with whips, the shouting, the blaring, the sun.

City Express Airline is due to fly to Kinshasa in two days.

The others checked into a hotel. I stayed behind to argue, pay extra, sign documents which claim to permit the bonobo on the short flight. I said, 'No, I'm not smuggling. It's dying.'

I cradle the bonobo. I talk to her and she responds to me. I stroke her hair. She luxuriates in it.

She holds my finger

————

Usually, Mr Nately perched on the edge of the desk – a typical teacher's place. Sometimes he sat there most of the afternoon, drinking tea; he talked, and sometimes Jo responded. But right now, he was staring at the window, watching fractal clouds surge past.

Jo sat in silence, unable to concentrate. Now and again she glanced at him. And at some point her lack of activity, like a clock that stops ticking, must have alerted him to a change in the atmosphere because he blinked and looked at her and said, 'Pardon?'

'Nothing.'

Looking up so sharply, he'd spilled tea. And now, irritated, he brushed at the wet spots on his thigh.

'Sir, are you all right?'

'I'm fine, yes.' Then, unknotting his tie, he admitted: 'Actually, I am a tiny bit tired.'

'Are you feeling sick? Should I go home?' She didn't want to.

Nately stretched his tie like a garrotte, then began to wrap it round his hand.

'Really, I'm fine.'

'Have you been staying up to watch Hale Bopp?'

He smiled – caught out – and Jo felt all right again. She felt herself relax.

'I've been interested in its progress, yes. The curse of the internet talkboard.'

That made sense. It's what Jo would be doing, too – if she had a telescope in her garden, and access to the internet. She thought how strange it was that this man, who had few real friends (if any), and who seldom left his house (if at all), was part of a community that girdled the globe like the lace of fat round a kidney.

He talked to people in Japan, South America. Lots of people in the United States – even someone at an Antarctic research station.

She said, 'Can I see them – the talkboards?'

He set the tightly-curled tie on the table and scratched at the crown of his head. A tuft of hair stood up. Curled up, the end of the tie came loose, like a snake's head.

'It's Hale Bopp,' she said. 'It's educational.'

Nately kicked his legs, thinking. Then he launched himself off the desk and landed flat on his feet. He clapped his hands, then rubbed them together.

'Let me make a cup of coffee and we'll have a look. Five minutes. Then back to work.'

He booted up and logged on and showed Jo a list of the talk-boards he visited. Most of them were soberly named, like *www2.jpl.nasa.gov/comet*, but there were others like FREAK SPACE! and DEVIANT SCIENCE and HAVOC ANALOG.

'What's that?' She pointed to HAVOC ANALOG.

'Light relief,' he said. 'A bunch of people who should know better, talking about things that don't exist.'

'Like what?'

'Well, right now, something called the SLO.'

'The SLO?'

Nately sang *The X-Files* theme tune. 'The Saturn-Like Object.'

'What's that?'

'A week or two ago, November the fourteenth, a man in Houston, an amateur astronomer, took a CCD photograph of the comet. And in the image, it seems to be *accompanied* by something. A UFO, apparently.'

He showed her the greyscale image. It revealed a bright spot, slightly pixelated, surrounded by a diffuse corona – that was the comet. Up and to the right was a second, smaller and sharper point of light. It had a ring around it.

'A giant flying saucer, shaped like Saturn,' said Nately. 'According to the photographer, it followed the comet for more than an hour. That night, he went on some freaky radio show to talk about it. The national media picked up on it, and then all hell broke loose.'

She leaned in close and frowned. 'What is it?'

'A bright star, probably. The Saturn effect is just an artefact. It happens sometimes, if you take a shot of a bright object using a spider.'

A spider was a secondary mirror system; metal vanes suspended it in the upper tube assembly of a telescope.

They looked at the image. He rubbed his jaw. 'Or it could be a software glitch.'

'So what's the problem?'

'A software glitch isn't what people want to see.'

Nately thought for a moment, then decided. He clicked on one of the talkboards, then gave Jo the mouse and left her to roam while he stood at her side, sipping coffee.

Hale-Bopp isn't just another comet; it's bringing a PHENOMEN-ALLY LARGE OBJECT which is DEFYING THE LAWS OF PHYSICS ... Hale-Bopp should be ORBITING THIS OBJECT which is 4 TIMES LARGER THAN EARTH ... but it's NOT ... what does that say to YOU??!!!

The object clearly has mass, but nothing we can comprehend at this time. Perhaps the object is hollow or composed of a matter we do not yet understand. Certainly its movements suggest possible intelligent control.

People are freaked out, obviously. Hey, the new millennium is almost here, and 'at forty-five degrees, the sky will burn'. That's what Nostradamus said in quatrain VI-97, right? Hale-Bopp will hit its perihelion in April '97 in the Northern sky at 45 degrees geographic latitude. And it'll be making the rounds about the same time Nossie scheduled Wormwood for a special guest appearance in the Apocalypse.

Jo read until Nately took the mouse from her and shut down *HAVOC ANALOG*.

He said, 'There are people on here – on the internet – who believe in all sorts of things: the Loch Ness Monster, alien bodies kept in American Air Force bases, big cats loose in Britain. Some of them believe the world is ruled by twelve-foot alien lizards.'

She giggled, and so did Mr Nately; and she thought of Patrick in the garden, erecting the cage.

'Right now,' said Nately, 'it's all about the comet. And the closer it gets, the madder they all become.'

Then he slapped his leg, once, resoundingly, and said, 'Right. Break-time over.'

*

The Anchorage Hotel had changed, because Chris McNeil had slept and woken and showered there.

It seemed miraculous – but miracles, like murders, changed places and her absence left the Anchorage corrupted by spoiled magic. It changed the light, made it yellow and creeping and old, and it seemed to change the physiognomy of the people who worked there; it made them sly and knowing and secretive, and Charlie feared them.

But he began to pull yet more double shifts – weeks of them, accumulating money, hardly caring. He just wanted to absorb any last, glittering, carcinogenic particles of Chris McNeil.

Making up the room she had once stayed in, he still hoped to come across some undiscovered trace of her – a whisper of scent, a pencil chewed and dropped. There was nothing. It was just a made-up hotel room. The sterility made him want to vomit.

During his lunch-break, he sat on the empty beach, scoured by the sand, the Anchorage behind him. He rehearsed their evening together; although it had been full of silence and shy grins and the clatter of cutlery, he wanted to fix it in his memory, to recall her face from every angle, as if from multiple cameras. The shadows in her laughter lines.

How old was she? He didn't know. But, meditating on the

details he had absorbed by staring at the visitor's book – her phone number, her address – he conjured a life for her: a dockside apartment, in which she lived alone, perhaps with a cat that sat on her lap, luxuriating in her touch as, in a white silk dressing-gown, she curled up on the sofa to watch TV.

Then, from nowhere, a suburban semi insinuated itself into his mind, devious as the reek of someone else's fart – a dog, kids. A husband. He doubled over the pain in his belly, hugging his knees, and returned to work with the wound still tender inside him.

In the laundry, Clive crept up on him and yelled *'Boo!'* and Charlie jumped and yelped.

Clive chortled and said, 'Wake up, dreamer,' booming and malevolent. And he stomped off on his flat feet, headed somewhere in the big, half-asleep hotel, his empty kingdom.

*

Patrick had cooked a proper meal, boar sausages and buttery mash and green beans, and local wine breathing on the table.

Jo was upstairs, asleep. Charlie was at work; these days, Charlie always was.

The door knocked, and Patrick answered, and it was the old vet, Don Caraway – the wind flapping at the skirts of his mackintosh and erecting his comb-over, as if electrified.

They had finished the meal and started on a second bottle when Patrick said, 'Don, I wanted to ask you something.'

Caraway showed compassionate, clerical dentures and cupped the ruby wine in liver-spotted hands.

'Is it Jane?'

Patrick tilted his head and scratched beneath his jaw. 'I don't know.'

He used an index finger to circle the rim of his glass. He looked into it. 'A few weeks ago – a few months back – I saw something.'

He was aware of Caraway holding his gaze, taking his measure.

'I think I saw a cat, Don. A big cat.'

He waited for the expressions of amusement, but they didn't come. Instead, Caraway sipped his wine.

'Where?'

'At the bottom of the garden. Where most people see fairies.'

But Don Caraway had grown more, not less, serious. 'What kind of cat?'

Patrick rubbed his eyes. 'Big. Black. Short legs, for its size. Rounded ears. Heavyish tail. A panther, I think. A black panther.'

Caraway crossed his arms. 'Why are you telling me this?'

'Who else am I going to tell?'

'The RSPCA? The police?'

'Come on, Don. Be serious.'

Caraway waved that away, dismissive.

Patrick said, 'Look, you've been here a long time. You know the farmers – you know everyone. You must've heard the rumours, the stories – the sightings, or whatever. I just need to know what you think. Am I going mad, or what?'

For a few seconds, Caraway sat tugging at a long, sandy eyebrow. Then he said, 'I did more than listen to the rumours. I saw some of those sheep, or what was left of them. I spoke to those farmers.'

'And?'

'I collected some faecal matter. It came back from the lab classified as canid. Dog shit.'

'But you don't think it was dog shit.'

'No. Is this why you bought the sheep?'

'What sheep?'

'Greg told me about it.'

Patrick groaned.

Caraway said, 'People round here don't have a great deal to talk about, Patrick. You turned up, out of the blue, on a Sunday morning – desperate to buy a sheep. Any sheep. I mean, really. You thought that wouldn't get round?'

Patrick scowled and made a vague hand gesture.

Don said, 'I suppose alarm bells should've rung, there and then. With the sheep. Are you trying to catch it?'

'Yeah. No. Maybe. Do you think I can?'

'Possibly.'

'But you believe me? You think I saw what I think I saw?'

'Oh, it's no secret the cat's here. Everyone round here knows it. I could take you to half a dozen people, right now – and they'd tell you stories to make your hair stand on end.'

Patrick shook his head. 'I'd like to keep it to myself. You know.'

Caraway straightened and his face, in the gloom, became eager as a schoolboy. 'You're a lucky man. I wish I'd seen it.'

'Oh no, you don't.'

'Oh yes, I do. A black cat crossing your path? – it's good luck, isn't it? Big cat – lots of luck. Stands to reason.'

Patrick had a buzz of giddiness, like a nicotine hit. He thought for a moment that he might pass out.

Don said, 'Are you all right?'

'Apparently, yes.'

'Listen. We'll wait for better weather. Gather up some

equipment. And – if it's come back – we'll go and find the sod. How about that?'

'How about that.'

Together, they drank a toast to the Beast of Exmoor and upstairs, Jo lay on her back with her eyes wide open. She had heard every word of Patrick and Caraway's conversation; it had been conveyed through the echoing air and through the spaces of the big, old, empty house.

Patrick and Caraway went when they could: Sundays, the occasional lunchtime. They took cameras – 35 mm, Charlie's old Polaroid, a bulky old Betamax. Don had packed his rucksack with sample containers, duct tape, plaster of Paris, lengths of rope. At his belt he carried a hunting knife, a compass. In his fist he carried, concertinaed, a map of the area.

They tramped through the undergrowth – the birdsong, the branches, the brambles, the twisting, hobbling roots.

Now and then, Don bent to examine some spoor – faeces or a pawprint, disturbed undergrowth.

But always came the slow, disappointed look. And always there was the determination to try again tomorrow.

And always, for Patrick, there were the daytime routines of Monkeyland. And these were followed by the vigil at the window, wrapped in a blanket for a shawl when, from the path, to any passing hiker – or to a big cat – he supposed he must resemble an observant ghost, waiting for all eternity for the killing sea to surrender up a long-dead lover.

*

They were at the computer, Jo standing at Mr Nately's side. His fingers were fast as he typed – he used all eight, including the pinkies, and didn't even look at them.

He said, 'I thought you might be interested in this, after our discussion the other day.'

The website took its time to download. It advanced spasmodically, jerking down from the top of the screen.

There was a field of stars. Then flashing, red words:

RED ALERT!

RED ALERT!

Jo wanted to giggle, because the screen reminded her of *DON'T PANIC* – which was so usefully inscribed on the cover of *The Hitch-Hiker's Guide to the Galaxy*.

Then there were more red words:

HALE BOPP

And the words became white on black, and made her eyes go funny:

Whether Hale-Bopp has a 'companion' or not is irrelevant from our perspective. However, its arrival is joyously very significant to us at 'Heaven's Gate ®'.

The joy is that our Older Member in the Evolutionary Level Above Human (the 'Kingdom of Heaven') has made it clear to us that Hale-Bopp's approach is the 'marker' we've been waiting for – the time for the arrival of the spacecraft from the Level Above Human to take us home to 'Their World' – in the literal Heavens. Our 22 years of classroom here on planet Earth is

finally coming to conclusion – 'graduation' from the Human
Evolutionary Level.

Last Chance to Advance Beyond Human, the website yelled at her,
against a starfield that hurt her eyes.

Mr Nately said, 'What are they like, eh?'

It made Jo giggle. But it was scary, too.

––––––––

<small>FROM JANE'S NOTEBOOKS</small>

At every intersection in Kinshasa stand lean young men,
chewing manioc root, selling cigarettes, wristwatches, birds in
cages, monkeys. Twice, we were stopped by the *garde civile* –
misnamed, of course. They shrieked for our papers.

Mobuto named this city in 1965. It was his triumph, his
showpiece. The Boulevard 30 Juin is a half-ruined testament
to that, garbage burning in the shadow of glass and steel
skyscrapers – wealth mocking poverty, poverty hating wealth.
And war, of course, on its way.

None of the big hotels would take us – not with a monkey.
All of them claimed, falsely, to be full. Richard sang 'Little
Donkey'.

In the end, a back-street place took me and the infant
while Richard and the others – close to rebellion – took rooms
in the Intercontinental, arranging to meet me tomorrow
morning.

We'll get the bonobo to the zoo, make sure she's looked

after. We'll get some footage, and then we'll get the hell out.

Kinshasa zoo is the worst place on earth.

They built a fake rainforest in the city, and they put a zoo in it. This grotesque pantomime hasn't been funded or maintained since the Belgians left.

The animals – chimps, leopards, lions – have been driven mad by hunger and boredom. They're locked up in under-sized, rusty cages; nothing but bars and concrete floors, barren but for accumulations of shit. To feed the animals, the staff raise chickens and ducks, and volunteers from Les Amis des Animaux au Congo bring scavenged bread, fruit, hotel scraps; none of it suitable, all of it better than nothing.

A few weeks ago a chimpanzee – balding, parasite-ridden, ready to grab at anything resembling food – attacked one of the keepers; she lost a hand.

The zoo director was happy to show all this to the camera. She's doing her best, they all are, but they need help, and there is none. Her biggest fear is a mass escape; starved animals predating on their keepers. It wakes her in the night.

Back in her office, she examined the bonobo and told us, on camera, there was nothing she could do. It will live, or it will die. There's no point bringing it to the zoo. This zoo is the last place in the world you'd want to bring a sick animal.

That was the end of it.

'Nobody will want to watch this,' said Richard. 'It's too depressing. It's not a bear in Greece. People understand Greece. This is just horrible.'

The others agreed. There was an air of sullen insurrection

about them. They looked schoolboyish and ridiculous; for all their filth and tangles of beard, unable to meet my eye.

Camra Dave said, 'We want to go home, mate. We just want to go home now.'

'We're not supposed to be here,' said Richard. 'This isn't why we came.'

The bonobo clung to me.

Mick said, 'It's only a bloody monkey. It's cute and every-thing, but who really gives a toss when . . .' He looked around, at Kinshasa. And he nodded at the horizon, approximately east, in the direction we've come from. Escaped from.

I said, 'I know you didn't sign up for this.'

'Too fucking right,' said Mick. Then he said, 'Sorry, mate.'

'Give the ape to the Belgian woman,' he said. 'The bonobo woman. She'll look after it.'

I said, 'Give me two days.'

'One day,' said Richard. 'I'm sorry.'

'It's not him,' said Dave. 'It's us. We've had enough. We're shitting it. Quite frankly, we're shitting it.'

The Belgian woman lives in an apartment block, half-deserted. The expatriates, the employees of logging companies, the teachers, they're all gone. The stairs are empty. The heat absorbs the echoes of our footfalls.

We knocked on the door and she answered: ebulliently red-headed, exhausted. Her flat stinks. It stinks because it's full of bonobos – half a dozen of them. She's bought them from local markets – babies. They retreat when we enter. They get behind her.

She did a brief interview for the camera. She wants to

publicize the plight of these animals, but she is disheartened, exhausted, and the atmosphere was strange – all of us huddled together in the small apartment, with all these apes.

I introduced her to our infant. She took it, tenderly. She stroked its brow with a gentle finger. Then she passed it back to me and said, 'What can I do?'

She meant, she has no more room.

I said, 'But we have to leave tomorrow. Perhaps you know someone?'

'I can make some calls, but this baby is very sick. I don't think it will live. I'm sorry.'

Dave put down the camera and Mick turned off the tape and we sat in the sweet, stinking ape heat.

I said, 'Okay.'

'I'm sorry.'

'Fine.'

She said, 'There are no vets. There is nowhere to take these animals.'

'And what about the people?' said Richard. 'There is nobody to care for the people.'

'People will die,' she said.

I stood, the infant clutching me. I could smell her. The musty, good smell of her, even in her sickness.

We left the apartment. The hot airlessness of the hallway was a physical weight, and the Kinshasa street it stands upon was like a vision of the future, a city gone chaotic under the swelling sun, the last days; the smoke from the burning garbage, the mad traffic, the money-changers, the police.

'That's it,' said Richard, kindly enough. 'What more can we be expected to do?'

I said, 'Take it back to England.'

He said, 'We can't do that. Can you imagine what it would take? The paperwork, the bribery. Dealing with the embassies, with quarantine. We can't do it.'

The others looked away. Richard said, 'Jane – it's dying.'

I reached up a hand and felt the shape of it, clinging to me; the nubs of her spine, the wiry tangle of her pelt; the humanity of her hands.

Richard bit his lip. Ruffled his hair. It needs cutting. In England he uses hair gel and mousse, and a mirror to get it looking right. But now it is a shaggy pelt, spotted with dandruff and sebum. His beard is weirdly orange, flecked with silver; it has crawled over his cheekbones and it bristles, orange and silver, just under his blue eyes.

They have given up, because this is too big for television. You need a wraparound screen, forty storeys high, 3-D glasses, the kind of sound-system that makes your eardrums bleed.

I said, 'I took responsibility.'

He said, 'For God's sake Jane, it's only an ape!'

I saw then that we have separated – Richard and Mick and Dave and me.

———————

Charlie was cleaning the rooms on the second floor when she found him.

He was finishing his next-to last room. The door was open. She passed by – backtracked two or three steps – stood in the doorway.

He was sticky-mouthed and sweaty. His hair was sticking up.

She leaned in the doorway. She looked the same. A different suit, different shoes, different shirt. But the same fine chain around the same throat.

She said, 'Hello again.'

'Hello.'

'I was wondering if I'd see you.'

There was a long mirror at the edge of his vision. He wanted to glance at himself: to see what kind of state he was in. But he daren't. He stood there with the Henry vacuum cleaner in his hand. It had a smiley face printed on the front of the red canister – the hose was its nose.

He said, 'Here I am.'

She half-lifted her little bag in strange salute, and the corners of her mouth flexed.

'Me, too.'

He had sweaty hair and he was wearing overalls.

'Well,' she said, 'I'd better leave you to it.'

She didn't appear to have blinked. It must have been an optical illusion – perhaps their blinks were synchronizing, the way the moon spun on its axis in perfect time with the Earth, always to show the same face.

But at dinner she was quiet, and prodded her food.

He tried to eat. It felt wrong.

She put down her cutlery and dabbed with a napkin at the corners of her mouth. It wasn't required; she'd eaten almost nothing. She said, 'I don't do this.'

'Do what?'

'This.'

'Eat dinner?'

She got the bill and he sat there, helpless.

They went to her car. She didn't offer her arm. He walked beside her.

He thought of the drive that lay ahead; all the way back to Innsmouth. Him staring at the passenger window, at the reflection of his own face. Chris at the wheel, following the radiant string of cat's eyes.

He touched her arm; her pointy elbow.

At his touch, she stopped. She faced him.

He said, 'Are you, like, married or something?'

She laughed. At first, he was glad; it was good to hear her laughing again. But then he heard that it was a bad laugh, a desolate laugh. It was like the Anchorage; it had been corrupted by bad magic.

'Yes and no. Not any more. It's complicated.'

She rooted in her handbag and produced her cigarettes.

'I'm twice your age. Jesus Christ.'

She booked them into another hotel; a better hotel. She showed Charlie her corporate credit card and made a face and winked.

Charlie blushed under the neutral gaze of the desk clerk, because often he had been in the desk clerk's position.

He followed Chris to the elevator and up to the fifth floor. And he stood while she opened the door and hung out the PLEASE DO NOT DISTURB SIGN and turned on the lights.

After he had come, a long and violent animal spasm, she stroked his face. She was crying. And he let her, because it made him feel strong. He buried his face in her neck and smelled her – different, even better now.

And he was still awake when the sunrise brightened the curtains and the Sunday traffic started outside, and he pulled the blankets over them and lay thinking.

He curled around her, thrilled by the astonishing intimacy of her kittenish snoring, the nape of her neck; her mouth slightly open.

He thought, *Don't sleep,* and soon he was asleep.

They woke just in time to check out. There was a rush of clothes-gathering, jumping into trouser and knickers: she hurried, topless to the bathroom and cleaned her teeth with an index finger, combed her hair with wet hands: produced make-up from her bag, scribbled some on.

The sunlight came clean and cold through the curtains. There was no wind.

He waited on the steps while she paid the bill. And in the car on the way home, he sat transformed. The cold air slipstreamed through the open window.

She pulled up opposite the house. And in the shadow of it, he felt the transformation begin to reverse.

He glanced at her knees, her ankles, her wrists. Thought of her, curled up asleep; her little snores. The way her naked breasts jiggled as she finger-cleaned her teeth.

He nodded and opened the door. He got out. She leaned over. Patted his hand.

He saw that, at the nearest convenient spot, she would pull over and lower the sun visor and she would correct her make-up. And then she would drive back to Manchester.

*

At his approach, the house loomed over him.

He opened the door – the peeling paint, the rusted lock, the disorder in the kitchen, the ancient pots and pans, blackened and never fully clean, and he smelled them for the first time – the family smell of them, penned up together.

He grunted hello, and stomped upstairs to his room and lay on his bed – his single bed, his *kid's* bed – and stared at the warped and damp-patched ceiling.

He stayed locked in his room all day, then lay awake in the darkness and into the dawn.

He masturbated four times, onto his stomach, but it didn't go away.

In the early daylight, Jo sneaked into his room and sat on the edge of the bed. Her presence edged Chris McNeil into another universe.

He pretended to be asleep.

Jo waited.

She shook his knee. He opened one eye.

'What?'

'*Shhh!*'

'What?!'

'I have to tell you something.'

'Tell me later.'

'I have to tell you *now*.'

'Is it about space?'

'No. Duh.'

He sat up, careful to cover with a blanket the dried, rice-paper flakes of semen on his belly. He saw she was wearing a sweater over her flannelette nightgown. She was sexless and thin.

'What is it?'

'Dad saw a panther.'

'A *what*?'

'A black *panther*.'

'Where?'

'In the garden.'

And Chris McNeil shrank to a point and was gone.

'When?'

'A while back.'

'What was it doing?'

'How am I supposed to know?'

'Wait, wait. Did Dad tell you this?'

'Duh, no.'

'Then how do you know?'

'I heard him talking about it.'

'Who to?'

'That weirdy vet.'

'The one with the teeth?'

'Yes. Mr Caraway.'

'What were they saying?'

'I don't know. Panther stuff. It's why Dad got the sheep.'

'He got the sheep to mow the grass because he's a lazy bastard.'

'That's just what he told us. He's using it as *bait*.'

'Dad actually thinks he saw a black panther?'

'Yes!'

'In the garden?'

'*Yes!*'

Charlie lay back on the bed and crossed his forearms over his eyes.

'Penis envy,' he said.

'It can't be penis envy, dork. He's *got* a penis.'

'Doesn't matter. Mum's left him, to look for some stupid monkey. He wants to prove her wrong by finding something better on the doorstep. Show her she should never have gone. Big white hunter. It's pathetic.'

'How would that prove her wrong? That wouldn't prove her wrong.'

'He's gone mad. Living here's driven him round the bend.'

He could hear that he was scaring her, so he uncrossed his arms from over his eyes and sat up again. She was wringing her narrow hands in her lap.

'Jo-Jo, he's wrong. He's seeing things.'

'Good,' she said. 'Good. Stupid thing.'

'But don't go out on the path alone.'

'Charlie!'

'Just don't, all right?'

She slapped his knee, and he slapped at her hand and tickled her in the ribs, and then they stopped.

'Do you think he's all right?'

'Who, Dad? No, I think he's gone mental. I think he's lost it.'

'But he's all right, though? Really.'

'Of course he is.'

*

Early December.

Patrick dropped Jo at Nately's gate, waved, drove away.

It was dark and wet and cold. Jo huddled in her red anorak, hood pulled up against the drizzle. She was a slash of colour against the mulchy browns and greys of the garden, the limewash of the cottage. Over one shoulder, she carried a rucksack; inside it was her packed lunch – some ham sandwiches and parsnip soup in a flask.

She opened the gate and walked down the path of dead winter roses and tangled wet grass. And on the brass doorknob, beads of rain had gathered.

Jo banged on the door three times, rat-tat-tat, and she clasped her rucksack in two hands as she waited.

After a few seconds, she turned and watched the rain, the travelling grey washes of it across the garden, the farmland, the hills, the distant woods.

She waited for a while, until she needed to pee. She was wet and cold, and her nose was running. She wiped it on the wet nylon of her sleeve – just about the worst fabric to wipe your nose on – and she knocked on the door, again, a bit louder.

Rat-tat-a-tat-tat.

Tat tat.

She needed to pee pretty badly by now.

She stepped back from the doorway – and when she moved, there was a wet throb behind her pubis: she *really* needed to go. It was beginning to *hurt*.

It was supposed to be full daylight, but the cloud cover was low, drifting like petticoats over the distant hills, and the morning sun was a faint opalescence behind it. The rain came at her in curly whipcracks that found the edges and seams of her kagoul; chilly water trickled down her spine and into the crack of her arse.

The house was dark.

She backed up to the gate, until the bony fingertips of the hedgerow prickled her spine; the screechy noises it made on her kagoul were amplified by the hood.

An empty house was not like an empty box. An empty house filled with something else – a primitive mind, maybe: or just primitive emotions. The cottage's windows were blank and reptilian.

The wind whipped at her kagoul, blowing long bubbles in it.

And she really, really needed to pee.

She didn't want to do it where the house could see her, so she walked round to the back garden, past the allotment, and found a corner between the shed and the border where the old orchard began; not far from where a blue tarpaulin flapped like a broken wing over a pile of old planks and damp bricks.

Hoiking up her kagoul, she lowered her jeans and squatted.

It took her a long time to pee because she felt watched, and the wind in the trees unnerved her. When she could finally let it go, the wind snatched at the piss and whipped it away from her. It spread and thinned in the rain, and she supposed some of it got to the apple trees; it would be sucked into their root system and then, minutely, into its apples. And Mr Nately would make apple pie and she would smile a secret smile – and he'd want to know why, but she would not tell him.

She zipped up. Her arse was cold, and under the hood it was becoming humid. But her hands were cold and wrinkling. And her feet were wet.

She was wearing Doc Martens, but only with thin socks – purple and pink striped ankle socks, actually, which she'd owned since she was nine and which were technically far too small to stretch over her long, knotty feet. But she liked them, because Jane had bought them for her on some inexplicable fancy – these girly, whimsical socks – and wearing them made her feel close to her faraway mother.

She walked once more to the front of the house. The house shifted like a head on a neck, to follow her. The wind whistled in the crooked chimney.

No smoke.

No lights.

She crouched and opened the letter-box – to call out a hopeful, 'Hello?! It's me!'

But, peering through that spring-loaded slot, the house extruded a vile rush of emptiness. It made her want to pee again.

So she put on her backpack – it had luminous yellow patches that would help drivers see her in the semi-darkness – and she began to walk to Innsmouth.

It was six miles. And she had walked two of them when suddenly she stopped worrying about the empty house, the long walk, the rain, and even Mr Nately . . .

. . . and remembered the panther.

She stopped, in the middle of the country road.

It was bordered by high hedges. It wound up and down the hill. There was no sound but the rain beating down on nylon. And Jo's heart began to trip with a bad rhythm.

She was fit enough. She could probably run all the way to Innsmouth, if she wanted. But to do that, to break into a *run,* would be to admit she was scared: really very badly scared now, out here all by herself.

She began to walk a bit quicker, and she thought about it logically. Would a big cat, adapted to the African savannahs, or whatever (she didn't know much about panthers) – would it come hunting humans on a filthy-cold morning like this?

Surely it would be holed up somewhere, out of the rain. Cats hated water.

Was that true of big cats, too?

What about big cats that *lived in rainforests*?

She adjusted her backpack, thumbs hoiked under the straps, and resolved not to think about it. She wiped her nose on her sleeve again, and walked on.

She tried to think of herself as the first human on a strange planet; the first observer of hills and billowing clouds. Because she wore the nylon hood, it sounded a bit like she was wearing a space helmet.

Normally, this was her relaxation exercise. In order to sleep when she was restless, she imagined violet skies and blood-red sands stretching to unguessed-at horizons. But here, now, wandering between thousand-year-old hedges, the thought just made her lonely. And the wet trudge of DMs in wet earth was depressing and earthbound.

A number of cars approached over the narrow, undulating roads, and one or two roared up, unexpectedly, behind her.

She could have stuck out her thumb, but she knew that kids her age (even really tall, and really clever kids), shouldn't be walking down lonely country roads by themselves, let alone getting into strange cars. So she kept her head down and pretended not to see, or to hear, and she hoped that, because of her height, the drivers would not think her a child.

She passed several farmhouses. Inside the gates were desolate collections of rusting carcasses of old vehicles, churned mud and corrugated sheds. And she ignored these too, because thirteen-year-old girls did not go knocking on the door of strange houses, not by themselves.

So she walked the whole entire way.

Not far from the edge of Innsmouth, one car did slow down and hiss to a stop. It was a black Golf, with a rain-jewelled sunroof. The passenger window hummed down. A woman was at the wheel, and she was frowning.

She leaned over and said, 'Are you okay?' and Jo said, 'Yes, thank you,' very politely, except she was too cold to speak properly and her voice came out shivery and she wiped her snotty nose on the back of her hand and walked on.

She could feel the car behind her, the woman at the wheel, watching her. The woman was pretty and seemed kind enough, but perhaps kind women – like grannies in a fairy tale – were wolves in disguise. Perhaps if Jo had climbed into that warm Golf, she'd have been abducted, taken to some faraway cottage and been given fudge cake and Coca-Cola and allowed to watch TV, and then when the sun went down and the moon came up, the woman would sprout hairs and teeth and claws and would bay at the sky and rip Jo to shreds and eat her – *gobble her all up* – and burn her clothes so that no trace of her was ever found – nothing but the faint relic of her urine, in Mr Nately's apples.

The silly thought called up a panicking child inside her, and Jo began to walk much faster, even though her legs were hurting and her feet were wet and sore.

The woman in the car was still watching her, quite still behind the steady pulse of her windscreen wipers, her intentions unreadable.

Jo walked until she found a small cluster of shops – a green-grocer, a butcher, a video-rental store and a Post Office. She went into the Post Office, because she had no money.

She queued with the hunched old ladies until she reached the front, and she asked the narrow-faced woman there to please, if she didn't mind, to please call her dad on this number and ask him to come and fetch her.

Patrick got the call shortly after giving Harriet a promotion that meant she could deal with the morning staff meetings he kept finding excuses not to hold.

He promised to get a new job description typed up by the end of the working day, but had no intention of getting round to it. Nobody at Monkeyland had job descriptions, least of all him. Or, they all had the same job description, which amounted to the same thing: *look after the monkeys*.

He made a quiet, triumphantly managerial cup of tea, and his phone rang.

The call had been put straight through by Mrs de Frietas, so he knew without asking that he had to take it. His first thought was of his wife, raped and dead in a burned-out Land Cruiser.

But instead, it was a woman called Esther Hivon who was, she explained, calling from the Post Office near the corner of Dagon Place and the main road. She had his daughter.

Patrick didn't think to ask any questions. He thanked Esther Hivon (she had the voice of a well-coiffed woman who wore spectacles on a chain) and hung up and hunted for his keys.

He drove into town at an unsafe speed, wipers beating at the rain, and he didn't so much park as abandon the Land-Rover on the corner of Dagon Place. He jogged to the Post Office.

He'd been wrong about Esther Hivon; she was an elderly and thin woman in a very tight polo-neck that made her look even thinner. She also wore an A-line, tweed skirt that didn't match. But she was waiting at the door for him, in the rain, and she greeted him and led him through the humid Post Office, back to the little staff room. It was hardly more than a big cupboard with a little window that overlooked a square of car park. And Jo was sitting there, hunched almost double, sipping from a cup of hot Ribena.

(The hot Ribena assaulted Patrick with a sense memory of his mother so powerful that for a moment his eyes pricked with tears and he felt briefly untethered and lost, as if he had walked into a dream.)

Jo's face had a sickly blue-white tinge, indigo round the eyes, like faded old Levis. Trailing curls of hair, the colour of cinnamon when wet, were plastered to her brow and cheekbones.

He knelt and brushed the wet curls from her eyes and said, 'Baby girl, what are you doing here?' and she put her long arms round his neck and squeezed him, and began to cry.

Esther Hivon let Patrick borrow the shop's landline; he'd left his mobile phone at the office, this time by accident.

It was a 1970s Trimphone – the sleek, modernist, beige kind that warbled like a canary. Seeing it, Patrick wanted to guffaw with astounded nostalgia. But he didn't – he dialled Nately's number instead, marvelling at the unhurried movement of the rotary dial. He hated to think what it must be like, to call 999 with one of those things.

Eventually, Nately's phone shrieked on the other end of the line. Patrick let it ring for fully two minutes. But Nately didn't answer.

So he drove to Nately's house with his knuckles white on the wheel and his jaw flexing.

Jo sat next to him, wrapped in a grey blanket. He'd turned the heater up to maximum, and the car was like a greenhouse. Rain exploded on the windscreen and made it worse. Patrick leaned forward in his seat.

The heat was soporific, and Jo was nodding into her chest. She'd have fallen asleep, had Patrick not taken the bends so hard, and had he not muttered impatiently to himself at every half-visible intersection.

Eventually, he pulled up to Mr Nately's gate, making a little cowboy noise (*whoa!*) as the Land-Rover skidded in the wet mud and stuck its fat arse into the road. Patrick struggled like a bus driver to correct it, cursing and heaving at the wheel. He told Jo to wait, then pulled the hood of his anorak over his head and climbed out.

Jo watched him.

He seemed to be far away – the steamy windows made him look like a memory, and the rain on the roof sounded like sleep.

Patrick's fingers were clumsy with nerves and anger, and he gashed his thumb yanking the gate open. He strode down the path sucking and biting on it.

He banged on the door with his other fist, still sucking his thumb. Three solid blows.

Bang.

Bang.

Bang.

Then he waited. He took his thumb from his mouth, and the rain diluted the blood to a thin pink that ran down the back of his hand.

He pounded on the door again.

Bang.

Bang. Bang.

He waited.

He noticed that the downstairs curtains had not been opened. Some of the anger left him.

Stepping back, he examined the front aspect of the house. The sodden grass wet his legs. His socks sponged up the water and wicked it into his boots. His feet squelched. He cursed.

Then he called out: 'John?'

He cocked his head, the anger all gone now. He stood in the front garden of the secluded cottage, and didn't know what to do.

He nibbled at his lower lip and made a decision. He glanced over his shoulder, making sure Jo was okay (she seemed to be asleep), then he tramped round to the back of the cottage. He stood in the long garden before the vegetable plots, the shed, the scratchy orchard, and called out once more.

'*John!*'

But the house was silent.

It felt haunted. The idea was silly, but it raised the flesh on Patrick's arms.

He squint-peered into the still-life of the conservatory, 1950s vintage; autumn fruit rotted in a ceramic bowl on Nately's breakfast-table.

Patrick hadn't even read Nately's references. He had simply listened to Jane rehearse them aloud, and agreed to everything she said. Jane had dealt with it all. And now look at him.

He called out once more – '*John!*' – and the sound fused with the wall of rain and vanished.

He considered calling Stu Redman, but he was too embarrassed. He knew Stu would keep him waiting out here, in the fucking rain, while he knocked officiously at the door.

So he said, 'Sod it', and kicked open the kitchen door.

It was a portal between worlds – the storm out here, the warmth and the stillness in there. It was like entering a painting. And then he stood in Nately's kitchen, with the rain outside.

He went to the kettle and touched it. It was cold. It hadn't been boiled today. The cold kettle made him scared to proceed.

He called out, once more – '*John . . . ?*'

But his voice was weak and the way it died in the emptiness unnerved him. The deep shadows, fading to reveal the antique furniture, the floral carpet, fifty years old. The ancient smells: Omo and Vim and other household chemicals that had evaporated from the shelves when Patrick was a child.

He passed the back room – Jo's classroom – the desk, the whiteboard, the bookcases, the computer.

He passed the downstairs toilet but feared to enter. He opened the door – just a crack – to make sure Nately was not inside. He peeked into the living room, although in this house it barely deserved that name. Smell of beeswax and starch.

No Nately.

He hesitated at the bottom of the stairs.

Then he went up; single stair by single stair. Into the bathroom. Heavy porcelain bath, lavatory and basin, dating to the first third of the century. The chemical did not exist that could blanch the stain of age from them.

The floor creaked underfoot.

He shut the bathroom door behind him.

The next door revealed a linen closet and Patrick closed it quickly, embarrassed by the intimacy of it – the folded sheets and blankets and spare duvets, smelling faintly of lavender and mothball and dust and spider carcass.

The next door opened onto a bedroom that seemed too big for the house.

As Patrick stepped inside, a squall of rain shuddered at the window. But he walked on in.

The curtains were closed. The light switch was a Bakelite nipple. He flipped it and the room fluoresced with a wan, nicotine glow. Against the far wall was a large double bed, and sprawled on the large double bed lay John Nately.

His eyes were closed and he lay quite still. His mouth hung open. A crust of dried saliva flaked from mouth to chin.

On the bedside table was a cardboard box containing Temazepam, which Patrick happened to know — because it was one of those snippets of information that his mind retained — was the best-selling prescription sleeping-pill issued in the United Kingdom.

12

Patrick needed help.

Charlie was missing, even on those few occasions he was actually at home. Patrick didn't know what was going on inside his head.

And Jo, too, was unhappy. She had no tutor, and Patrick was taking her to work, where she fretted and moped – as if it was Patrick's fault that Nately had tried to top himself.

Patrick took her to meet the people who'd be running stalls when the market opened in a couple of weeks. They showed Jo the things they made, the cloth they wove, the candlesticks they wrought, the wine they brewed, the specialist ales, the venison sausages, the boar steaks. Jo was polite and distant; she didn't understand these people, and when Patrick drove her back to Monkeyland, she moaned, 'Why do people just have to *sell* things all the time?'

'I don't know. Human nature.'

She looked at him sideways, because he wasn't an expert on any kind of nature, least of all human. He waited for another question he wouldn't be able to answer, but Jo just frowned to show disagreement.

They jostled in the Land-Rover. He wished the radio worked.

He supposed he'd have to find her a school. But the local comprehensive wasn't local. Just getting her there and getting her back again; dropping her off at the right place, at the right time, and picking her up again, was logistically vexing. Until Jane got home – if Jane ever got home – he was a working single parent.

Nately had been a good tutor, and Jo liked him. But right now, Nately was in the nuthouse, shuffling round in carpet slippers.

Jo said, 'I want to see him.'

'You can. As soon as the doctors say it's okay.'

He was lying.

He was angry at Nately. And he was angry at Jane for choosing Nately as Jo's tutor. And he was angry at Jo, for pining for Nately so acutely. And he was angry at himself, for being so uselessly fucking angry.

Who could he ask for advice? It was easier, looking after chimpanzees. He bared his teeth in a big, happy bark when he thought that, and wished there was someone to whom he could explain what was so funny.

So in the evening, they sat alone together in different rooms. Patrick in the kitchen, trying to read *20,000 Leagues Under the Sea*. Jo upstairs, mooning. Charlie in the living room, staring at *Top of the Pops* on the old TV with the fucked-up colour balance.

There was the sound of a vehicle, slowing down in the driveway.

In the living room, Charlie hit the mute button.

In the kitchen, Patrick looked up from his book.

In her bedroom, Jo sat up.

They weren't expecting anyone; they never were – not unless

it was Don Caraway. And Don never came after sunset. They heard:

A car door slamming.

Crunchy footsteps. Hesitating.

A knock at the door.

Patrick unfolded from his chair. Set down his book.

Went to the door. Opened it.

And there was Richard. He was dressed in clean, new clothes – Levis, trainers, nylon parka, nylon shoulder bag. His hair needed cutting and he had the makings of a pretty good beard.

Nausea billowed up inside Patrick, and all the dreams came rushing at him – he stood in a howling tunnel of them. And then they'd passed, like a ghost-train, and Richard was still there, on the doorstep.

He said Patrick's name and extended a hand. But Patrick was holding onto the doorframe because his legs had weakened and he thought he might fall over.

He was aware of the kids, behind him. A hand – tentative – crawled into his, like a hermit crab into a shell. Jo's. He squeezed. Relaxed.

He could feel Charlie's energy, at his shoulder.

Patrick said, 'Is she all right?'

'She's fine.'

Before Patrick could speak, or think what else to do, Richard had reached into his shoulder bag and removed from it a dilapidated Jiffy bag, ripped in places to show the grey wadding.

Patrick took the Jiffy bag. Its flap was open. Inside was a notebook. Attached to the notebook with a thick, rotten, multi-wrapped elastic band, was a piece of paper.

Patrick inspected it. It was a letter.

Then he looked, uncomprehending, at Richard. Who said, 'You'd better read it, mate.'

'I don't want to.'

'I'm sorry.' Richard had the night behind him. He was a shadow.

Patrick stuffed the Jiffy bag in his pocket.

He said, 'Richard. Christ. Do you want to come in? Have a drink or something? A hot chocolate. You look—'

Richard shook his head. 'I'd better – you know. I'd better get home. I haven't been home.'

He re-set the nylon bag on his shoulder.

'I'm sorry, mate.'

He nodded a shamefaced goodbye to the kids and walked back to his car.

Behind the white glare of headlamps, Patrick could see the boxy shapes of Richard's luggage, piled haphazardly onto the rear seat, like Christmas gifts in a sentimental old movie.

They went inside and sat round the kitchen table.

Patrick blew out his cheeks. Exhaled. Took the Jiffy bag from his pocket. Removed the elastic band. It was perished and it snapped and uncoiled on the table like something dying.

Patrick unfolded the letter. It was fragile, stained, like an antique.

Jo said, 'Read it out.'

He scanned it, first. Then he licked his lips:

These notes started as preparation for a script, maybe even a book – a bit of local colour, a bit of political background. But they turned into something else. Not even a diary.

  It would be pointless, telling you this over the phone, because

I wouldn't be able to do it. You have to be here to understand, and you can't be here. You can't come here, and I can't leave.

I'd be betraying myself if I walked away from this, from those animals in that terrible zoo.

I don't know how long I'll be here. Not long, I hope. I'm not even sure, yet, what I can do. But I have to try.

Does this make any sense?

Write to me, c/o the International. Richard has the details. I'll write when I can. Keep safe. I will. I'm not alone here; there are aid workers and journalists and God knows who else. I'll be safe.

Look after each other. I miss you. I love you.

'And there are,' Patrick counted, 'twenty kisses.'

'Let me see,' said Jo, and Patrick passed her the letter. 'There are eighteen, actually.'

'There are eighteen kisses,' said Patrick.

For a few moments, they stared at the scarred surface of the old table. Then Jo said, 'Excuse me,' and pushed back her chair and went up to bed.

Patrick waited for a while. Then he muttered something to Charlie – a soft grunt more than a word – and followed her.

He and Jo sat on the bed together, hands clasped in their laps.

He said, 'Are you okay?'

She was looking at her lap. 'She still loves us.'

'She does,' he said, not knowing if it was true.

And Jo told him, 'Love is like maths.'

He'd been stroking her hair. Now he let his hand fall. 'Is it?'

'Like – is it real? Is it a *thing*? Or does it just describe the relationship between things?'

He looked at the wall. It was an old wall, and beneath the

peeling paint in the 60-watt lamplight, it was a landscape of lumps and bumps that cast odd, mauve shadows.

'I don't know, baby.'

She said, 'I would like to go and see Mr Nately.'

'I know.'

She cuddled his arm, sniffing. Her hair brushed his face and a few strands caught against his stubble. The weak light shone on the hair that joined them, and he knew the answer to her question: love *was* real, and if you were lucky you walked inside it.

And everything – the planets, the combusting, wheeling suns, the impossible galaxies, the dreadful spread of the universe: everything was inside it. And he realized that his daughter had made him believe, for one moment, the only moment in his life, in God.

He said good night, and she lay down, fully dressed, and he turned off the light.

He wanted to touch her brow and take it away from her. He wanted to heal her. But Patrick couldn't heal things. Never could; he blundered and said the wrong thing and made things worse. So he hesitated in the doorway. She was a bundle of sturdy twigs, bound together with a shock of rough wool, and he knew what it meant, when people talked abut a heart breaking. A broken heart swelled until it exploded in your chest, like a universe being born.

Downstairs, Charlie was still at the table. In the background, the TV was still on. *EastEnders*.

Patrick went to the fridge and got out two cans of Guinness. He cracked them and poured them into a couple of glasses.

He was trying to think of a story – an anecdote, something about when Jane was young, not yet a mother. The anecdote would illustrate how she'd always been the same, and would never change – and how that made her the person they loved.

But he couldn't think of any anecdotes. So he sat down and sipped Guinness.

In the end, Charlie spoke first. What he said was: 'I think she's sleeping with Richard.'

Patrick sighed. 'I know.'

In the quiet that followed, Charlie seemed to condense and solidify.

Patrick told him, 'It doesn't matter.'

'How can it not?'

'Well, sometimes it *feels* like it matters. But it doesn't. Not really.'

Charlie was still gazing down at the table. Patrick could see the sandbar pattern on his forehead, the place permanent wrinkles would some day appear.

'You should have done something.'

'Done what?'

'I don't know.'

'Hit him?'

'No. Yeah. I don't know.'

'Hit *her*?'

'No.'

'*Left* her?'

'No.'

'Then what?'

Charlie was looking at the table.

Patrick said, 'We're not animals, mate.' Gently, he turned a knuckle into his son's skull, like turning a key. 'We've got this,' he said, 'In here.'

Charlie didn't speak, or move.

Patrick said, 'It's not about not *having* urges like that. Violent urges. Stupid urges. It's about overcoming them.'

'*She* doesn't overcome them. *Her* urges.'

Patrick covered his mouth with a hand. Speak no evil. He took it away.

'I love her, Charlie.'

Charlie was whispering now. 'How do you do it?'

'I don't know. You just do. If you have to.'

Charlie nodded, once. His fingers were splayed wide on the table, as if to anchor it, to keep it from floating away.

*

Another letter arrived. This one had been addressed to Patrick at Monkeyland, and Mrs de Frietas had placed it – sarcastically? hopefully? – at the summit of his in-tray.

He took it down, creating a small landslide. The envelope was handwritten with, by the look of it, a pretty decent fountain pen. He opened the envelope, put his feet on the desk and unfolded the letter.

North Devon District Hospital
12 December

Dear Patrick,

Firstly, an apology. I can only imagine how alarming it must have been, finding me like you did. Secondly, I must thank you for your prompt action.

And an explanation: it was an accidental overdose of Temaze-
pam, which I have prescribed to help control a mild sleep disorder.
I almost wish it could be more dramatic.

Naturally, I accept that this incident has altered the nature of
our relationship, in that you almost certainly will no longer
require my services as Jo's personal tutor.

It has been a great pleasure, teaching Jo over the last year. She is
an exceptional young woman. I hope you have no objection to my
writing her a letter, to explain the circumstances? I would hate
for her to think I let her down deliberately, or callously.

Affectionately,

John Nately

Patrick folded the letter and put it in his pocket. He made a cup
of tea. He was chuckling to himself, at Nately's priggishness.

And the next day, he took Jo to see him, in hospital.

On the way, Jo nibbled fretfully on a pulpy hangnail. Seeing it
made Patrick wince, and he kept slapping at her hand to make
her stop. But she was still nibbling as he parked the Land-Rover
and they crossed to the hospital entrance.

Jo was wrapped up in winter gear, her Doc Martens and her old
man's overcoat. Her hair exploded from beneath a knitted beanie.

A nurse led them to the day room which, apparently, was full
of mad people. Patrick could tell they were mad, but he didn't
know how.

He was ashamed to recall that seeing the panther had caused
him to doubt his own sanity. Now he saw this had been a romantic
ideal – insanity as an excess of passion. The people in this room

didn't behave like that. There was no excess of emotion here; just a sense of gloominess and winter light.

Nately was alone, reading.

They waited until he looked up. It took him a moment, then his face opened up. He beamed. He stood, putting down the book. 'Well! Hello.'

Jo blushed. Patrick thought Nately might be about to cry.

Instead, he blustered, 'How nice to see you.'

Patrick laid a hand on Nately's shoulder and let it rest there for a long moment. Then he pulled up two chairs, one for him and one for Jo, and they sat down to join him.

After being treated at the Accident and Emergency department, Nately had been interviewed by a young woman from the hospital's psychiatric liaison team. She asked a great many questions – about his sleep pattern, his eating, whether he'd had thoughts of harming himself, or feelings of helplessness.

('Who doesn't?' said Patrick.)

Had Nately heard voices when no one was around? Did programmes on the television relate specifically to him? Did he feel that other people were putting thoughts into (or taking thoughts out of) his head? Were other people out to harm him?

Nately told them no, nobody was out to harm him, not that he knew of, and nobody was controlling his thoughts, not even, apparently, him. And that nervous little joke led to a Section Assessment.

Then two psychiatrists and an Approved Social Worker assessed him again, by asking exactly the same questions – which he answered, this time without humour. Nevertheless, they decided to apply Section 2 of the Mental Health Act; he could be held for yet more assessment – and possibly treatment – for up to twenty-eight days. He might then be taken to a mental hospital to be assessed even more.

But he was hoping to have the Section rescinded by the ward's consultant psychiatrist. Then he would be allowed to go home.

Patrick said, 'For God's sake – this is bullshit, isn't it? Wasting time and money, keeping you in here. Let's get you out, soon as we can. Come and stay with us. Come and stay for Christmas.'

He became aware that Nately and Jo were gazing at him with identically affectionate expressions.

He said, 'What?'

And in the car, he said, 'You owe me for this.'

'I know,' said Jo.

'Well,' he said, 'I hope you do.'

*

Monkeyland held its first Christmas market that weekend. The stall-holders arrived when it was still dark, when the chimps were still huddled in groups, vigilant and full of night.

The stall-holders, in their woolly hats and Puffa jackets and ponchos and boots, queued at the van for Styrofoam cups of coffee and tea, and they sat crushed together on cold benches and low walls, smoking roll-ups and wrapping themselves tighter in their winter clothing.

The stalls went up: the candlestick-maker, the organic baker. The faux-ethnic cushions and throws, the jams, the wines, the cheeses. The cold sun rose behind a bank of mackerel cloud. The stall-holders flapped their arms and looked at the sky.

To get an extra fifteen minutes in bed, Patrick hadn't showered, and now he regretted it. He felt dirty and his beard itched in the cold. But gradually, the morning's motley air cheered him up – all these cold, sleepy, excited people with their steaming breath and their woolly hats and their polite and nervous conversations, hoping to sell the things they'd made.

And there, in one of the centre stalls, Sarah Lime sat on a bar stool. There were rips in her Levis and on her feet were tatty tennis shoes, and she wore a grey overcoat and a scarf round her neck. The scarf was the colour of raspberries, and set with dozens of little mirrors. Her hat was some kind of South American weave. It had flaps that hung round her ears, like Sherlock Holmes or Deputy Dawg.

All that morning, they caught each other's eye and made little faces; little grimaces of anxiety, acknowledgments of their half-established intimacy, topped-up in case it should weaken in the strangeness of the morning.

At nine o'clock, Patrick opened the gates. He was greeted with a smattering of applause, and that was good.

Half an hour later, Sarah brought him a hot dog in a paper napkin and a cup of tea with a plastic lid.

He said, 'What's this?'

'Breakfast. Lunch. Brunch.'

They half-squatted on a low wall by the rubbish bins; in summer, these bins were buzzed by a constant, slow vortex of wasps. Patrick hated wasps; they scared him more than any animal alive – except panthers.

He bit into the hot dog. Vinegary ketchup and yellow mustard smeared over his bristles and cooled there.

She said, 'So. How you feeling?'

'All right.'

She nodded.

He said, 'Where are the nude self-portraits then?'

'You.' She nudged him in the ribs. 'It's too cold for nudes.'

'It's too cold for anything. I wish I was in bed.'

'Well, let's see how it goes. Have you heard from Jane?'

'Not really. We watch the news, but you know.'

'Me too. I watch the news.'

He finished the hot dog. Wiped sauce from around his mouth with the napkin. Scrunched it, threw it away.

He said, 'It's in Africa. So who cares?'

'She'll be all right.'

'Oh, she'll definitely be all right. She's always all right.'

And now she turned to face him. 'I didn't know you were that angry.'

He kept his eyes forward, her frown a milky blur on the edge of his vision. He could feel her breath.

'I'm not angry. You love someone, you have to let them – y'know. You just have to let them.'

She drained her cup, crushed it, dropped it into the empty, waspless, winter bin. She was breathing steam. Her feet looked small and cold in the tennis shoes.

By five o'clock the visitors had trickled to nothing and it had become impractically frigid – fronds of mist rising in the sodium lights. Most of the stall-holders had long since begun to pack up, stripping their stalls down to skeletal cubes.

That last, quiet hour was cheerful – Christmassy. So Patrick closed the gates a bit early.

He approached Sarah Lime, packing up, and asked her; 'So. How did it go?'

'Really well.'

'The nudes?'

She pouted, between the flaps of her hat. 'There was a lot of looking. But nobody took the plunge.'

'Shame.'

'So. A bunch of us are meeting up, later tonight. Are you up for it? A drink?'

She looked almost comical in the Deputy Dawg hat. But Patrick thought of the scar that ran into the neck of her T-shirt: of tracing it with his fingertip. He thought of her body beneath him. He thought of making Sarah Lime cry out, dig her nails into him.

And then he thought of Jo, alone in the house. She'd keep the windows and the doors locked, and the telephone to hand. But she might wish to observe something interesting in the night sky; and there was *always* something interesting in the night sky. A marching band could sneak up on Jo while she watched the familiar pitted moon, arcing across her eyes.

And then, unbidden, he thought of his wife: he thought of her bad temper in the mornings, her disorganization, and he smiled, and loved her.

He said, 'Best not.'

Sarah Lime kicked her feet. 'Fair enough. Catch you in the week, then.'

'Catch you in the week. Don't drink too much.'

She turned and backed away, making a fish-face at him from beneath her Deputy Dawg hat.

'Some hope.'

She made another funny face and Patrick sat there, watching her go; it was dark and it was cold, and he was happy.

*

Monday morning, the rain hung cold and heavy on the fences, the trees; the snaking, naked hedgerows. Livestock that had churned the fields to a rich, fudge brown stood, unmoving and miserable.

As the Land-Rover came down towards the salt flats, Patrick could see the field below. He squinted; frowned. Slowed. Stopped the car.

The cattle had moved to the field's muddy edge. Some of them were nuzzling at the concrete trough. In the centre of the field, twenty magpies stood in a circle.

In the middle of the circle stood a single crow. It made no effort to fly away – it stalked, pompously, up and down within the circle. It was barking and clacking its great beak.

The magpies watched, unmoved, until one of them took a waddling step into the centre of the ring. It pecked the crow. The crow called out; harsher now. But still, it did not fly away. Instead, it faced its attacker and tilted its head.

Then the circle closed: the magpies rushed in, and the crow disappeared in a boil of white and black and iridescent green.

Patrick waited at the wheel.

The magpies attacked for perhaps a minute before, as one, they erupted into the air, scattering and separating.

The cattle at the trough raised their heads when Patrick opened the door and jumped out of the Land-Rover. He trudged through the squelching mud, climbed over the fence and crossed the field. He was nervously attentive, in the distant trees, to a raggy audience of crows and rooks.

The crow was a bloody scrap, smeared and folded into the mud:

there were no eyes in its skull. Black feathers had been churned in the mud, had caught in the heavy, wet grass; they blew in the morning breeze, blood-tipped, whipping into small vortices.

Patrick's feet were cold in his boots: caked with mud to the ankles. The wind cut through his jacket. Feathers caught in his hair: he brushed blood across his cheeks, over his lips. He spat, angrily, coughing it up.

He looked at the crows in the trees. And he looked at the cows at the feeding trough. And he looked at the sky, which was slowly billowing white-grey and indifferent: the sun shone through it, a perfect, perfectly white sphere.

'I've heard of it,' said Don Caraway. 'Reports back to Chaucer. But it's uncommon. Obviously.'

Patrick shifted in his office chair, the phone hooked between his neck and shoulder. He had his muddy feet on the desk; a cup of tea balanced on his stomach. He had the blinds closed on Monkeyland, and he had draped his jacket over most of his landslide in-tray.

'It was weird,' said Patrick.

'It sounds weird.'

'Is that it?'

'What do you want me to say?'

'I don't know.'

'Perhaps they were punishing it.'

'For what?'

'Thievery. They're thieving buggers, crows.'

'And magpies aren't?'

'I don't know, then.'

'This conversation is mad.'

'You started it.'

'Yeah, yeah. Cheers, Don,' Patrick said, and hung up.

*

Nately sat happily in the back seat of the Land-Rover, watching the fields – the cows, the sheep, the woebegone December.

As Patrick pulled up to the house, Jo leaped from the front seat and, like a gangly bodyguard, ran round the car to open Nately's door. She took the larger of his bags in two hands and carried it to the house, leaning hard to compensate for its weight.

All the way, she continued an unbroken commentary that had begun when they met Nately at the hospital. 'It's very old,' she told him, 'seventeenth century, I think. It was a farmhouse originally, but it hasn't been for a long time. You can see that it's old because none of the lines are straight, so Dad calls it Higgledy House, which is pretty funny, and Charlie goes on about it being haunted although of course there are no such things as ghosts. I told Charlie this when he was trying to frighten me one time, and he just made a loud noise and said "BUT THEY'RE WATCHING YOU" and actually I was pretty frightened, but I didn't tell him.'

They had reached the door. Patrick dangled his keys and said, mildly, 'Jo, shall we let Mr Nately get inside?'

She blushed. 'Sorry.'

They entered, and Jo asked Nately, 'Would you like a cup of tea or a cup of coffee? We have some herbal tea if you'd like.'

Patrick said, 'Herbal tea?'

'It's Mum's. Top cupboard.'

'Is it?' He made a face: who knew?

Nately was looking round the kitchen. Patrick said, 'Sorry about the mess, John.'

Nately blinked at him.

Jo said, 'Would you like to see your room?'

Patrick held up a hand in surrender, and let Nately go. He lit the gas ring and listened to them clump upstairs and there was a small lurch in his heart.

Jo had been preparing for days. She had washed bedding from the airing cupboard, and she'd taken the posters from her wall – Hubble starscapes, stellar maps, red exploding novae, a picture of the sun – and Blu-Tacked them to the spare-room wall.

She'd hoovered the threadbare carpet and opened the window, trying to air out the smell of damp. She'd pinned one of Jane's African wraps over the mouldy patch in the high corner of the ceiling. She'd put scented candles in empty drawers that had been rickety when Patrick and Jane bought the chest, years ago from a flea-market in North Wales. And she had selected a number of her favourite books and laid them on Mr Nately's bedside table, so he would have something to read.

Now Nately entered the room with his bag in one hand, and Jo's insides felt funny.

He stood in the doorway and took it in. The posters, the African cloth, the single, damp-warped low window that overlooked the garden and the coastal path and the woods beyond it.

Mr Nately set his jaw. Flexed it.

Jo waited. 'Don't you like it?'

'No,' said Mr Nately. 'It's great.'

He sniffed and made a brave, happy face, and Jo understood – or thought she did – and she nodded like a butler and stepped backwards out of the room, and went downstairs.

Patrick was waiting in the kitchen. He heard her clumpy shoes on the loose stairs.

She came into the kitchen and saw Patrick's face.

'What?'

'Nothing.'

Patrick was reaching up and, with his fingertips, hunting for the box of herbal tea. He found it; it was camomile.

*

In the lead-up up to Christmas, the Anchorage had hosted a series of works parties, Christmas karaokes and other events. Charlie worked them all. The parties were desperate and grotesque, but he belonged in the Anchorage now, with its tat and its baubles; its blood-red bar and its tawdry orgasms.

Christmas morning, he was there to serve breakfast to the hungover and the childless. They hunched like gargoyles over their plates. He hated them, and he hated Christmas, and he was shambling, in a daze, not quite present – tormented by thoughts of Chris McNeil; of whom she might be with, on Christmas Day.

When he thought of her, lonely in a clean white bathrobe, watching the Queen's speech, something inside him went wrong. And when he imagined her at a Christmas dinner-party, it got worse. The other guests at this party were unclear to him – he didn't know who they were, or how old, or what they did or how they spoke. He just saw crystal glasses in elegant hands and hands touching thighs under tables.

He saw Chris McNeil lying beneath an anonymous man, being invaded, and he saw her legs tense in time with his thrusts.

And that was physical pain, pressure in his head like a great, oil-clogged engine.

A week before, in revenge, Charlie had sex with a Minehead office girl. She was pissed, at a works-party, and Charlie had been working the bar.

He went to her room. The unfamiliar smell of her breath and her breasts in his hands; the colder flesh of her arse when she undressed. The sodium glitter and slow-shifting of the tinsel.

Charlie was mechanically aroused but unable to orgasm. At first, that was okay. But it became maddening, like a dream where you can't run from your pursuer.

He thought of Chris McNeil, grinding her hips below someone else, and the orgasm that followed was quick and violent and followed by an engulfing roller, a breaker of shame. He had to bury his head into this strange girl's neck — suffocated by her perfume and her tickly hair, her sweat and her tits squashed against him, her legs wilting like flowers at the small of his back — in order not to sob. She muttered something, some squalid joke, and she played with his hair and he saw her engagement ring.

That was five days ago. It felt like a hundred years. Charlie felt ancient; a creature of the Sumerian desert.

Now it was Christmas Day, and he got home to a noisy house. The kitchen was full of people — Don Caraway, the toothy vet with the comb-over, Jo's mad teacher. Patrick. All of them were doing something — peeling potatoes, topping up glasses, mixing stuffing.

They looked cheerful. And when Charlie walked in, Patrick called out 'MERRY CHRISTMAS!' And Jo said, 'Whoooo!' And the vet and the teacher looked at him bashfully.

Charlie said, 'Merry Christmas,' back, then made himself yawn and said, 'I might have a kip.'

Patrick's face softened, as if he knew something.

'Get your head down, mate. We'll keep your dinner warm.'

Patrick was about to make a joke – the same non-joke he made every year, about whether Charlie wanted breast or leg, but now Charlie beamed it out through his eyes: *Please don't*.

Patrick didn't. And Charlie raised a limp hand and went upstairs and crawled into bed. He was back at the Anchorage by 8 p.m.

*

Round midnight, Patrick carried Jo up to bed. It wasn't easy; she was taller than him, and he was a little drunk.

Downstairs, he found Don Caraway stoking the fire and John Nately in the tatty embroidered armchair, drinking whisky from a heavy tumbler. The TV was on but silenced, and the shadow of the flames licked at the higgledy walls, made them seem close and low and alive.

Patrick eased himself onto the sofa. He made a series of con-tented little groans and picked up his drink. The fire warmed and fascinated him. All three men, tending their drinks, stared into it.

Nately said, 'She told me about the panther. Jo.'

Patrick looked at him. 'Oh.'

'She overheard you, discussing it with Don.'

Patrick remembered the meal, the two bottles of wine, their plans to capture the beast. His growing excitement. Perhaps they hadn't been as quiet as they supposed.

'She felt she had to tell me. She was worried it might eat me.'

Patrick wasn't angry at Jo for telling Nately. He was too warm, too drunk, too amiable. It was good, to be content for a while, to have no secrets.

'It's funny,' said Nately.

'What's funny?'

'Once upon a time, I discussed these big cats with a friend of mine.' He leaned forward and turned his head to Caraway. 'ABCs. That's right?'

Don nodded. 'Alien Big Cats.'

Nately settled back into his chair and watched the fire.

Patrick thought of the beast, crouching at the border of his land. And how it had flowed onto his property like ink, and then disappeared.

He glanced at Don, but Caraway too was staring into the fire.

Nately went on, softly, 'A few years ago, he was walking – my friend – not far from here, and he saw a black shape spring over a fence. An impossible leap. He'd seen a big cat.'

And now both Patrick and Caraway were looking at him.

'He was scared. Terrified, actually. But he's inquisitive; a scientist. Or anyway, a psychiatrist. So the next week, he went back. Same time, same place. And the week after that. He kept a vigil. It took him three months.'

'And?'

'And he took a photograph.'

Caraway and Patrick leaned closer.

'Of a dog. A mastiff cross. Leaping the unleapable fence.'

Patrick and Caraway groaned like Christmas ghosts.

'The strangest thing was, he had a very distinct memory of a tail. But the dog had no tail – it'd been docked. So he began to look into it; why he'd seen what he'd seen. Apparently, eyewitnesses often go on to insist they've seen a big cat, even when a dog is *proven* to be responsible.'

Don grunted reluctant confirmation.

Nately said, 'It's because we were preyed on, once; mostly by felines. And now, certain stimuli – especially quick movements, on the edge of our vision – fit a mental template, a default setting that causes us to see big cats. It's better to be safe than sorry; better to think *Cat*! And run, and find out three months later it's a mastiff cross. So our minds fill in the details for us. The whiskers, the long tail . . .'

They watched the fire.

'But John,' said Patrick. 'I really did see a panther.'

Nately's face was cast in flickering shadow; it hollowed out his cheekbones and eye-sockets, and the fire shone on his corneas. Patrick saw no challenge there. But he did see fear.

*

That night, because he was drunk, Patrick actually went to bed. It felt unfamiliar – lying down with his head on a pillow. He stared at the ceiling and thought about the cat, and about something Jo had told him once about the fractal nature of nature, and how the Fibonacci series expressed itself in leaf patterns, in seed heads. He saw the world, briefly, as a series of numerical attributes, flowing towards and away from him. And he wondered if that was how his daughter saw the world, all the time.

And he thought of his wife, who had sidestepped into a different universe. He thought of making love to her on the wet grass beneath the rotting umbrella of stars. And he thought of women he had loved before – girls, really – and how that love had seemed eternal and now he could not remember what it had been like, to have those strangers in his heart.

Everything was connected to everything else. The iron in his blood was formed by exploding stars. His molecules had once belonged to other living creatures. He was made of borrowed life, from borrowed materials. Eating, he turned death into life. And when he died, his body would disperse – like the matter of an exploding star – and become part of other living systems; trees and foxes and worms and grass. And they would die and become still other things; he would pass into other people, as other people had passed into him. The rain that fell on him contained molecules of water that, as a child, he had sweated away. Everything was one thing; everything had once been compacted into a single point that discharged existence.

He took no comfort from this.

*

On New Year's Day, Patrick and Caraway set out to hunt the black panther. Don carried an old canvas knapsack with leather straps; it had a picnic inside. And he'd brought his 35 mm camera. It bounced on a strap round his neck.

They crossed onto the South-West Coastal Trail, and they walked for some miles north, towards Minehead. They returned with the sunset.

On 2 January, they repeated the excursion, walking some miles south – through the woods, and over the cliffs, and down to the salt flats, and past Innsmouth.

But they found no trace – no stools, no paw prints. There had been no reports of livestock damage, or of mysterious growling in the night. There had been no sightings. There had been nothing.

A mile south of Innsmouth, they watched a fat man on the desolate beach, throwing a stick for a black Labrador. The dog chased the stick into the surf, barked, returned it.

The sight of it brought Caraway and Patrick to a halt. They watched the Labrador for a while, silently. They watched the happy man who was walking it, stopping to throw sticks.

They felt old and stupid.

Patrick said, 'It's not here, is it?'

And Don Caraway said, 'No.'

Don snapped a shot of the man and his black dog, its barrel torso low to the ground on stumpy legs, and they pulled up their hoods against the drizzle coming in off the ocean, and they turned inland and headed for home.

13

God, we've had some strange Christmases! You remember the first years back in Wales, how you got carried away? We said we'd keep it all to one present each, something constructive, nothing commercial, nothing plastic, and you drove into Liverpool and came back with about two dozen Woolworth's carrier bags. And I was angry and we argued, and then when I saw the kids on Christmas morning I cried because you were right – although you did spend too much, and always did.

How many Christmases have we spent together now? I can hardly work it out. I keep forgetting what year we met. Isn't that funny? I remember myself when I was five and it seems you're there.

The bonobo died on Christmas Day. You won't be surprised to hear it. The infection cleared up, but she was too weak. She slipped away in my bed.

I held her in my arms, dead, and I sat in this crappy hotel room and sobbed. And it was so hot, and I could smell myself. So I went downstairs and got a pair of kitchen scissors and cut my hair.

I thought I should let you know that, in case you don't know me when I come home.

There's an American school in Kinshasa. Enormous grounds, covered in acacia trees. It's very beautiful; stupidly so, really, given the rest of it.

I've been speaking to them about the bonobos, about the idea of a sanctuary. God, I mean I've been talking to everyone. Embassies. Hotels. Anyone I can think of, who might help. We've grubbed up a little money; enough to keep them fed for a few months. But the situation is so unstable.

We huddle round the radio at night. Every day or two I pop into the Internationale: they've got CNN there, and a decent bar, and journalists.

It's not easy to keep account of the factions, of who's doing what to whom, but it's bad. I can't see Mobutu walking away from it, but that could mean months and months more of this. It could mean anything, really.

But we're hanging on, and things are looking good with the American school. A few more months, I think, and we can do some real good and I can come home.

God, I want to come home. Homesickness is what children suffer from at camp, or during sleepovers. But I've got it now. It's not funny. Homesickness.

I love you.

Patrick read it a dozen times, then made an appointment at the bank, where he begged a young man with too much gel in his hair, to be allowed to raise a small mortgage on the house.

And he wired the results – a few thousand American dollars – to Jane via the Internationale. Then he phoned the American school in Kinshasa. When he got through, at some length, he left a message.

It was, *Happy New Year*.

*

In a dark garden on the western edge of England, under a bright and hollow sky, Patrick stood pointless guard over Jo and Nately. Wrapped in coats and scarves and hats, they were taking it in turn using Patrick's field-glasses to observe the comet.

It was visible even to his unaided human eye – a bright star with a hazy tail, like a wandering ghost in a wedding gown.

Patrick stamped his deadened feet. His fists were buried deep in his pockets. His ears were numb. He cast wary sidelong glances into the shadows at the end of the garden – the stile, the woods behind it. He could hear the sea, a slow wave of white noise. There was nothing there.

The sheep stood with them. It, too, was looking up.

Jo told him, 'Some people believe there's a spaceship coming with it.'

'I bet they do.'

Craning his neck, Nately said, 'Have you ever seen a UFO?'

Patrick scoffed. 'No. Have you?'

'Yep.'

'Really?' said Jo. 'Where?'

'Here. Or near enough.'

'What did it look like?'

'Like a UFO.'

'And what does a UFO look like?' said Patrick.

'Glowing. Moving. That sort of thing. It was a weather phenomenon. Some kind of weird weather.' He passed the field-glasses
to Jo.

'I've seen some weird weather,' said Patrick. 'In Africa. Weird
weather.'

'Or it was a military aircraft.'

Patrick narrowed his eyes and looked askew at Nately. 'John,
are you pulling my leg here?'

'Not in the slightest.'

'You saw a spaceship. In Devon.'

'You saw a panther.'

Patrick liked this waspish new Nately. Or perhaps it was the
waspish old Nately; perhaps it was how Nately usually was, in the
privacy of his mind.

'The difference is, John, at least I know for certain that, somewhere in the world, panthers actually exist.'

'Oh, what I saw *existed*. It wasn't an illusion, it was definitely
there. But what it actually was – that I don't know.'

'But you don't believe it was a spaceship?'

Nately squinted at the comet. His breath steamed in the cold.

'I don't believe in spaceships.'

Patrick didn't want to keep standing out there, night after night,
one eye on the shifting forest while Nately and Jo scanned the skies,
ignoring his solicitations of hot cocoa followed by hints that it was
time to go inside.

So, after feeling stupid five nights running, he arranged to drop them at Nately's house, to use the telescope. He'd pick them up round midnight. He waited at the wheel until they were safely through the red door, grey in the darkness, and he drove away – pleased at last, to have an evening to himself.

Jo and Nately entered the dark cottage. It felt very empty. Its residual heat had leached into the winter ground and the light bulbs, in the downtime, had lost their power to illuminate; their thin glow edged the darkness into the corners; it crouched there, licking its chops.

Nately went upstairs. Jo followed at his heels.

He opened the bedroom door. Dampness had settled into the candlewick bedspread from which Patrick had lifted Nately's head, to check for a pulse. The bedding was still disordered.

It was a strange, to look at it. They still had their coats on: they felt like explorers.

'Well,' said Nately. 'Here we are.'

A few days later, Nately moved back home and their lessons began again.

Twice a week, Jo stayed late to comet-watch. And Hale Bopp, the Great Comet of 1997, grew brighter in the sky, and brighter still, until – as it began to close on the sun – it sprouted two tails.

*

The Anchorage had shed its festive-seasonal staff, leaving behind a low-season skeleton crew. So Clive agreed that Charlie could put in all the night-shifts he wanted.

Jo phoned him a few times, and so did Patrick. But it seemed to Charlie that they sounded painfully distant, like voices carried by fading radio waves across galactic distances – and, on the far other side, they heard the strangeness in his voice and took it for indifference, or hostility, and did not bother to call again.

He worked alone at night, serving the creatures the Anchorage drew to it, and he slept all day.

Tonight, he took some clean towels to Room 11 just after closing time. He could smell the vomit even before the door opened.

At 2 a.m., the adulterous couple in Room 27 ordered sandwiches and Asti spumante. The man – hairy, wrapped in a white towelling dressing-gown – met Charlie at the door. He blocked Charlie's view of the room and peeled a fiver into his hand.

At 3 a.m., with Charlie nodding off at the desk, the buzzer went.

Sometimes, drunks pressed the buzzer, or kids on their way home from nightclubs. Sometimes, it was half of a newly separated couple, looking for somewhere to see out the remains of the night. Now and again, it was men with hookers. Charlie wasn't supposed to let them in, because Clive didn't want the Anchorage to get that kind of reputation; it might put off the respectable adulterers. But Clive didn't understand the Anchorage.

If it was early enough, if Charlie could get them out in time, he let the room, cash, by the hour, and replaced the bedding when they'd gone. He wasn't really interested in the money; it was what the Anchorage expected of him.

Sometimes, he answered the buzzer and was met by silence. And that's what he liked the least; it made his skin crawl. He feared robbery, murder, restless spirits.

Tonight, it was Chris McNeil. She was hovering at the door like a vampire, unable to enter without an invitation.

He said, 'What are you doing here?'

'Open the door and I'll tell you.'

'I can't.'

'Open the door.'

His body felt far away. She had on a long coat, belted at the waist. Earrings, necklace. Little clutch purse on a thin leather strap.

He opened the door and she came in.

'Sit at the desk,' she said.

'No.'

'Sit at the desk.'

'Be quiet.'

'Sit at the desk.'

He sat at the desk. She walked behind it. She set down her little handbag, next to the computer monitor. She crouched. Pulled at his zip.

'What are you doing?'

'Apologizing.'

She rubbed his cock and kissed it; made famished noises. It took about five seconds. And when it was over, it withered in his lap and she grinned, sated, and swallowed. Then she perched on the edge of the desk. There were beads of semen in her hair, just behind the ear. And that's what he knew his mind would return to: Chris McNeil hovering at the door like a vampire, begging to be invited in, and opening her mouth and sucking out his life-force. And now, perched sideways, going through her bag, with his semen glinting in her hair, pearl-grey.

She put her cigarettes on the desk and wrote something on the back of her business card; the name of a hotel and her room number.

And she left without speaking, pushing the green *exit* button and pushing then pulling the door, and letting it swing slowly shut behind her. And she pixelated in the night, and was gone.

He met her at sunrise, on Minehead beach.

There were two early-morning joggers, some dog-walkers, some old people out for their widowed stroll. The wind blew off the sea and scoured his face.

Chris was hugging her knees. She was hungover, wincing. She hadn't slept. She smelled of booze and cigarettes; and his semen, dead on her breath. She was looking at the water.

He was next to her, still in uniform. They sat there like owls.

He said, 'Are you married?'

'No, I'm not married. Not for a long time.'

'So you were married once.'

'I'm thirty-eight years old.'

He shrugged, surly and chimp-like. He dug in the sand with a length of driftwood: curls and patterns.

'Married ten years. Separated the last three of them.'

He thought about her on her knees, wolfing at him. He needed to go and masturbate; then he could think straight.

She lit a cigarette and flicked away the match. Charlie had an urge to reach out and grab it. Pocket it.

'He got ill. The woman he was with, she couldn't cope. Didn't want to. And he had no one else. There was a sister; she's in New Zealand now.'

Charlie didn't care.

'I kept working. Had to; you don't get time off to nurse dying exes. And even with your friends, it's complicated. And you get to a point where there's nothing to . . .'

He wondered if he was expected to touch her. She would drain him like a battery.

'It's funny, my job – you get smiled at a lot. And I spend time in hotels, so there's always men. Propping up the bars, thinking because you're a woman on your own ... But, the night I met you: that was the first time anyone had smiled at me for a million years. I mean, really smiled. Actually smiled.'

And he thought of her, swizzle-sticking her glass at some hotel bar: the fat men in cheap suits all around her. Her naked breasts swinging as she finger-cleaned her teeth.

'I thought – a bit of fun. Where's the harm. He's young.'

'Thanks.'

She guffawed at herself, mercilessly. Puffed on the cigarette.

'Have you ever been to a funeral?'

'No.'

'They make you feel strange. They make you feel like sex. That's all it was meant to be. Sex.'

He held up his hands in surrender and walked away and never saw her again.

He stayed on the beach. He flexed his toes inside his trainers.

'I keep meaning not to come back. And I keep rehearsing this – what I'm going to say to you. And each time, it made me sound like a *teacher*. And that makes me feel sick. That thought. Jesus.'

He wasn't looking at her.

He said, 'So is that it?'

She was watching the sea.

He said, 'So now you can fuck off and leave me alone.'

She flinched, then pursed her lips, as if about to whistle. Instead, she blew, once – a long, sad exhalation. 'Oh-kay.'

And then she stood and brushed the sand from her arse. He

looked at her shoes and there were scuffs on the toes; the heels were worn down. She put her bag on her shoulder.

She said, 'Oh-kay,' again, and drew a shaky hand through her hair.

He kept looking at the water. What people took for the electric smell of ozone was just the smell of rotting seaweed. It was why people thought the seaside was good for you; the sea air. But it was just the smell of decomposition.

Her shadow fell over him. She was casting a shadow like a sundial. And then her shadow moved. And he listened to her footsteps, on the sand, moving to the promenade and he surged inside, as if the ocean had entered him.

He knew when she had gone: it was a light blinking out, behind him.

14

FROM A LETTER TO JO

Today I was speaking to a teacher at the American school and of course I mentioned you, the way I mention you to everybody. And he was very excited because of your comet; he told me it would be brightest on April Fool's Day and I told him how much you would appreciate that – and that you'd be out there, watching it.

———

Clive summoned Charlie downstairs to the laundry. This time of night, it was the most silent room in the silent hotel – windowless, underground. Clive leaned against the wall and leered, a great wet split across his circular head.

'This hotel is not your personal messaging service. Tell your bird to call you on your own time.'

'What bird?'

'I don't know what bird. The bird who keeps calling.'

'When did she call?'

'Half a dozen times.'

'What did she say?'

'Not much. Left a message for you to call her.'

'Why didn't you tell me?'

'I told you. We're not your personal messaging service.'

'For fuck's sake, Clive.'

'Hotel policy.'

'Since when?'

'Since I said so.'

The leer widened. Charlie thought about stuffing Clive's head into the great, rolling dryer they used for the bedding. See how wide and flat the leer could get.

Charlie said, 'Fair enough,' and Clive regally inclined his head to indicate the basement audience was over.

Upstairs, still shaking, Charlie went through the guest's register. He took Chris's number from it.

Once, her details had contained magic, a certain voodoo potency. He had visited them often, just to look, and think about calling her. But now they were dismally pragmatic, grave words and figures on a green-screen monitor.

He went to his room and called her mobile. He paced the room; up and down the narrow strip of carpet between the end of his single bed, the entertainment unit and the trouser press.

She answered on the sixth ring. She'd been digging around her bag, looking for the phone.

She said, 'Chris McNeil,' in case it was a client calling.

'It's me.'

'Is that you, Melanie?'

'It's *me*.'

She paused. There was noise behind her – a song, people's loud voices. She was in a bar. Or at a party. Three buttons undone, a fine silver necklace that glinted in the tender scoop between her clavicles. She was drinking a gin and tonic.

'Charlie?'

He listened to the background noise, and wondered who she was with.

He said, 'Well. You sound all right.'

In the background, someone laughed. The line rustled like a paper bag as she pressed the phone closer to her ear and headed away from the noise, turning her back, but it was too late – he'd heard it.

'Say that again. Sorry.'

'I said, *You sound all right*.'

She'd left the loud room. And now it was quiet on the line.

'What do you want me to say?'

'Nothing. I don't want you to say anything. I want you to stop phoning.'

'I just wanted to know you were okay.'

'I'm fine. Stop calling. Just leave me alone.'

He heard her lighting a cigarette. Exhaling.

She said, 'Fine.'

He waited for words to puke up into his throat; something vicious. But there was nothing. So he hung up, and then he went to the bathroom. And after cleaning his teeth, he got himself a glass of Coke from the minibar, and went back on duty at the main desk.

He sat there all night, now and again taking a sandwich or a bottle of wine to one of the old and ugly couples fucking in one of the cheap rooms it was his duty to protect and serve – like someone condemned for a sin he had certainly committed, and never repented, but had now forgotten.

*

Patrick was reading in front of the open fire when the phone rang. He slouched into the kitchen to find the handset.

'Hello?'

'Patrick?'

'Yeah?'

'It's Richard, mate. How's it going?'

'I'm good, I'm good.'

Patrick moved his lips and tongue in a silent, vile curse. He looked urgently around the kitchen, as if for an escape route. There was none, so he sat heavily in a kitchen chair and put his elbows on the table. The kitchen was cold and draughty and the windows were black.

Richard said, 'Just wondering if you'd heard from her?'

'Jane? A couple of letters. You?'

'Not a sausage. But we didn't part on the best of terms.'

'She hasn't mentioned.'

Patrick felt sorry for him; that was the worst of it.

He said, 'You were okay though, you two? It's not like this is going to cause, like, longterm problems?'

'No, no. Not much chance of that. The problem is . . .'

'What?'

'The show – the Monkeyland show. There's nothing we can do with it – not while she's out there, in a frigging *war* zone. We can edit; we've put together the first few, and it looks good. It's a good show. But it's lost its slot. We can't show it. Not when we don't know if – when she's coming back.'

'She's coming back.'

'I know. Of course she's coming back. Of course she is. But when? That's the problem.'

'When she's ready.'

Richard made a noise on the line. Patrick didn't know what sort of noise it was.

'And you don't, I suppose – you really don't have any idea? When that might be. I suppose.'

'Your guess is as good as mine, mate.'

'Well. Okay. Look, keep in touch. Keep me up to date. I'll send you some tapes.'

'Will do. Thanks.'

'No problem. Cheers.'

'Cheers.'

Patrick hung up and said, 'Fucking prick.'

Then he walked to the living room and lay on the sofa and opened *The Count of Monte Cristo*. But he couldn't concentrate on the words. His eyes moved over them, and saw nothing.

In the heat of the wood fire, he fell asleep, and dreamed of Jane.

*

Charlie pulled a woman on a hen-night. *Woman!* She was a girl, really – about his age. And she was shit-faced drunk, and he wasn't even sure if he pulled her, or she pulled him, or if the group of screeching women at the table had pimped them to each other.

The girl sneaked back to his room and stumbled as she kicked off her shoes, and she left the door open when she went for a piss, and when she came back he grabbed the hem of her skirt and hiked it round her hips and they were kissing and they fell back on the bed and he helped her wriggle from her knickers and he went down on her, buried his face in her, and she squirmed and hissed and tugged at his hair, and she grabbed at his shoulders and pulled him up and he kissed her, her tongue slathered round his mouth and she fumbled at his buttons and he pushed her away but she moved back, and she pulled down his zip, and her fingertips snaked inside his underwear and she cupped him, and she groaned when she found the cold putty of his flaccid penis and he whispered give me a minute and she gave him a minute, but a minute wasn't enough and neither was two minutes or three minutes and he could feel the sex leaving the room like a presence, like a third person who had been watching, and he tried to go down on her again, murmuring an apology, faking hunger, making hungry noises, but she closed her thighs and pushed him away and she stood and hunted for her knickers and stuffed them in her handbag and slipped her feet into her shoes; she didn't know what to say and he sat on the edge of the bed with his flies undone and his shirt untucked and his feet bare and cold on the hotel carpet. And he said sorry and she said don't worry about it (but that was not what she meant) and he had nothing more to say, there were no words and she left.

*

28 March.

Jo arrived at Nately's cottage and knocked on the door.

At length, Nately shuffled to the door like a pensioner – like the old man who was supposed to live here. He was unshaven, in pyjamas and dressing-gown and carpet slippers. Jo had never seen him unshaven before; let alone in pyjamas. And he smelled sour and yellow, like vegetables left to spoil in a basement.

'Sir? Are you okay?'

He squinted and whispered, 'Migraine.'

She phoned Patrick. He wasn't answering his mobile – he never did – so she left a message with Mrs de Frietas. Five minutes later, Patrick called back and promised to come and get her, right away.

Mr Nately's head hurt too much; he shambled upstairs to lie down in darkness. Jo made him a cup of cocoa and carried it to his room.

He was lying down with the curtains closed and a pillow pressed over his eyes.

She said, 'Get some sleep,' and she walked backwards and closed the door, and went downstairs and waited for Patrick to arrive.

And then the gate squeaked open and Patrick appeared, in his parka and boots, his greying shaggy hair, far too long, and his unravelling woolly gloves, and for some reason she wanted to cry.

She opened the door to him.

'How is he?'

'Sleeping.'

'Okay. What do you want to do? Go home, watch some TV? Come to work with me?'

'Come to work.'

'Cool. Get your coat.'

Jo watched him go upstairs. And she waited at the foot of the stairs, by the rotary dial telephone, in her coat, with the hood up.

*

Patrick had climbed these steps once before. Now he hesitated at
the bedroom door.

'John?'

'Come in.'

Nately was lying with a pillow pressed to his eyes. Patrick
approached him like a burglar.

'You okay, mate?'

'Fine. A bit below par. Sorry.'

Patrick nodded, slowly. The room seemed very cold to him.
He glanced at the curtains, drawn against the morning. Touched
the cold, dusty radiator.

'Can I get you anything? Lemsip? Some fruit?'

'No. Thank you. Really.'

'So you're okay?'

'Yes.'

'You're not having – trouble? Sleeping?'

Nately shook his head – once, very slowly.

'Okay. Well. Look after yourself. If you need anything – you
know what to do.'

'Thank you. I will. I'll call.'

*

Jo sat at Patrick's desk and opened his newspaper.

Patrick leaned over her, closing his pirate novel to reveal the
wages spreadsheet he was supposed to be working on.

He went to make tea.

Jo made a weird noise.

He turned, a dry teabag pincered in each hand. 'What?'

She nodded at the newspaper.

Patrick had already read the paper. He'd seen this story and rolled his eyes and tutted, and he'd turned the page, seeking out news of Zaire. Five days ago, American troops had arrived in the country. Patrick hadn't heard from Jane for a long time.

So he'd given no attention to this silly, sad, pre-millennial farce. Now he said, 'I know,' and rolled his eyes again, to show how silly it all was, and how sad, and he clicked his tongue.

Jo said, 'Dad.'

And Patrick put down the tea bags and came and took the paper from her.

In a rented mansion in San Diego, thirty-nine corpses had been discovered. They belonged to members of the Heaven's Gate cult: they had committed suicide by drinking phenobarbital mixed with vodka, then had plastic bags secured to their heads. The bodies had been lain out on bunk beds, neat as you like – then covered with blankets, from the lower end of which protruded box-fresh Nikes. Women and men had shaved their heads. Some time before, most of the men had castrated themselves.

Patrick thought of Nately, lying down in that chilly, darkened room, with a pillow pressed to his eyes.

Each of the Heaven's Gate pilgrims had packed a suitcase for their trip aboard the Hale Bopp comet. Among the dead was Thomas Nichols. He was the brother of Nichelle Nichols, who played Uhura in *Star Trek*. The one with the communicator in her ear.

The night before, Patrick had an urge to call Jane, care of the Internationale. But he couldn't get through. There was noise on the line, and mysterious clicking, and what sounded like the echo of a distant phone, ringing in some unglimpsed room. So he put down the receiver.

Now he looked at Jo, swivelling in his ratty old office chair.

He said, 'Let's go and look at the capuchins.'

She gave him a strange look.

'Come on. They're great. They're *evil*.'

So they left the office together, and followed the double loop of Monkeyland's main path – past the A Compound, past the Bachelor Group; peaceful now, but sullen with the recall of past violence, and the contrivance of violence to come.

Jo slipped her hand into Patrick's, as she'd not done for a very long time. And, cuddled up together against the cold, they sat on a bench, next to a rubbish bin, and watched the capuchins.

*

Richard addressed the box of video cassettes to Patrick at Monkeyland, but Patrick waited until he was home and Jo had gone to bed, before opening it.

He dumped the box on the kitchen table and opened the tool drawer – cluttered with rusty secateurs, blunt scissors, old hammers and chisels, assorted, mismatched screwdrivers, ends of wire and string, a dented yellow can of lighter fuel of unknown provenance – and took out a carpet knife. He unzipped the box with it (he thought of Rue, on the slab, unzipped from throat to pubis) and removed the uppermost cassette. He went into the living room and opened a bottle of whisky and put the tape into the old player

And there they were. All of them. The apes, the capuchins, his family. Jo and Charlie and Jane.

There was Charlie with Rue, trying to talk as she groomed him: Charlie gently slapping away her insistent hand – then allowing the old matriarch to embrace him.

And there was Jo, talking about smelly chimps. And there was Patrick, talking to Meredith, as the new jungle gyms were erected.

And there was Patrick again, in his muddy jeans and frayed sweaters, drinking tea and brushing the greying fringe from his eyes.

And there was Jane, in the office, and Jane visiting the compounds, and Jane chatting with elderly visitors, and there was Jane with the corpse of Rue.

Seeing it on screen made it less real. None of it resembled his memory. The film came from different angles. The colours, the light saturation; the voices. It was all wrong.

When the tape had finished, he sneaked upstairs and went digging around the small VHS library they kept in an Argos bookcase – in the marital bedroom, ha ha.

It took him a while, but eventually he found the programme about the bear – the triumph of Jane's first programme as presenter.

The bear was elderly, toothless, shabby as a cheap sofa. Name of Koukla. They'd filmed her being poked and prodded and jeered at, forced to perform a grotesque little parody of a dance.

'The bears live a nomadic existence,' Jane whispers to camera, *'being dragged from village to village by their owners. Usually, they travel in horse-drawn carts, perched on tiny wooden platforms. It's like being transported back to the Middle Ages. When Koukla isn't performing, she's chained up through a ring in her nose. She has no*

shelter from the sun or the rain, no chance of exercise and not enough food and water. It's a miserable experience for such a beautiful creature.'

Later, they filmed a meeting with the bear's owner. Although Richard had brought along an interpreter, on camera he had Jane speak to the owner in English. His thick-tongued hesitancy, his toothlessness, his grey stubble; all these things accentuated his villainy.

Jane requests that Koukla be released into her custody. The owner refuses; the bear is his livelihood.

The next scene – before the break – shows Richard and Jane, despondent, staring wordlessly into the middle distance as the Mediterranean sun sets behind them.

And then, after the commercials, there is a hustle of activity; phone calls to and from Britain; the arrival of an animal charity's Land-Rover; another meeting arranged with the bear's owner, a fraught financial negotiation.

And finally Koukla is led, stumbling like a drunk, to freedom. The charity vet shoots her in the loose, sagging arse with a tranquillizer. She is removed to a straw-lined transport carrier, an aluminium cage secured to the inside of a ventilated truck. And she is taken to a bear sanctuary.

All this is followed by an epilogue. Two months later, Jane stands once again in the bright sunshine, watching as Koukla, her coat glossy, her frame heavier, frolics at the edge of the water, runs with other bears.

Close-up on Jane, hair teased from her pony tail by the warm breeze. A final shot of Koukla, in slow motion. Fade to credits.

*

Two weeks ago, Laurent Kabila's forces captured Kisangani. A stormfront was moving towards her, this woman on the VHS, to whom Patrick was married, but who seemed farther away than it was possible for a human being to be.

He watched the video twice. By then, the bottle was nearly empty and he was good and drunk.

When he stood, he swayed. He was unsteady on his feet. In his anger and club-footed drunkenness, he was swaying exactly like this toothless old dancing bear his wife had long ago rescued. And that made him snort, to be lurching like a toothless old bear with an imaginary ring, punched right through his nose.

*

When Jo had gone home, Nately sat in the empty classroom, irradiated by the blue light, accessing his chatrooms:

This planet is about to be recycled, refurbished, started over

Our current best estimate for the diameter of Hale-Bopp's nucleus is 40 kilometers (= 25 miles)

The SLO (Saturn-Like Object) is many times larger than Earth. And the way it shadows the comet, it's obviously under intelligent control . . .

He stayed late into the dark of the morning, typing, reading, shifting the mouse. As sleep skulked up behind him, he squinted closer at the monitor. His lower back and buttocks ached. He drank strong, instant coffee that scalded the surface from his tongue.

Nately was having trouble with sleep again. The same trouble he'd had since he was child.

It wasn't insomnia.

One night, at the age of eleven, John Nately awoke in the smallest bedroom of this cottage. His skin was buzzing like a wasp and his teeth were chattering like a wind-up monkey. And he couldn't move. He lay there, cemented to the bed –

– as the *door opened*.

He knew he'd closed it, because he always did. He often stayed up late, reading, and the light kept his grandparents awake. They were light sleepers.

But the bedroom door snicked and swung slowly open. And into the room stepped the Squasher.

John's mouth was clamped shut, juddering like a drill. He could do nothing but look at the ceiling. The Squasher came close. He heard the slow pad of its footsteps. It radiated evil.

The Squasher sprang like a cat onto Nately's chest. It was very heavy. John croaked as the breath was forced from him. Talons closed round his slender throat. Began to squeeze.

He couldn't breathe. Couldn't move. Couldn't even scream. He passed out.

And woke in the bleached morning. He knew it hadn't been a dream – because John Nately was a clever kid, who knew the difference between dreams and reality. But clever kids also knew that Squashers didn't exist. So John told nobody; not his teachers, nor his grandparents – not even his diary.

But the Squasher came back. Not once, but many times.

Only when John turned nineteen did the Squasher at last reveal itself. He lay in bed, fearfully paralysed, as a group of extra-terrestrials clustered round his bed. They were naked. Large heads on small grey bodies.

The leader tilted its head like a puppy – and as it approached, it narrowed its black almond eyes. In its hand, it held a spindly, metallic instrument.

At twenty-one, Nately sought psychiatric help. The psychiatrist didn't laugh, or commit Nately to an institution. Instead, he gave a name to these events, and that was the first relief – if it had a name, it existed. Nately had spent a decade both fearing he was insane, and fearing he might not be.

The name he was given was this: *sleep paralysis with hypnagogic and hypnopompic hallucinations*, and it wasn't even uncommon. If the psychiatrist was right, it was experienced at least once by half the population of the planet.

But – because it wasn't a commonly *known* phenomenon, the people who endured these terrible hallucinations tended, just like Nately, to classify them as supernatural. And, on the whole, people who believed they'd been visited by ghosts, demons or angels, often did what Nately had also done, and kept quiet.

In fact, paralysis while asleep was normal. The human body secreted hormones that prevented movement – it was a protection against acting out your dreams. Sometimes in old men, this paralysis didn't occur. You might find them fighting off tigers, or playing soccer, or walking an imaginary landscape, or waltzing with some long-dead sweetheart.

John Nately sometimes woke when this hormone was still functioning, or the hormone began to function before he had quite gone to sleep. So he lay, genuinely paralysed, and dreaming, but in some strange way awake. The Squasher, the alien, was a manifestation, a broadcast from the animal side of Nately's brain; the Squasher was a manifestation of all his primitive fears.

The things John Nately experienced were real. But the things he saw weren't. They were twentieth-century demons.

Beyond naming it, not much could be done; but naming it was powerful enough. And Nately began to research his condition. He learned that sleep paralysis was common to all cultures, at all times. Historically, the attacks were given to monsters like *Lilitu*, the Sumerian Hag-demon who attacked men while they slept, squeezing the life-breath from them.

In Ancient Greece and Rome, the terrible presence was identified with demons of the forest and woodland. One of them was Pan, from whose name was derived the word panic – the emotion begotten of Nately's night-time visitations.

In St Lucia, the Squasher was the malevolent spirit of a dead baby. Similar child spirits, unbaptized, haunted the Irish. In Thailand, the experience was known as *Phi um* – being *ghost covered*. In Japan it was *kanashibari*: to tie with an iron rope. Those thus bound could commune with the dead. In Germany, the perpetrator was an *Alp,* a word related to *elf*. And in England, it was known as the *Night-hag*, or *Night-mare*.

Only recently had Europeans and North Americans – who no longer much believed in faeyries and night-walking devils – been obliged to find a new interpretation for this experience. It was only when the forest had been emptied of its evil spirits that people such as John Nately began to receive in their bedrooms visitors from outer space.

The Greys clambered in his room like baby mice, while he lay paralysed before them. They took him elsewhere, he could never remember quite where. They took semen, and faeces, and samples of skin.

He knew these were episodes of hypnagogic hallucination. He had a name for it! He knew its history. He knew these were not real extraterrestrials, any more than they were a manifestation of Lilith, Adam's first, demonic consort – whom God formed from filth and sediment, instead of dust; and who then spawned all the demons which infested the skies.

But he also knew he was awake when the aliens came.

Conceivably, he sometimes thought, the aliens *were* real, and had always been here. Perhaps ancient humans, other cultures, simply observed these extraterrestrials through the distorting goggles of culture – and made gods of them, and fairies, and devils.

Perhaps sleep paralysis really did give a name to something. But not to what it thought.

It was difficult, sometimes, not to think these things. And although Nately knew the comet had no *companion,* there *had* been a night, long ago, when he'd seen those lights in the sky behaving like lights shouldn't be able to.

And it *wasn't a* cloud formation, and it *wasn't* ball lightning, and it *wasn't* a military aircraft. And he stood and watched it – alone, perfectly sober and perfectly awake and perfectly sane.

And still he visited those chat-rooms, full of intelligent, articulate and sometimes lonely people who seemed perfectly con-vinced that the comet – a lump of ice the size of a mountain, approaching the sun – somehow *meant* something.

And sometimes, he got a feeling. And he had the feeling now.

Scrolling through those pages. Through the cables and the underground, through the wires, he felt connected to something.

The atmosphere around him shimmered with aliens and demons: half-hidden, half-real. And at the bottom of his garden, an orchard shushed in the night wind, and John Nately was very afraid.

15

The day of the comet's perihelion fell on Tuesday, 1 April.

John Nately was still downed by migraine, so Jo went to work with Patrick. They ate lunch together, a sandwich by the capuchins: Jo too had become eager to witness them capture a passing duck.

So they sprawled on the bench by the empty bin, and the capuchins – habituated by now to their daily visits – ignored them and got on with the foraging and squabbling and avoidance of the murky water of their moat.

And they also ignored the maudlin, honking ducks that now and again sailed past, heads held high, oblivious.

*

Charlie woke, and wanted to go home.

He looked at his little room, the hotel TV with its pay-per-view movies and porn and sport: the minibar fridge, the miniature kettle. And he thought of the months he'd spent here. And now he was done. There was no sense of relief, but there was a good feeling of something ending. He took a shower and felt it wash away.

And he whistled as he cleaned the rooms and pressed the sheets, and wheeled the laundry baskets past the reps queuing to check out, their cheap baggage at their feet. It all felt like nothing to him: and so did the narrow-eyed, gossiping staff who'd been trapped here with him: the cleaning girls, Mad Mervin in the laundry, the tattooed casuals in the kitchen who had once so frightened him.

He thought of hitchhiking from Bath, and saw how it had been a preparation for this: for Chris McNeil, for the Anchorage. Nothing was wasted.

He saw Clive that afternoon and asked for some time off. Clive wasn't pleased; he saw the glint of freedom in Charlie's jackdaw eye. But there was nothing Clive could do; he could see that Charlie had escaped.

At lunchtime, Charlie went outside and stood on the edge of the crescent moon of beach, whipped into eddies and whirlwinds by the Fool's Day breeze, and he saw it was a patch of desert, and he closed his eyes and stepped onto it. His feet sank a little into the soft sand and he was scoured clean; the sand hurt his cheeks and his ears.

He walked down to the edge of the sea. It was small and polluted – but further out, it was deep and green and clean, teeming with life.

There wasn't much to pack, but he packed it all, because he was never coming back.

He passed through the main door of the Anchorage, popping out like a bubble from a mouth. He walked round the corner, to where his rusty old VW estate was parked. It was older than him, and he got in and settled into the cracked leather seat. The gear-stick fitted perfectly into the cup of his palm.

Behind him, the Anchorage Hotel shimmied and disappeared – it would reappear, he knew, when its next inmate arrived.

He drove home and the route had no memory, or meaning, or significance. It was just a road.

*

Patrick was making dinner when the key scratched in the lock. His heart thumped, and he saw Charlie in the doorway, setting down his bag.

He said, 'Mate!' and walked up to his son and hugged him. Charlie hugged him back.

Patrick ruffled his hair. 'What's this? You want your laundry done?'

'It was a hotel, Dad. They did my laundry.'

'Duh.' He slapped Charlie's arse, resoundingly. 'Shall I put the kettle on?'

Charlie nodded, dog tired.

'Go upstairs,' said Patrick. 'Dump your bag. Then come down and tell me how you've been. We thought you'd dropped off the face of the earth.'

On the landing, Charlie bumped into Jo.

She said, 'Hello. Are you okay?'

'Yeah. I'm fine. I'm excellent.'

She hugged him. Her coarse hair tickled his cheek. 'Welcome back.'

'I hope you didn't go nosing round my room.'

'What would I want in your smelly room?'

He grinned, and moved on. Good to be back.

And later, they sat, the three of them, round the table. Charlie told them stories of the Anchorage Hotel, or as many as he was able. But Jo wasn't listening. She kept glancing at the kitchen window, the way lovers glance across crowded bars.

Charlie nodded at her and raised his eyebrows.

Patrick told him, 'It's this bloody comet. It's closest to the earth today, or something.'

'To the *sun*,' said Jo. 'It's the perihelion. It's closest to the *sun*.'

'Well, excuse *me*.' Patrick waggled his eyebrows at Charlie. *See?*

Jo scowled, pissed off – as the phone rang. Patrick answered. It was Nately.

'John! How are you?'

'I'm fine. Much better.'

'That's good. That's good.'

'So.'

Patrick was aware of Jo, at the table, pricking her ears up like a rabbit.

'Do you think Jo should come over?'

'Ah, I don't know, John. It's getting late. She's got the binoculars.'

The rabbit ears wilted, and Patrick felt bad. He was joking. He had no intention of standing in the field all night, guarding Jo against imaginary predators – not when he could be drinking a beer with his boy, at the warm fireside.

He rested the phone on his shoulder. Jo was pleading with silent, puppyish intensity.

He put the phone back to his ear. Asked: 'What time's good?'

'Anytime. Soon as. Tell her to dress warm.'

Jo was already halfway up the stairs.

In the roaring Land-Rover, chasing the headlights, they sat in silence. Patrick had on his old parka, Jo her stripy beanie cap.

Jo said, 'He's okay. Mr Nately.'

Patrick shifted gears. Heavy as a bus.

'I know he's okay. If I didn't think he was okay, I wouldn't be taking you.'

'I know he's strange.'

Patrick glanced at her as he drove. Her face was angelic with knowingness and love.

*

Alone, Charlie wandered room to room, reckoning the source of the house's unfamiliarity. It felt lifeless, unanimated – the opposite of haunted.

He examined photographs of his mother and father. And of him and his sister, much younger, squinting under African skies. He remembered everything.

And he went downstairs and turned on the TV. He settled into the sofa. He felt safe and warm.

There was a knock at the door.

*

Nately was waiting at the window. He opened the door before they were halfway down the path, and the yellow light cast him into silhouette.

Patrick stamped his feet. It was a cold, clear night; the sky vast above them, making them small.

He said, 'What time shall I pick her up?'

'Hey, come on. Stay for a look.'

'I've seen the comet, John. Several times.'

Jo shook his wrist. 'Come on.'

'Come on,' said Nately.

Patrick sagged, powerless. He wanted a beer with Charlie. But this night was important to Jo – and Nately, too. Importuning Patrick to stay had been an act of considered, if peculiar, hospitality.

So he surrendered – 'Okay. Five minutes' – and followed them inside.

*

Charlie rolled his eyes, hit *mute*. He put down the remote control.

'Coming!'

The hallway was shockingly cold, cold enough to make him gasp a little; the flagstones made his feet numb. He opened the door.

It was Chris McNeil.

*

Patrick followed them to the little observatory. Nately had killed all the lights, and Patrick was troubled by the quality of the darkness. He looked up, at the slow-spinning starscape – and was able to locate the comet with his naked eye; a bright star drawing a diaphanous tail behind it. It made him think of Jane, and he was overcome by a sudden, terrible yearning; a kind of homesickness.

Jo pulled down the noisy rolling shutter, exposing the fat telescope.

Patrick and Nately exchanged a glance. There was something in Nately's face.

Jo said, 'Do you want to go first?'

'Go on, then.'

Patrick squeezed himself into the shed, settled himself into the chair, and squinted into the eyepiece.

*

Chris McNeil shuffled her feet.

'Can I come in, then?'

Charlie stepped aside, and she entered the hallway, delicate as a cat in her dove-grey coat and cranberry scarf. He said, 'Come through to the kitchen.'

He didn't want her in the living room.

She nodded and followed, unwrapping the scarf as she went.

*

Patrick was moved by the comet. He understood its loneliness.

Very softly, he said, 'It's amazing,' and when he moved back from the eyepiece, he blinked.

Jo was almost sitting on his knee, she was leaning in so close. 'You see?'

He kissed her. 'Yes. Now your turn.'

They swapped places. It was like manoeuvring inside a submarine. Jo put her eye to the telescope and Patrick joined Nately in the garden.

Nately said, 'Why don't you stay?'

'I'd love to. But I can't, mate.' Patrick turned to face him. 'Are you okay, John?'

Nately was going to say *yes* – he was so close to it that Patrick actually saw it pass across his face, like an after-image. But the after-image faded.

'John?'

Nately shook his head. 'Stay. Just for an hour.'

From the shed, Jo called out, 'It's *fantastic*!'

'You stay there,' Nately called to her. 'Take notes.'

Patrick shuffled, awkward. Then he checked his watch. 'I'd best be off.'

Nately scratched the nape of his neck. And then he did something he'd never done: he offered Patrick his hand.

'Goodbye, then.'

Patrick shook the hand.

He looked up at the sky.

He left.

*

Chris said, 'I can't believe I'm here.'

She still had on her coat. It was cold; the Aga wasn't lit because they never used it.

'Charlie, I know I said it before. But I really am sorry.'

Behind her, the air boiled with sprites and demons that belonged to the Anchorage Hotel. She was a herald, an emissary. She'd been sent to take him back.

'Don't worry about it.'

'Can't we have one adult conversation? Just one.'

'Whatever.' He thought of her, on her knees, gulping at his cock: then sitting drunk on the edge of his desk with his semen glinting like pearls in her hair.

'Okay.' She found her cigarettes and passed the pack from hand to hand. And then she said, 'I'm pregnant.'

He jerked his head – shocked and birdlike – to look at her.

She lurched away, as if to avoid a head-butt.

'Sorry?'

She popped a cigarette into her mouth and lit it. 'I'm keeping it. And whatever.'

The world was making a noise like a vacuum cleaner. Thinking was difficult. His body beat with the rhythm of his heart.

Eventually, he said: 'You're having a baby?'

'People do.'

He laughed out loud, because she was stronger than him. It was a terrible feeling. Oppressive, incarcerating.

'Do you want it?'

She hugged herself. 'Actually.'

She reached over the table, to touch the back of his hand. He withdrew: her touch would suck the life from him.

She said, 'This isn't your problem.'

They each had their back to the cold, stone walls of the kitchen; outside, England wheeled all around them. The fields, the sky, the sea, the yellow bubbles of the cities.

He stood. 'I need a drink.'

She crossed her legs. Tapped a nervous foot.

'I don't *want* anything from you,' she said. 'Or anything like that. But I thought – you know.'

He went to the kitchen drawers.

She had her back to him. There was a knot of cells inside her, dividing. He thought of the walls in the Anchorage Hotel bar; throbbing, womb red.

He opened the tool drawer and took out the claw hammer. He took a step. Then he hit Chris in the head with the hammer. Its claw pierced her skull and entered her brain. The impact nearly broke his wrist.

Chris McNeil fell over. The chair landed on its side next to her. She made a strange noise, baby noises.

Her hands and feet were moving in circles, like someone making a snow angel. The hammer jutted from her skull like a handle. She was trying to grab it, but she couldn't control her hands. Her eyes were white.

Charlie ran the tap and splashed his face with cold water.

Chris was moaning and trying to kick herself along the floor, towards the door.

And then the thing inside Charlie curled up and shrank down, leaving him an empty shell.

Charlie vomited. Everything came up with it. But when it had,

Chris McNeil was dead anyway. And, although the little thing inside her lived for a little while longer, soon it, too, was dead.

Chris was lying on the floor with her arms more or less at her sides, and one of her legs askew, as if she was dancing the Charleston.

Charlie hadn't moved, except to drape a dirty dishcloth over her face. He was still sitting in the kitchen chair when Patrick walked in.

Patrick stood there for a very, very long time.

*

Inside Nately's house, the phone began to ring. Out in the garden, Nately turned towards it and Jo followed his gaze.

'Who's that?' she asked.

'Wrong number.' But Nately stared at the dark house, as inside, the phone rang and rang and rang.

Eventually, he said, 'Wait here.'

'Okey-dokey.'

As Mr Nately scuttled away – why so fast? – Jo became aware of his absence. But, although she felt weak and frightened, looking up at the cold indifferent sky, she kept her eye to the viewer, following the comet's progress; the tumbling mountain of ice, its skirts of vapour trailing in space behind it.

Nately didn't turn on the lights. He didn't need to. He went to the phone.

'Hello?'

'John?'

Something had gone from Patrick's voice. Nately shivered and turned on the spot, wrapping the telephone cord around himself, the better to look into the shadows.

'Patrick. Are you all right?'

'Yeah. John, listen. Could Jo stay at your place tonight?'

Nately consulted his watch. It was still 1 April.

'Of course.'

There was a noise on the line, and for a moment Nately wondered if Patrick was weeping. He thrilled with terror. And on its heels, there was a kind of relief.

'She can stay as long as she likes. She's welcome.'

'Great,' said Patrick. 'See you in the morning.'

*

After Patrick had vomited, then wept, then threatened to kill his own child, then wept again, he got himself together.

He opened a bottle of whisky. Then he sliced a lemon in half, tilted his head back and squeezed the juice of each half down his nostrils.

He snorted, choked, coughed, cried out.

Then he drank off a quarter pint of whisky, wiping at tears with his forearm. When that was done, there was a moment of violent disorientation. But then his head cleared.

He looked at his child. Hating him

Then he went outside and looked at Chris McNeil's car. He had the bottle of whisky in his fist.

Charlie followed him.

'Have you touched this car?'

'No.'

It looked very solid in the moonlight, like an ingot.

Patrick turned and stalked inside.

In the kitchen, he stared at the corpse and began to cry again. 'Who is she?'

He'd already asked it a hundred times, and had not once waited for an answer.

He wiped his snotty nose on the back of his hand and then took a swig of whisky. Then he knelt and opened the bottom drawer. It was the carrier-bag drawer. He took out a carrier bag. Tesco.

Charlie hung over him. Patrick looked up and snarled. For a moment, crouched there, he resembled a wolf.

'What did you touch?'

'Nothing.'

'Her handbag? What?'

'Nothing.'

Patrick swallowed a mouthful of sour whisky vomit. He looked briefly at the floor.

'Go and get some gloves. And some boots. And a coat.'

Charlie went upstairs to get his boots and his parka. He put them on. He found his gloves. He put them on, too. Then he went downstairs.

In the kitchen, Patrick had worried and strained at the hammer until he was able to remove it from Chris McNeil's head. Then he set it to one side, on a carrier bag. He was kneeling. He had lifted Chris McNeil's head into his lap and slipped a carrier bag over it. Now he was Sellotaping the carrier bag; wrapping the tape round and round the dead woman's throat.

He was muttering under his breath.

Charlie tilted his head; a question.

'It's for the blood,' said Patrick. 'You little prick. It's for the blood.'

Chris McNeil was heavy. It was like carrying a sofa, or a mattress, and it took them a long time just to get her to the stile, and a great deal of heaving to get her over it. By then, it had gone midnight: it was 2 April.

They lugged her through the oak forest, and onto the clifftop; the place where, in the summer, Patrick sometimes liked to come and read a book. Here, they laid her down.

Their backs and arms and legs hurt. It was hard to breathe. They were muddy and scratched.

The night sky was still very clear. Patrick could feel the comet, although he did not look at it. He knelt and removed the carrier bag from Chris McNeil's head. He had been careful, so that none of the tape's adhesive had stuck to her throat. He scrunched up the bag and put it in his pocket.

There was a hole in her skull; the shape of a hammer-claw. The shape went into her brain; the police might take a cast from it. So, on his knees, Patrick felt around for a rock, something that would fit the palm of his hand.

In the darkness, on his knees, it took a while. When he had the rock, he knelt beside Chris McNeil.

He said, 'Oh God,' and brought down the rock on Chris McNeil's head. He felt it break, like an egg. But not enough. So he did it again, and again, until he was sure.

When he was finished, he turned his face away and stood. Stooped. Grabbed her wrists. They were slender.

Charlie grabbed her ankles.

Patrick counted quietly to three. Then, keeping their backs straight, they hoisted her. And then they swung her – one, two, three! – like a hammock, and tossed her over the edge of the cliff.

Chris McNeil was broken up by the rocks below. And soon the tide would send out fingers to dislodge her from the rocks, take her with it, wherever it was going.

They heard nothing. Just the sound of their own breathing.

Charlie sat and hugged his knees.

Patrick stooped to pick up the rock. It was speckled with wet matter. He was glad he was drunk.

He reached back his arm, as far as it would go, and he launched the rock into the sea.

They walked back. The night spoke softly.

Outside the house, Patrick ordered Charlie to strip naked. When Charlie protested, Patrick struck him, open-handed across the face. Charlie fell to his knees.

Patrick wanted to hit him again; but if he started, he wouldn't stop. He waited with fists clenched at his sides, until Charlie stood like a stamen in a bloom of a muddy clothing. He was naked in the moonlight, hairless and tuber-pale, this murderer, and Patrick turned the hose on him.

Charlie screamed, because the water was shockingly cold. Patrick grabbed his neck and forced him to his knees and passed the cold surge of water through his hair.

Then Patrick stripped and turned the hose on himself.

And dripping, he went into the house and got two bin bags and took them outside, and into the bags he stuffed their muddy clothes.

Patrick stood, naked, shivering, in the kitchen. He dripped on the flagstone floor, big fat splats. Wet footprints. His hair curled, wet, at his nape.

He picked up the whisky and drank the rest of it. He waited until the fire passed through him.

He put the bloody hammer into the sink. He ran the tap, so the hammer was covered with half an inch of water. Into the water, he emptied half a container of Drano – it was in a cupboard under the sink, among a jumble of other unused cleaning products. The water began to foam and boil. It would destroy the blood and dissolve the hair.

He went upstairs, to get dressed. He passed Charlie's door. Charlie was sitting on the edge of his bed.

Patrick stood in the doorway.

Charlie didn't move. Patrick expected his eyes to glow yellow in the lamplight. But instead, they had the pleading mildness of a kitsch Christ, rendered in Catholic tat.

*

Before sunrise, Patrick set out in the Golf. He ordered Charlie to follow fifteen minutes behind him, in the VW.

He drove all the way to Bristol; to a council estate called Knowle West. He remembered it from his time on the *Evening Post*. It was notorious. He left the Golf parked by the kerb.

He headed down the street, aware of the pit bulls and German shepherds growling behind flimsy gates. He reached the main road and waited outside a corner shop until a bus came to take him into town.

He met Charlie outside a Mall called the Galleries. Charlie had dumped the binliners in the wheelie-bins behind a McDonald's – and in another bin were Chris McNeil's handbag and credit cards, carefully shredded.

Patrick let Charlie take the wheel on the way back to Devon. It wasn't a long trip, fifty or sixty miles south-west, but Patrick soon lost his sense of position.

He unwound the window and smelled the sea. It did not make him happy. That man was gone.

That man had been a sidekick. This man was an accomplice.

*

They parked in the sunlight outside their house. They got out of the car. They stared at the house. It had not changed.

Patrick said, 'You killed Rue.'

Charlie swivelled his head. And at last, Patrick saw the creature that lived behind Charlie's eyes: the hyena.

'And the letters. Those terrible letters to your mum. The photographs. That was you, too?'

Charlie stared at the house.

'Why?'

'I wanted to stop her.'

'Stop her *what*?'

'Sleeping with Richard.'

Patrick roared and raised his fist. He grabbed his son by his tender throat and squeezed. He backed his son into the door and roared into his face. Charlie cringed and trembled.

And when the roar didn't empty Patrick, he let the boy go and watched him sink to his knees. Then he punched the door, and punched it again, and punched it again until the panel splintered and the skin of his knuckles ripped and the bones bruised inside him and the urge to kill had gone.

Patrick sucked at his bleeding fist while Charlie knelt in the shadow of the house, coughing green bile upon the stone threshold.

We were adapted to live in the shadow of predators. It was fear of the beast that made us human. Beasts were simply the product of forest and grasslands – the urge to kill, to live, to create life. Beasts were part of natural history.

So were monsters.

Patrick bound his swollen fist in an athletic bandage and they drove to Minehead and had their heads shaved; Patrick was concerned that brain matter and blood had dried in there. He sat in a nylon cape and watched curls drop into his lap; he looked at an unfamiliar face: haggard, older than he expected, with raw, red ears.

Charlie's hair was like suede; his skull was a fine shape. His eyes were big and harmless. He looked like a wigless prince.

*

Shaved, Patrick wandered the infinite double loop of Monkeyland.

His ears and his scalp were chilled by the wind. He stood and watched the capuchins.

They stopped capering. For an extended moment, they raised up on their hind legs and stared at him. He dropped his eyes in shame; moved on.

*

Patrick drove to Nately's house, still drunk, with Jo's things in bags and boxes: her books, her clothes, her posters, her only CD, *Nevermind*.

He wanted her never again to set foot in the house Charlie had contaminated. It was filled with black radiation. It would ruin her. It would blacken her teeth and poison her hair; it would riddle her with tumours.

Nately's garden was just entering into bud, and Nately and Jo stood together in the doorway. They saw Patrick – thinner, shaved, deep vertical scores in his cheeks, holding a box of Jo's stuff in his arms.

Nately took the box from Patrick, took it and stepped inside. He said nothing.

He left Jo on the doorstep.

'Dad?'

And their last moment was gone; it had been a long time ago. He thought of their morning runs; of her determined slog, her comically flailing limbs. And he loved her, terribly and acutely, as something lost to him.

He kissed her forehead. He ran his hands though her dry tangled hair, as he once had, when she was a toddler and he was soothing her tears.

'I love you, baby girl.'

'Me, too. And it's not for ever, is it? It's not like it's going to be for ever.'

He crushed her to him. She was so fragile; her long thin bones.

'Nothing is. Nothing's for ever.'

But he was lying, and in the terrible nights that followed – alone with Charlie, full of whisky and hatred and ghosts – Patrick thought often of the night of the perihelion, in Nately's garden: how Nately had asked him not to go. And how he'd tapped his watch and said no.

And he hated Nately, for if there had been no comet, the woman might still be alive. And when he remembered his daughter, safe and uncorrupted in the haven of Nately's cottage, and Nately's goodness, he clenched his helpless fists and ground his helpless teeth for the creature he'd become.

When the morning came for Charlie to leave, Patrick grabbed his son's shirt in his fist – so violently that Charlie nearly lost his footing – and stuffed into his pocket a wad of cash. Charlie didn't need the money; he'd saved so much, pulling all those double shifts at the Anchorage Hotel.

Patrick growled, 'Go to Greece, France. Whatever. Go where kids go. Get a job. Stay away.'

Charlie touched the wad of folded, dirty cash. 'When can I come home?'

Patrick barked, and flecks of his spittle wet his son's face, his eyelashes.

'If I ever see your face again, I'll smash it with a fucking rock.'

Charlie burned with resentment and self-pity. He hoisted his rucksack.

Patrick said, 'I *made* you.'

But Charlie didn't understand. With watering eyes, he dumped his rucksack on the back seat of the orange Volkswagen estate, with its Greenpeace and WWF decals, and drove away.

He left the car at Heathrow airport.

*

Now it was two weeks later. Jo was still at Mr Nately's. Patrick was at his desk, putting his paperwork together. He was preparing to sell Monkeyland, and with it the house. It would bankrupt them.

Mrs de Frietas put through a call. It was Don Caraway. The line was bad: thin, with loud bursts of white noise.

Caraway said, 'Patrick?'

Patrick was distracted; he was shuffling papers, leaving them in a neat pile for Mrs de Frietas to file.

'Yup?'

'You'll never guess where I'm calling from.'

'No.'

'Minehead.'

'That's lovely for you, Don.'

Patrick's flatness dimmed Caraway's excitement for a moment; then it flared again.

'Aren't you going to ask what I'm doing here?'

'What are you doing there?'

'Attending an autopsy.'

Patrick stood up. There was no paperwork to knock from the desk. He looked at the clean corner where it should be.

'What autopsy?'

'A body.'

'Whose body?'

'Some suicide.'

'Man? Woman?'

'Woman. Can I get to the point?'

'Sorry.'

'She's not a drowner, apparently. She's all smashed up. A jumper.'

'Definitely suicide?'

'Looks like. Can I actually finish?'

'Sorry.'

'Well. Guess where they found her?'

'Where did they find her?'

'In the *woods* – back of your house.'

Patrick dropped the phone. It lay, meaningless, on the floor, buzzing like an insect.

He sat and opened the lower desk drawer. But his hand was shaking too much to open the bottle he found there.

He walked to the centre of the office. He replaced the phone on the desk.

When it rang, he cried out in terror. Then he snatched it up.

'Something happened,' said Don. 'We got cut off.'

'Yeah. Sorry.'

'Anyway. Don't you think it's *amazing*?'

'Yes. How did she get there? To the woods. Did she crawl? Walk? What?'

There was a silence.

Don said, 'Are you all right?'

'Fine. Why?'

'Have you heard a word I'm saying?'

'Yes.'

'How could she walk? She's a *jumper*. Dead as you get. Dead as a dodo. All smashed up.'

'Right.'

'So how did she get into the woods?'

'I don't know, Don. That's what I'm asking. How did she get to the woods?'

'Something *dragged* her there. She jumped, got pulled in by the tide. Washed up on the beach – fresh meat – and something dragged her off the beach and up into the trees.' Patrick sat down. He was slipping out of his body.

'And whatever dragged her into the trees, it *ate* her.'

Feedback squealed on the line.

'They called me out,' said Don, 'to examine the bite radius and whatnot. Bit icky, but I wasn't even thinking about what lay on the slab – what there was of it. I was thinking – what could've eaten her?'

'And?'

'It's out there,' said Don Caraway. 'You're not mad, Patrick. It's definitely out there.'

Patrick thanked him and hung up.

He placed his hands on his clean desk. He felt that he was floating to the ceiling; spreading like a gas. His body was there, below him.

16

On 1 May 1997, Britain elected a new government. Just over two weeks later, Laurent Kabila declared himself president of the Democratic Republic of the Congo, the former Zaire.

He was sworn in before 35,000 people who had gathered in the dreadful, wet heat of a Kinshasa sports stadium.

Kabila wore a dark safari suit, and took his oath before twenty-two justices, all of them adorned in scarlet robes trimmed with leopardskin.

The oath of office was administered by Mungulu Tamaigane, Mobutu's former Chief Justice. Perhaps dazed by the appalling heat, Tamaigne confused Kabila with the deposed dictator, and the old country with the new. He referred to Kabila as Joseph: once, that had been Mobutu Sese Seke's name.

*

Together with Camra Dave, Sound Mick and Richard, Patrick hitched a ride to Congo on a UN Hercules. They were in the company of print journalists and aid workers.

They arrived in steaming darkness. They struggled and argued through customs, then met an old minibus that drove through the hive of Kinshasa – the stink of burning garbage, the glow of fires, the presence of soldiers.

And later, in the early hours, Patrick sat at a table. He was in the bar of the Hotel Internationale.

His shirt was open. He was sweating. Beads of it gathered in his softening crew-cut, his greying beard.

Richard was with him. Patrick had demanded it; had growled it as an order.

And Richard waited, not speaking, while Patrick worked his way through most of a bottle of Johnny Walker. He was surly, drunk and – Richard thought – dangerous.

Now Patrick sighed. Rubbed his face. Richard heard it; the scrape of palm on bristle.

Patrick leaned over the table, towards him. His eyes were hooded, lazy, raptorial.

Richard leaned back; far from the whisky breath, the sleepy hatred in the eyes. It occurred to Richard that Patrick might be dying.

Patrick said, 'You and Jane.'

'What about me and Jane?'

'It's all right. I just want to know, when and where?'

But it wasn't all right, not really. Richard knew when to be scared; and he knew when to back off from a growling dog and when to stand your ground. Sometimes, if you moved too quickly, or in the wrong direction, a dog would have your throat.

Richard began very slowly. He said, 'Okay.' And then he said, 'A long time ago.'

Patrick didn't move. He looked at Richard from under his brow.

'A long time ago. After we'd grown close. Jane and me.' He stopped, to draw a shaky breath. 'She's an amazing woman.'

Patrick's face and head were overgrown with greasy, sweaty, silvery stubble. He'd lost a great deal of weight. His chest was bony, glistening. He looked like a convict.

'We were in a hotel. Greece. Filming the bear programme.'

'Koukla.'

'Koukla. Exactly. It was a nice hotel. And we knew we had a good show: we knew we were going places. As a business.'

Richard's throat was dry. He had to take a drink. He lifted his glass and sipped, swilled, like a man in a dentist's chair.

'We drank some champagne. Quite a lot of champagne. And we were laughing, and she was looking good. Very beautiful. Very happy. And we were drunk.'

Patrick blinked, slowly.

'We said good night.' And now, as Richard lifted and tilted his glass, his hand was shaking. 'I went back to my room. I couldn't sleep.'

'You were horny. You had an *itch.*'

'So I got dressed, got another bottle of champagne and knocked on her door. She asked who it was, and I said, *Who do you think?* and she opened the door.'

'Go on. Finish.'

'She was wearing . . . she was wearing underwear. She was a bit drunk. But she didn't seem, you know – to object. She just said, *What do you want?* and I walked in and closed the door, and she said *Richard*, and I put down the champagne, and I kissed her.'

Richard's breath came in a shudder. He ran his hands through his hair. The hair fell back into place. Well cut.

'She pushed me off, and she said, *What are you doing?* And I said, *What do you think?* And she said, *Richard, don't be so fucking silly.* And she sent me back to my room with my tail between my legs.

'I tried once more, a few days later – and, if you want to know the truth, once again about a year after that. But she didn't want to know, Patrick. She didn't want to know – about me, or about anyone else. Only you.'

Patrick stared at him through those newly dead, convict's eyes. And then he guffawed.

And then he hid his face in his hands, his elbows on the table. He was making a noise; he was laughing or he was crying.

When Patrick took the hands away, his eyes were wet, red-rimmed, swollen. He craned back his head on his neck and bared his teeth at the ceiling.

Then he composed himself. He looked Richard in the eye.

Richard said, 'So what now? Where does this leave us?'

Patrick topped up their glasses. He touched the rim of Richard's glass with the base of his own.

Clink of glass. Bright, clean, in the humidity.

Patrick said, 'To my wife.'

He first emptied his glass in a single swig, then raised it in salute.

*

Her hotel was on a side street. On the pavement outside were spilling heaps of garbage. He walked through the high stink of it.

He slipped the receptionist five American dollars, and then he walked upstairs, alone. He came out of the stairwell, and walked along the hallway, counting doors.

He stopped and straightened his shirt. He blew through his mouth, like a preparing athlete, then knocked.

From inside, a sense of sudden stillness.

Her voice.

'Who is it?'

He looked down at his chest. Ran his tongue over his teeth.

'Room service.'

There was no room service. Not in this hotel.

And now there was movement inside. Coming close on bare feet. She hesitated behind the door. He measured the quality of it, the shape and intention of the pause.

He knew she was cocking her head. Frowning.

Curious.

And then, the door. Opening.

17

Jane and Patrick spent a year in the Democratic Republic of the Congo. They worked hard, and successfully, to arrange the evacuation of many animals from Kinshasa zoo.

Richard, Camra Dave and Sound Mick were there to record most of it. It made a good show.

Patrick dreamed of Charlie, sometimes. He dreamed of Beacon Batch, the day he learned of Charlie's existence. And he dreamed of 1 April 1997, the day of the perihelion, when he understood for the first time what Charlie was.

Sometimes I get pressure in my head, Charlie said, and Patrick woke.

And in those dreams he must have mewled and reached out for his wife, because Jane was always awake when he opened his eyes. And Patrick folded into the warmth of her neck and arms and breasts and belly, and she wrapped around him, and he breathed her in, and sometimes – although she did not see – he wept.

*

Patrick never returned to England. But, in the years that followed – always in the company of Richard, Camra Dave and Sound Mick – he and Jane visited every continent.

As a team, Patrick and Jane worked well on camera. They had good chemistry.

Usually, the shows they made were shown by one of the satellite channels. But even this was enough to make them passably wealthy; wealthy enough to absorb the fabulous loss they suffered when Monkeyland finally closed its doors, late in 1999, having never found a buyer.

Patrick is buried in Australia.

He and Jane were there hoping to track down and possibly film a cryptid known locally as the Yowie.

Jane was at the wheel of a white jeep, open-topped. Patrick came sauntering up. He was suntanned, grinning, wearing khaki shorts and a bush hat; from beneath it curled his long hair.

He stood, under the Australian sun, grinning – as he had grinned at her once, long before, when they were strangers meeting at Bristol Zoo.

Then something in his brain burst. He whispered, 'Oh Christ,' and touched his eye.

He sat down on the red earth, blinking. And then he was gone.

I stayed in England, with John Nately. I took my A-levels early. Then I took some more, because I wanted to stay with him a little bit longer. At eighteen, I went up to Cambridge.

Occasionally I flew out to visit my parents, wherever in the world they happened to be. But not too often. I liked it in England.

John Nately made a good *in loco parentis*, and a better friend. The day I passed my first A-levels, he bought me a bottle of Asti spumante and we drank it together in deckchairs, in the garden.

People wonder about him. They always want to ask the same question, although they never do. But John Nately never laid a hand on me; didn't even *look* at me that way, not once. To tell the truth, I don't even think he was gay. I think he was asexual, like angels are supposed to be. Or aliens.

He cried when I left for Cambridge. I think he hated the idea of being alone in the cottage again. In all the years I lived there, the aliens never came for him – and sometimes that convinced him they'd been hallucinations all along. And sometimes, of course, it convinced him of just the opposite.

Because Mum and Dad paid for a flat, I never had much cause to visit Devon. But, during my undergraduate years, John and I wrote frequently; never by email. Thinking about it, he only faded away when David came on the scene, which was – what? – early 2004?

He still writes, of course. But not so often.

It makes me sad, to think that. It makes me wonder why.

Although Don Caraway was eager to testify that the bites on the unidentified woman's remains were felid, the coroner disagreed. Officially, the animal that gorged on her was canid; a dog, a fox, a combination of the two. As to how her corpse got itself into the fork of a tree – that remained open.

Maybe kids did it.

For a while, Stu Redman and Don Caraway dined out on the story – but it became embellished, year on year and telling on telling, until nobody believed it any more.

Once, during a morning jog (I kept it up, and got better) I thought I heard a low growling from under the hedge. But I thought then, and I think now, that it was the wind, whistling in off the Bristol Channel.

Jane visits me twice a year. I am older now, she often takes care to remind me, than she was, when she met my dad.

We never mention Charlie.

He wrote to her, for a few years – from Greece, India, America. He married at twenty-two, divorced at twenty-five. Married again a year later. He was living in England then; Manchester. After that, the letters stopped.

Sometimes I read a newspaper, and see that this woman has disappeared, or that girl was found dead, and I wonder. But really, there's no point. There's no point thinking about it.

Two years ago, on the anniversary of Patrick's death, Jane drove me to Monkeyland.

It's empty now, of course, and more desolate than it ever was, with that bright signage faded almost to white and pocked with airgun pellets.

We sneaked in – through the hole in the fence round the back of the adventure playground – and trod past the glue bags and the cider bottles.

We passed all the empty compounds, the place where the A Group had been, the Bachelor Group, the capuchins; all of them since moved to other zoos. Some of the chimps might live another twenty years.

The empty enclosures are defaced by graffiti; stupid, obscene, childish scrawls. Every window has been smashed. Inside Patrick's old office, a fire had been lit. The spoor of the indigenous wildlife.

Jane stood where she'd once stood, supervising the construction of a new jungle gym.

She said, 'Just look at it.'

I looked at it.

Then we sneaked back out, through the same hole in the fence, and she drove me home.

The last naked-eye observation of the Hale Bopp comet was made in December 1997. It had been visible without aid for 569 days. It's still being tracked by astronomers. I'm one of them.

It'll be visible with large telescopes until perhaps 2020, by which time it'll be nearing 30th magnitude. By then, it'll be difficult to distinguish it from a very large number of distant galaxies of similar brightness.

Around the year 4380, it'll be back.

I kept a single souvenir of Monkeyland: a painting. It was Patrick's, bought for him as a gift – although Jane neglected ever to tell him that. He only looked at it once, and briefly. He saw a woman with a storm behind her, then he turned the canvas and propped it against the office wall, promising to hang it when Jane returned.

But he never did. Patrick never hung a painting in his life. So he never knew that Sarah Lime had written, in very small script, bottom left of the canvas, the painting's name. It was called *Natural History*.

I took the painting from his office, and I hung it for him. I hung it on the wall of my little bedroom in John Nately's house. Then I hung it on the wall of my student digs; my first flat; my house. Now I am in Houston and it hangs above my desk, above my laptop.

I think of Patrick when I look at it. I remember him, how he was, midway through our morning jogs in Devon. He was wincing, out of breath. And holding on to that signpost.

Clutching it, like a captain at the mast.